THE COMANCHEROS

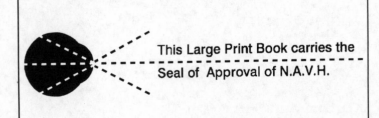

This Large Print Book carries the
Seal of Approval of N.A.V.H.

CHARLEY SUNDAY'S TEXAS OUTFIT

THE COMANCHEROS

STEPHEN LODGE

WHEELER PUBLISHING
A part of Gale, Cengage Learning

GALE
CENGAGE Learning

Farmington Hills, Mich • San Francisco • New York • Waterville, Maine
Meriden, Conn • Mason, Ohio • Chicago

GALE
CENGAGE Learning·

LIBRARY OF CONGRESS CATALOGING-IN-PUBLICATION DATA

Names: Lodge, Stephen, author.
Title: The Comancheros by Stephen Lodge.
Description: Large print edition. | Waterville, Maine : Wheeler Publishing, 2017. | Series: Charley Sunday's Texas outfit | Series: Wheeler Publishing large print western
Identifiers: LCCN 2017001709| ISBN 9781410499967 (softcover) | ISBN 1410499960 (softcover)
Subjects: LCSH: Large type books. | GSAFD: Western stories.
Classification: LCC PS3612.O34 C66 2017 | DDC 813/.6—dc23
LC record available at https://lccn.loc.gov/2017001709

Published in 2017 by arrangement with Pinnacle Books, an imprint of Kensington Publishing Corp.

Printed in the United States of America
1 2 3 4 5 6 7 21 20 19 18 17

THE COMANCHEROS

PROLOGUE

1961

"Hold your horses, I'm coming!"

The youngest Pritchard child, Noel, stuffed a piece of half-eaten, jelly-covered toast into her mouth, turned around slowly, and backed off the couch. She'd been sitting there while watching a Saturday morning television program with her two brothers. Now she was on her way to answer the doorbell. Without taking her eyes away from the television screen, she shuffled to the front door, still in her robe, pj's, and Flintstone's bedroom slippers. She passed the Christmas tree, decorated to the hilt and all lit up. When she reached her objective, she had to struggle with the latch for a few moments until the door finally opened. A sharp blast of cold, icy air burst through the open portal, as Noel stepped back to let her great-grandfather, Hank, enter. The old man gave her some help getting the door closed behind them, and when he knelt to give her his greetings, Noel's eyes were still glued to the television set across the room. Her two brothers, Caleb, the middle sibling, and Josh, the oldest, hadn't moved an inch from where they had been sitting when Hank had first rung the bell.

Hank leaned forward to give his great-granddaughter a kiss and got a grape-jelly imprint on his white-stubbled cheek in return.

"What kind of a greeting was that?" he said, confronting not only the girl, but also the two boys. "That must be a pretty special TV program you're watching for you to treat me like a secondhand uncle."

"It's *Fury,* Grampa Hank," said Noel. "It's all about a boy and his horse, living on a ranch. And even though it's a rerun, it's still my favorite TV show."

"Mine too," echoed both of her brothers without looking away from the TV screen.

"Well," Hank went on, "I can understand you kids liking anything about living on a ranch with horses. So, go on back to your TV. Can I get you kids anything? I'm assuming your mother's in the kitchen."

When he got no answer from any of them, he turned and walked over to the kitchen door.

With a quick knock, Hank entered the room. He found his granddaughter-in-law, Evie, with rollers in her hair, on the rotary phone, deep in conversation. She took a sip from her cup of hot chocolate, then looked up. She smiled, held up her index finger and mouthed *one minute,* then she went back to her conversation.

Hank nosed around, looking at things on the counter: Evie's keys, a small bowl containing some coins, and a couple of ballpoint pens beside a notepad. He blew some dust off a plastic flower display, then opened the refrigerator door. He checked out the contents of the fridge before closing it. He neared the stove where he found a Hershey's hot chocolate container beside a simmering pot of water. He removed a cup from the cabinet above the stove, where it hung, and mixed himself his own cup of cocoa. He returned to the table where he sat opposite Evie. She was still talking on the phone. He noticed the daily newspaper, front-page up, on the table facing her, so he began to read upside down, mumbling the words to himself.

"Coldest Winter Since the Turn of the Century Hits Texas," he read out loud. He feigned a shiver as Evie concluded her phone call.

Evie stood up, placed the receiver back in the cradle, then bent down, throwing her arms around Hank's neck.

"I'm so glad you could make it for Christmas, Grampa Hank. I've already made their lunch. It's in the refrigerator, just under and to the right of the milk. I made y'all tuna fish sandwiches. There's some potato chips on the counter, in case anyone wants any. Everything else you might need is in the fridge — milk, cookies for dessert. You know where it all is. Oh," she remembered something. "If I'm running late, there's some TV dinners in the freezer — Salisbury steak and chicken. The kids love 'em. I hope you do, too."

"Can I let 'em eat their lunch off of paper plates, Evie? Makes it a whole lot easier when I'm cleaning up."

"Whatever you want to do, Grampa Hank. You're in charge until I get back later this afternoon. Oh . . . That was Ronice Thompson I was talking to on the phone. She'll be by to pick me up in a few minutes, so I'd better go get changed."

She turned and disappeared down the hallway.

Hank was left alone in the kitchen. The only noise he could hear was the muffled soundtrack of the TV show in the living room — a horse's whinny and a kid's voice saying *Good boy, Fury, good boy.* Hank took a final sip of his cocoa, set down the cup, then he stood up and went back through the door and into the living room.

The show was over. The final credits were rolling as Hank crossed the room to where the three children were still laid out in a trance. He wove his way through the maze of human flesh that was stretched out on the couch and two chairs that had been pulled up close to the nineteen-inch screen. He turned off the set. The black-and-white picture whirlpooled itself away, leaving a blank screen.

"Hey, what's going on?" said Josh.

"Why did you do that?" asked Caleb.

"Grampa Hank's here," said Noel, having come out of her TV stupor much sooner than the other two.

"Hi, Grampa Hank," said Josh, jumping up to greet his great-grandfather, along with his younger brother, Caleb.

"When did you get here?" asked both boys at the same time.

Hank moved to his great-granddaughter, lifting her up into his arms.

"A little bird let me in," he said, tweaking her nose.

He winked.

Noel grinned. "Tweet, tweet," she said. "That little bird was me. Are you here to babysit for us, Grampa?" she added.

"I like to think of it more as ridin' herd if you don't mind, sweetheart. Makes your brothers feel better having me around when I call it that."

"Mommy's going to a Christmas party."

"I know that, darlin'."

"She won't be back until it's dark," said Caleb.

"Did that ever happen to you when you were a kid?" asked Noel. "Did your mother ever leave you with someone while she went away?"

"Can't rightly say that she did," said Hank. "Oh, wait. Wait just a minute. It did so happen to me. But not quite for the same reason your mother is doing today. Believe it or not, it was around Christmastime, too . . . *and* it happened in the middle of a record-setting cold spell, just like we're going through now."

Sensing that one of Hank's stories was about to be told, the boys turned their chairs around to face their great-grandfather, who still held Noel in his arms.

The double-tap of a horn honking came from outside. Everyone looked up as Evie, dressed in rubber boots and a calf-length, heavy wool coat, made her way to the front door. Before leaving, she turned to the others who were all looking her way.

"You all know where I'll be. I left an emergency number by the phone in the kitchen, Hank, if you think you need it."

She opened the door to the icy wind, pulled her wool scarf tighter around her neck, then she slipped out as fast as she could, pulling the door closed behind her.

"Anyhow," said Hank. "Where was I? Oh, yeah, I remember now. It all started one day, on my grampa Charley's ranch, when he received a letter from my mother . . ."

Chapter One

1900

A sharp wind was blowing as a single horse, pulling the local U.S. Post Office delivery wagon, trotted its way up the road toward Charley Sunday's Juanita, Texas, ranch house. The frisky animal blew steam from its nostrils after every breath taken. The postman who drove the *mail wagon,* as it was called back then, had passed the all-metal mailbox, secured to a wooden post that stood beside the entrance gate. Charley and his partner, Roscoe Baskin, had shed sweat and tears over that mailbox when putting it in during early fall. It replaced the old, paint-peeled, all-wooden mailbox that had been doing its job just fine for more than eighteen years.

Roscoe Baskin was cleaning his wire-rimmed spectacles with a dishcloth when he heard the noise outside. He peeked through the curtains, then wiped at the

15

steamed-up window glass to watch the postman jump down from his buggy and tie off his horse. He climbed the steps to the back porch, where Roscoe met him at the screen door, having pushed it open to greet the frigid little government worker.

"Mornin', Roscoe," said the postman. "I got a letter here for Charley . . . it's from his daughter, Betty Jean, in Austin."

"Why don't you tell me what she wrote, Toby. You seem to know so much about what's in it."

"I get all my information from the return address on the corner, right there. You know me better than to accuse me of snooping inside the envelope."

"Implying," said Roscoe. "I only implied that you was snoopin'."

He turned and called back inside the house.

"Charley! . . . Toby's here with the mail, an' he's got a special letter here for ya from yer daughter."

Charley's voice echoed from down the hall.

"I'll be right there, Roscoe . . . and don't let Toby leave just yet."

Roscoe turned back to the postman.

"You heard him, Toby. He'll be right here."

The sound of the indoor toilet flushing

could be heard, then Charley appeared, coming from the hallway. He was still buckling up his trousers, pulling his lime-green suspenders up over his shoulders. When he reached the back porch screen door, he took the envelope from the post-man's fingers and circled back to the kitchen, where he sat at the table and called out, once again, for Roscoe.

"Roscoe," he yelled. "Can you bring me my magnifiers?"

Roscoe was at his side in an instant with the reading glasses in hand.

"Thanks," said Charley, taking the wire-rimmed reading spectacles from Roscoe and slipping them on, one ear at a time.

"Danged woman," he mumbled to himself. "I don't know why she insisted that I have a telephone put in here when she never uses it."

By then, Toby, the postman, had followed along into the kitchen, and he casually pulled up a chair on Charley's left. Roscoe took the right-hand seat, then both men leaned in as Charley slit open the envelope with his pocketknife.

"What's she say?" said Roscoe.

"What does she say?" echoed Toby, the postman.

Charley threw back his arms, puffing his

17

chest, to give himself more room before he started reading.

"She ain't going to be saying nothing until you two nosy old maids learn to mind your manners and give me the proper space a man needs to read, for heaven's sake."

The two observers slid their chairs back a few inches on both sides.

"That's better," Charley announced. Then he pulled the one-page letter out of the envelope, shook the paper to get the folds out, adjusted his glasses, and began reading out loud.

"My dearest daddy," the letter began. He hesitated when he noticed Toby, the postman, leaning in from his side, trying to read along with him.

"What are you doing here, Toby?" he asked.

"It was you that asked that I stay," said Toby.

He started to get up.

"But I can leave any time you want me to, Charley," he said. "It's just that . . ."

"Just what?" said Charley.

"Just that . . . there'll be no one to spread the news around town unless I hear what your daughter has to say in her letter."

"Oh, all right, Toby. You can stay. Just be quiet while I'm reading, that's all."

Charley started again.

My dearest Daddy

I know it's unusual that I'd be writing to you again . . . so soon after we both agreed on our plans for the Christmas holiday. But sometimes plans must change. Something very important has come up for Kent. His employer has requested that he be in Kansas City on Christmas Day, and I have decided it is my wifely duty to accompany my husband wherever he must go. Unfortunately, our son, Henry Ellis, has a different idea when it comes to where he'd like to spend the holiday. His wishes are to be with you, Daddy, on your ranch there in Juanita.

His school allows the students a month off for Christmas vacation. That is because it is a private academy, and most of the pupils live such a great distance away, and must travel many miles to reach their homes for the holiday.

Kent and I have discussed this matter, and we both feel that Henry Ellis has proved he is capable of traveling by train all by himself.

Please let me know how you feel about this, Daddy. I think it would be proper if you telephoned me. In our house, that service is paid for by Kent's company, so, you calling me is the better idea. That way, Kent's company won't be charged for the call.

Sincerely,
Your loving daughter,
Betty Jean

After Charley finished reading, there was silence for a few moments while he refolded the letter and tucked it back into the envelope.

"Well," said Roscoe.

"Well, what?"

"Are we gonna be havin' a guest here over Christmas, or not?" asked Roscoe.

"Now, what do you think?"

"I think I'd better finish my route," said Toby.

"You do that," said Charley. "And make sure you tell everyone howdy from Roscoe and me."

"Oh, I surely will," said the postman.

"Oh, I bet you will," said Charley.

The two old Texans watched through the window beside the back porch door as Toby, the postman, untied his horse and climbed into the buggy. Once he was settled into the leather seat, Toby backed the horse, then turned the little wagon around before retracing his path down the entrance road to the farm to the market road that ran parallel to Charley's property line.

"Reckon I'd better telephone Betty Jean so we can make plans concerning Henry Ellis's visit," said Charley.

"Before you make that call," said Roscoe, "don't forget we're supposed ta take the train to San Antone next week anyway so we can pick up the new surrey."

"Damn," said Charley. "I'd nearly forgotten all about that. Maybe we can work it out so we meet Henry Ellis at the train station in San Antonio, and he could ride back here to Juanita with the two of us."

"He'd like that, Charley. He really would."

CHAPTER TWO

Charley Sunday's grandson, Henry Ellis Pritchard, dressed in his brand-new winter suit and overcoat, made his way down the aisle of the passenger car until he found an empty seat toward the rear. It was a window seat, which seemed to brighten his day. He removed a dog-eared dime novel from his side coat pocket, settled back, and began to read.

Something was wrong. He was too warm. He started to take off his overcoat, but a thought stopped him: *If I take off my overcoat, everyone will see that my mother still makes me wear knee pants and stockings, instead of ankle-length trousers like a man.* His thinking was interrupted by a well-dressed gentleman sitting in the seat behind him.

"I don't think removing your overcoat is such a good idea, son," said the man.

Henry Ellis turned around to see just who

it was that was talking to him. He came face-to-face with the middle-aged gentleman in the seat behind him. The man was slight of build, foppish, and wore meticulously trimmed sideburns, plus a well-groomed mustache. A handsome woman was sitting beside the man, and she nodded in recognition of the boy.

The man continued.

"Once this train gets moving," he said, "every unsealed crack between wood frame and glass, both doorways at each end of the car, and the abundance of loose floorboards beneath our feet will let in a tremendous amount of freezing air from outside. As you can see, both my wife and I find it much more comfortable traveling in this weather with our topcoats on. Sorry, let me introduce myself and my wife."

He leaned in closer to the boy.

"I am Dr. Benjamin J. Campbell, and this is my wife, Eleanor. You can call me Ben."

"Pleased to meet you, Ben . . . ma'am," said the boy. "I'm Henry Ellis Pritchard, from Austin, Texas."

"On your way for a Christmas visit somewhere, it appears," said Ben.

"On my way to meet my grandfather. I'll be staying with him over the holiday."

"How long has your grandfather lived in

San Antonio?" asked the woman.

"He doesn't live in San Antone, ma'am," said the boy. "I'm just meeting him there. You see, he and his partner, Roscoe, ordered a new surrey, and they're picking it up in San Antonio. They're picking me up there, too. Then we're all riding back to Juanita together."

"Juanita?" said Ben.

"That's where my grampa lives. I stay with him on his ranch whenever I get the chance."

"It's such a small world we live in," said Ben. "We're on our way to Juanita, as well. My wife just inherited a ranch from a distant cousin, and we're on our way there now to sign the final papers before we take possession."

"Sounds like you're going to be our new neighbors," said Henry Ellis. "What was your cousin's name? It's possible my grampa and I knew him."

"Uh . . ." said Eleanor. "He was such a distant cousin that I never actually met him. But, if your grandfather is from Juanita, I'm sure they must have known one another."

"Yes . . . sure . . . I suppose they did," said Henry Ellis, aware that he hadn't gotten the answer he was searching for.

The train had picked up some speed by

then, and just as Ben had told him, Henry Ellis could feel the icy cold from outside creeping in around them.

"Is there anywhere else on the train where it's a bit warmer?" he asked.

"We spent some time in the gentlemen's car before we arrived in Austin. It may be full of cigar smoke and slick gamblers, but it is a lot warmer than here."

"They have two stoves in the gentlemen's car," added Eleanor. "That's one good reason, I suppose."

"Is it all right if a kid . . . I mean, am I old enough to be in the gentlemen's car?" asked Henry Ellis.

"I don't see why not," said Ben as he started to get to his feet.

Eleanor followed along with him as he moved away.

"Why don't you come with us? No one will bother you. They'll just think you're part of our family."

The three of them entered the gentlemen's car, passing the conductor who was on his way out. He welcomed them all to the car, paying little attention to the boy.

Even though he'd been advised about it, Henry Ellis was still surprised by the amount of cigar smoke hanging low over almost everything. There was a faro wheel, a roulette table, which was closed, and several card tables, with only one being used for a poker game in progress. And even though there were two wood-burning stoves at each end of the car, just the presence of all those bodies jammed into such close quarters kept the car much warmer than the passenger car they were seated in previously.

All the spectator chairs had been taken, so Henry Ellis just stayed close to Ben and Eleanor Campbell. They stood behind the cardplayers and observed while the game was being played.

Something drew the boy's attention to Ben, who stood a few feet away from him. The gentleman's eyes seemed to be glued to one particular cardplayer, a man in a black cutaway coat with red piping, who was sitting with his back to the car's side windows while the barren winter scape passed by outside.

Before too long, two of the players threw in their cards, checking out of the game. The man in the black coat, and the man opposite him, continued to play.

It wasn't but minutes later that a squabble broke out between the two remaining gamblers, with the man nearer the center of the car accusing Black Coat of cheating. Within seconds, both men drew their guns. Seconds later, both pistols discharged, and as the black powder smoke enveloped the entire scene, another shot could be heard. Henry Ellis glanced over to Ben, just in time to see him pocket a small derringer.

By then, there was too much confusion for anyone to know what was happening, and as the smoke finally began to disperse, two bodies could be seen draped over one another, on top of the poker table.

Someone shouted, "By damn. They've shot each other."

"Sure looks that way," said someone else.

"Get the conductor," shouted yet another voice.

Henry Ellis just stood there. He was not watching what was going on around him like everyone else. Instead, his eyes were focused on Ben Campbell's pocket, where the boy knew a murder weapon was now safely hidden away.

The conductor entered the car. And as the crowd spread itself apart to reveal the two bodies, Ben Campbell put his hands on both his wife's and young Henry Ellis's shoulders. "Eleanor . . . son, we don't need to be a part of this. Follow me. We're going back to the passenger car, if no one objects."

Steam hissed from the locomotive's escape valves. It was now stopped on one of the two sidetracks beside a yellow depot. On each end of the building, there were signs that read:

SAN MARCOS, TEXAS
POP. 152

In the dining car, for some late-morning refreshment, the Campbells, along with Henry Ellis, were being joined by the local constable and his deputy, who had come aboard an hour and thirty minutes ago, when the train had made this emergency stop to report the shootings.

" 'Scuse me, ma'am, sir . . . son," said the constable, sliding into a chair opposite the threesome. "My name's George Smithers. I'm the constable here in San Marcos, and this is my assistant, Harry Goodfellow. We're interviewing those who were in the gentlemen's car at the time of the shootings. The conductor said you were there. This shouldn't take long."

"I'm actually his deputy," said Goodfellow. "The constable thinks it sounds more important if he calls me his assistant."

"Thanks for your explanation, Harry," said George Smithers, "but I'll do all the talkin' from now on, if you don't mind."

"Yessir, Constable Smithers," said Goodfellow.

Smithers smiled, then turned his attention to Ben and Eleanor, sitting across from him.

"Did either of you actually see the shooting?" was the constable's first question.

Henry Ellis's face brightened as he leaned forward to speak. But he had second thoughts as he realized the question hadn't been directed to him but to the adults sitting next to him.

"It was very crowded," said Eleanor.

"And we weren't that close at all," added Ben. "But I do think I recognized the man who wore the blue suit. Actually, I have only seen a flyer . . . a poster . . . a wanted poster with a drawing that pretty much resembled the man. You see, in my previous employment, I worked as a clerk for a shipping company in Fort Worth, and we would get those posters all the time, advising us of who might be out there waiting to rob one of the company's cargo wagons."

"So, who was it?" said the constable. "I mean what was the name on the poster with the drawing that looked like the dead gambler in the blue suit?"

Ben took a moment to think before answering.

"Speer," he sputtered. "The first name was something like Melvin . . . Marvin . . . something like that."

"But you're sure of the last name. Speer, was it?"

Ben shook his head.

"I saw that poster more than a year ago, Constable. You must understand that I just can't be sure."

The constable turned to his deputy who was busy taking notes.

"Go back to the office, Harry. Then get over to the telegraph office and contact the central filing office in Austin. See what they have on a Melvin Speer . . . or a Marvin Speer."

"Or maybe it was another name entirely," said Ben. "Like I said, it's been over a year."

Harry was halfway out the door when the constable called for him to stop.

"Harry . . . you may as well forget about that telegram. Just go back to the office and find all the posters we've received in the last few years, and —"

Ben cut him off: "My wife and I will not be here in San Marcos long enough to look through stacks and stacks of wanted posters, Constable."

"Oh," said the lawman. "Those stacks and stacks are gonna be for me and Harry to go through, once you're gone. Right now, we'll go ahead and compare 'em to the dead man in the blue suit, since both bodies are now the official property of our undertaker. I wouldn't think of putting you two through such an ordeal."

"Why, thank you, Constable," said Eleanor. "That's very kind of you."

Henry Ellis watched as the lawman and his deputy excused themselves, then moved on to the next car.

Henry Ellis stared into a void, realizing that what he had to say wouldn't be of interest to anyone, except, maybe . . . his grampa Charley.

CHAPTER THREE

Because of the freezing hailstorm that engulfed the city, Charley Sunday and Roscoe Baskin were watching from inside the San Antonio railroad station for the train carrying Charley's grandson, Henry Ellis. While the hailstones bounced across the wooden planks between depot and tracks, doing an inharmonious tap dance on the station's loading platform, the locomotive pulling the car that carried the boy chugged to a stop.

Charley waited until the engineer released the steam pressure before he went outside. He spotted Henry Ellis preparing to disembark. Using his hat and sheepskin jacket to shield himself from the hail, Charley turned up his collar, then ran down the steps and over to the passenger car where he took charge of his grandson. Charley took the boy's one piece of luggage and told him to get under his jacket, then he marched him back to the depot where Roscoe was waiting inside for both of them.

Charley and Henry Ellis joined Roscoe at a small table near a wood-burning stove, where he had already purchased two cups of coffee and some hot chocolate for Henry Ellis. Charley shook the excess water from his hat and coat as he sat down.

"If it gets any colder, I'll be trading my cattle in for some sheep," said Charley with a wink to Roscoe. "With the wool sheep produce, I could become a millionaire overnight in the wool-blanket business. Or maybe I'll just buy me a blanket farm, outright."

"What's a blanket farm, Grampa?" Henry Ellis wanted to know.

"It's a farm where you plant fleece bales in the spring and harvest wool blankets in the fall," said Charley.

"That's a big windy if I ever heard one," said the boy.

"Well, where do you suppose blankets come from?"

"From wool," answered Henry Ellis. "And wool comes from sheep, like you said."

"I musta meant to say that I'd buy a sheep farm," said Charley.

"Here," said Roscoe, shoving the cup of steaming hot chocolate toward the boy.

"Drink it down so you won't catch your death."

He shoved one of the cups of coffee toward Charley.

"You, too, sheep man. Drink up."

Charley nodded. His hat was still dripping. He blew on the steaming liquid before taking a sip.

At that moment, Henry Ellis happened to see Ben and Eleanor Campbell entering the concourse. He waved.

The Campbells waved back. Then they were on their way.

"Who was that?" asked Charley.

"Just some friends I met on the train from Austin," said the boy. "They are real nice people; I had my noon meal with them today. They're moving to Juanita, you know. Gonna be your neighbors, Grampa."

"Is that a fact?" said Charley. "Is that so?" he said again as he watched the couple disappear through a side door.

"There is something strange about Dr. Campbell, though," said the boy.

"What's that?" asked Charley.

"Well," Henry Ellis began. "There was a shooting on board the train —"

"Shooting?" said Charley, cutting him off. "What kind of a shooting?"

"Two gamblers in the gentlemen's car got

into a fight and shot each other."

"What were you doing in the gentlemen's car?" demanded Charley.

"The Campbells took me in there. They said it would be warmer."

"That's no place for a youngster is what I'm saying," said Charley.

"Do you want to hear about what I saw, Grampa?" said Henry Ellis, "or not?"

"All right, son," said Charley. "Go ahead. Sorry I interrupted you."

Henry Ellis went on.

"Before the men drew their guns, Dr. Campbell looked at one of them like he knew him from somewhere before," said the boy. "Then, when they both went for their guns, Dr. Campbell pulled his own pocket gun and shot the one he appeared not to know . . . at the very same time the two of them shot each other."

"Kinda like he wanted to make sure the guy he was familiar with didn't miss?" said Roscoe.

"Kinda like that," the boy agreed. "Anyway, as soon as Dr. Campbell fired his shot, he put the gun back in his pocket."

"Did you tell the conductor about this . . . about Dr. Campbell being involved, too?" asked Charley.

"I couldn't," said Henry Ellis.

Charley frowned.

"Why?" he asked.

"I couldn't, because I could tell no one else heard the shot, and also because I was still with Dr. and Mrs. Campbell. Besides, later on, Dr. Campbell did tell the constable he recognized the man he had shot from a wanted poster."

"That's still no reason to shoot him . . . even though the man was about to be shot by someone else."

"But he did shoot him, Grampa. Please believe what I say. No one else will even listen to me."

"When they find two bullets in the dead man's body, maybe someone will start believing your story, son," said Roscoe.

"I wouldn't count on that, Roscoe," said Charley. "No one checks out a dead person's body for evidence like they should. In a case like these two gambler fellas killing one another on the train, I'll bet no doctor ever sees those bodies. They'll just lay around in some jail cell until the constable decides to close the case . . . or the smell gets too bad. Then they'll bury both of 'em in the same grave in a potter's field."

"So you're telling me that I should probably just forget what I saw?" said the boy.

"Don't forget it, Henry Ellis, just tuck it

away somewhere in your head until someone does want to hear about it someday."

"In the meantime," said Roscoe, "we got a brand-new surrey waitin' for us to pick it up, and a hotel to check inta, so why don't we get a-goin'?"

"A man told me a while ago that we can pick up a trolley car on the other side of this building that'll take us into the city."

"So, what are we waitin' for?" said Roscoe. "Follow me."

The surrey Charley had ordered stood bright and shiny in the display window, in front of the wagon builder's shop on West Crockett Street near Alamo Square. A matching set of well-behaved bay horses had been hitched to the tongue of the surrey, awaiting their new owner. Someone had tied two large red bows around the horses' necks, which, because of the damp weather, were looking rather droopy. Plus, two shop workers were still busy installing the heavy-duty isinglass curtains that hung down all the way around the slick-looking vehicle, to be used in the same kind of weather that was presently battering the area.

"Did you ever give any thought to getting one of those fancy, newfangled motor cars instead of a surrey to replace your old two-seat buckboard, Grampa?"

"No, son, I reckon I never did," said Charley. "And it'll be a cold day in July before you'll ever hear of me owning one of those cantankerous contraptions."

"Ahh, Grampa," said Henry Ellis. "I sure wish you would change your mind about getting an automobile. It's the turn of a new century. Everyone else seems to be adjusting."

Charley pointed a snubbed finger at the boy.

"If you want one of those funny-looking horseless carriages, son, you go ahead and buy one for yourself," he said. "Otherwise, don't bother me about it again, or wait until you're old enough to drive one yourself."

"Yes, Grampa," said the boy. "Sorry, Grampa."

Roscoe nudged the boy.

"Your grandfather means what he says, Henry Ellis," whispered Roscoe. "He had hisself an experience with one of them whoop-n-bangers a while back, an' he still don't care much ta talk about it."

With that, Roscoe moved on up to where Charley had stopped — directly in front of the shiny new surrey. All Henry Ellis could do was scratch his head.

"Well, here she is, Roscoe, Henry Ellis," said Charley. "Since I knew we'd be driving

38

her back to Juanita, I gave 'em permission to buy me a nice matched set of American trotters, sight unseen. A man looks good when he's being pulled by trotters . . . makes certain folks think he might be a gentleman."

"Can I help you folks?" said a man in a derby hat and work apron, as he stepped out of the barnlike structure behind the surrey.

"Yessir," said Charley. "I'm Charles Abner Sunday from Juanita. I ordered this surrey from you by mail order."

"Oh, yes, Mr. Sunday," said the man. "Why don't you come inside outta the rain and we can complete our transaction."

Not more than an hour later, the trotters trotted down Crockett Street pulling the brand-new surrey behind them. Henry Ellis and Roscoe sat in the rear seat while Charley worked the reins — and oh, yes, a steady drizzle was coming down all around them.

"So, what do you think?" said Charley to the others.

"It's a good ride," said Roscoe.

"Good ride, hell," said Charley. "It's the best damn ride you ever had in your life, Roscoe Baskin."

"I bet an automobile would be more

comfortable," said the boy. "And faster."

"Now, there you go again, Henry Ellis. Didn't I tell you not to be talking about motor cars?"

"Yes, sir," said Henry Ellis. "You sure did. I was just making a comment, that's all."

"Well, keep your comments to yourself, and enjoy the ride."

They were about to make a left turn into the rain-slicked Alamo Plaza when Roscoe saw the warning sign.

"Sign says it's one way around the plaza, Charley. In the *other* direction."

Charley reined up quick, causing the driver of a buggy going with the traffic's flow to rein his horse to the left. It slightly clipped the wagon next to it, leaving no damage — except to the pride of the teamster who was driving. He yelled down to the drivers of both conveyances.

"Don't neither of you two know nothing about workin' yer ribbons? I seen better horse drivin' by a first-time dirt farmer plowin' a rocky field."

And he was gone, whipping his four-up team into another lane, then disappearing into the crowd of other vehicles in front of him.

About then, a traffic cop in his gray uniform, wearing a slicker to keep him dry, saw what was happening, and he moved over to the confused Charley.

"Anything I can help you with, sir?" asked the policeman.

"All I want to do is get from here across to that hotel over there," said Charley.

"You ever driven this rig in a big city before, sir?"

"Bigger cities than this one," Charley answered back.

The cop took Charley's answer with a grain of salt. He knew perfectly well that the old man was not being completely honest with him.

"How about I slide in there next to you, sir. Let me have the leathers and I'll get you and your friends over to your hotel quicker'n a duck on a June bug."

Charley leaned in closer to the cop so those in the rear seat couldn't hear him.

"Thank you, but no thank you, Officer," said Charley. "I'm afraid that would be a little too embarrassing for me. In front of my grandson," he added with a wink.

He nodded toward Henry Ellis in the rear seat. The boy was too busy watching the surrounding activity — vehicular and pedestrian — to deal with the traffic, let alone the bad weather.

"Seriously, Mr. . . ."

"Sunday," said Charley. "Charles Abner Sunday. I just bought this here surrey. Gonna drive her all the way back home to Juanita, I am."

"That's fine, Mr. Sunday," said the cop. "That's country driving. What you're in the middle of here is city driving. But for now, I just want to get you over there to your hotel. What would you say if I walked in front of you and stopped some of the other wagons and buggies . . . just to make sure you get yourself, your friend . . . and your grandson, over to the hotel?"

"I don't think you doing that would bother me so much, Officer," said Charley. "I thank you. Lead on."

The cop held up his wet, white-gloved hands, then he stepped out into the plaza — and its puddles. He put a whistle between his lips and used it in synchronization with his arms to stop all the traffic moving around the one-way concourse. When he was sure he had the attention of every single driver, he moved out slowly — avoiding the deeper pools of rainwater — with Charley driving the surrey across the wide cobblestone square, until he reached the other side. Once there, the cop suggested that Charley pull the surrey to a stop directly in front of the Menger Hotel, an elegant, stone structure that appeared to take up the entire city block.

The crack of a gunshot rang out, and a voice screamed from inside.

"I'm being robbed! They're taking everything I have in the shop."

Three men came running out of a jewelry store — one shop out of many doing business in the storefronts that were a part of the elaborate hotel's stone facade.

Behind them came the jeweler, a partially balding man in his late forties, still wearing his jeweler's eyepiece. He spotted the cop.

"Help . . . Police. I've just been robbed."

As the escaping thieves continued to run right at him, the traffic cop reached for his side weapon — which wasn't there, because he was directing traffic and not walking a beat.

When the robbers saw the officer was unarmed, they slowed down. Then they aimed their weapons at him.

Three shots in quick succession exploded from behind the cop. The robbers clutched their wounds and pitched forward, one of them dropping the bag of stolen loot as he slid along the cobblestone gutter at the curb. His body came to rest just inches from the cop's feet. The other two robbers landed not that far away.

The cop looked down at his empty hand. Then he glanced behind him.

On the other side of the trembling horses, Charley sat smiling in the surrey's front seat, his smoking Walker Colt in one hand, the horses' reins in the other.

The cop could only stare at the old man in the surrey with the large revolver. He didn't say anything, because his jaw had dropped four inches when Charley's bullets whizzed past his head before burying themselves in the three jewelry-store bandits.

After a long moment, the other drivers in the plaza whipped up their teams. Traffic resumed to normal within minutes.

Someone inside one of the shops who had witnessed the shooting must have called the police, because it wasn't that long before the clanging bell of an approaching police wagon was heard growing closer and closer.

By the time the law enforcement vehicle arrived, the traffic cop had recovered the bag of jewelry and was standing over the wounded robbers on the boardwalk, talking with Charley, who had gotten out of the surrey. The hotel doorman had joined the two. Roscoe and Henry Ellis remained in the surrey's rear seat waiting for a reason to disembark.

Charley called over to his partner.

"Roscoe," he said. "Take Henry Ellis inside. There's no reason for him to be seeing this. And have a bellhop come out for our luggage, what little we got. I'll be there in a minute to get us registered."

Roscoe helped Henry Ellis out of the surrey, skirting the crime scene with the boy. They entered the hotel through another entrance several yards away.

"I shoulda known you'd been in law enforcement just by looking at you," the traffic cop was saying.

"What I can't figure out is why a member of the San Antonio City Police Department ain't toting a gun," said Charley.

"That's the way they're doing it nowadays in most big cities," said the cop. "We're what they call 'departmentalized.' And the rules are, the traffic department don't carry weapons."

"You realize that if I hadn't been there, you'd be dead, don't you?"

"I sure do, Mr. Sunday. And that's something I'd like you to talk to my chief about, if you would."

"It'd be my pleasure," said Charley. "But, I don't have the time to be going to your station."

"That's all right," said the cop. "The chief's with the bunch that just pulled up in the wagon. Matter of fact, he's coming this way right now."

"You'll have to excuse me for just a minute, though," said Charley. "I gotta run inside this here hotel and register. My friend and my grandson need to get to our room."

He turned away quickly, almost colliding with a bellboy who was carrying their luggage toward the hotel entrance.

"Here," he said. "Let me give you a hand with that, son. It's only right that I do, because most of it belongs to me anyway."

He took the largest carpetbag of the three, turned, and went inside.

The bellboy just stood there for a moment, while the quizzical look in his face turned into a wide grin. In his hand was a shiny ten-cent coin, slipped to him by Charley during the luggage extrication.

The lobby of the Menger Hotel was large and airy, with a huge longhorn steer's head and horns mounted over the main entrance. The floors were solid marble, causing voices and footsteps to produce hollow echoes throughout the enormous expanse.

Charley saw Roscoe and Henry Ellis sitting on a circular divan near the front desk. He waved to them as he passed on his way to deal with the desk clerk.

The clerk stood at attention behind the

desk, a room key held to the proper height in front of him.

"Welcome to the Menger, Mr. Sunday. You're in room three oh four, as requested."

"Folding bed for my grandson?"

"Already in the room," said the clerk.

"Well, thank you, James. You tell the bellboy where we are, an—"

He stopped, setting his personal carpetbag on the counter in front of the clerk. "And you can give him my bag, too. He's already got his tip."

An hour later, the three of them had settled into their hotel room. Two brass beds, plus a smaller fold-up, took up most of the floor space. Roscoe lay on one bed, the boy rested on his fold-up. There was a muffled flushing of a toilet, then Charley emerged from the bathroom, pulling his lime-green suspenders up over his shoulders.

"Ain't nothing like indoor plumbing is what I say," said Charley.

He glanced around the room and saw the others stretched out on their beds. Charley could sense that Roscoe was about to start snoring.

"Hey!" he shouted. "It's still daylight outside, to hell with the nasty weather. We promised to show Henry Ellis this historical city, Roscoe Baskin. And if you don't have the energy ta go out again today, I'll take the boy myself."

The surrey, with its isinglass curtains still rolled down against the weather, traveled along another San Antonio byway. The trotters were moving briskly as the rain had let up some, and they were now on the outskirts of town where the traffic was much lighter. Roscoe was sitting in the rear seat by himself. Henry Ellis was up front, beside his grandfather, pointing at everything they passed. Charley drove the team.

"Where are you taking us, Charley?" Roscoe wanted to know.

"I thought I'd start out by showing the boy the San Antonio River. If you want to see how it's supposed to look, you have to get out of town aways. Back in the city, the river has darn near become a sewer, with everyone using it as a garbage pit, or a place to toss their junk. Don't you worry yourself, Roscoe Baskin, we're almost there."

Within minutes, Charley had pulled the surrey over to the side of the road and was pointing out the San Antonio River to both Henry Ellis and Roscoe. They all stayed inside the vehicle because the rain had started to beat down harder, and the air was becoming much colder.

"I thought she'd be bigger," said Roscoe.

"She's bigger than usual right now because of the rain," Charley told him. "Though there've been times when folks have dammed her up in places to collect the water in big ponds for their livestock."

A bright flash of lightning filled the sky overhead, followed by rolling thunder. The rain was now coming down in torrents.

"Well," said Charley over the pounding rain on the canvas top. "I wanted to stop by the missions of San Antonio on the way back, but in this weather, I reckon I'll just hafta point 'em out to you as we drive by . . . if we can even see 'em."

"There's a lot of history right there in the Menger, too," said Charley. "And you don't have to get all wet seeing it."

He leaned forward and wiped away some condensation from the inside of the isinglass in front of him.

"We'll be home before you know it, Roscoe. I'm getting kind of hungry, too."

The three of them sat at a small table in the Menger Hotel bar, eating roast beef sandwiches.

"Sorry it's so dark in here, Henry Ellis," said Charley. "But everything being made of dark wood, like it is, doesn't give the available light anything to reflect from."

"Plus, it's a dark and dingy day to begin with," added Roscoe.

"But it sure is pretty," said Henry Ellis. "It's exactly what Rod told me it'd look like. The hand-carved wooden support posts, the bar itself, the narrow stairway leading to the balcony upstairs, even that big ol' moose head hanging over the door." He pointed. "And just being in the same room where Teddy Roosevelt signed up a bunch of the men for his Rough Riders is enough to keep me happy for the rest of the year."

"This bar is famous for more than just Teddy Roosevelt signing up the Rough Riders, Henry Ellis," said Charley. "This bar is where Roscoe Baskin faced off with three dangerous outlaws back in 1878."

"Really?" said the boy.

"It was two drunken trail hands, not no dangerous outlaws, Charley Sunday," said Roscoe. "An' it was a fistfight, not no gunfight. They punched me until I was too tired ta hold my hands up. And then they stole my badge."

"They got away with your Texas Ranger badge?" said Henry Ellis.

"I'd'a never got it back without Charley's help," he said. "Charley buffaloed 'em both with his Walker Colt. Then he made 'em apologize to me an' pin my badge back on my vest."

"Wow," said the boy.

"An' another time here in the Menger bar," said Roscoe, "your grandfather caught up with a three-man gang of bank robbers, who'd stopped in for a belly-warmer before makin' their getaway."

"That's right, son," said Charley. "I chased 'em as far as Pipe's Creek, and then some, before I caught 'em. Some folks still like to say that they were remnants of the old Jesse James gang come to Texas to try their luck in a new territory, but after we got 'em behind bars, it turned out they were just a bunch of war veterans, about my age, trying to put a little excitement back into their lives."

"An' what about the time ol' Feather Martin got hisself so liquored up in the Bull's Head Saloon up in Waco that he didn't remember how he got here when he woke up under a table in the Menger bar? Even today, old Feather don't have no recollection about the ride that brung him here."

A bright flash of lightning illuminated the small window in the outside door. That was followed by a loud clap of thunder that rattled the old bar's wooden structure.

The bartender came out from behind the bar, cracked the door, and peeked outside. The rain was coming down in sheets.

"I don't think we'll be going out anymore this afternoon," said Charley.

"Not unless one of those lightning bolts strikes this hotel," said Roscoe.

"Hell," said Charley. "We're wasting good sleeping weather. Why don't we all go upstairs for a nap until suppertime?"

"You'll get no argument from me on that one, C.A.," said Roscoe.

All Henry Ellis could add to the conversation was a big, wide yawn.

CHAPTER FOUR

They left San Antonio a little before six in the morning. The rain had stopped for a while, but the temperature outside was still in the low twenties.

By seven, they were beyond the city limits, on the road that paralleled the railroad tracks all the way to Juanita. As usual, Charley drove the surrey, while Roscoe sat beside a still sleeping Henry Ellis, both covered with heavy blankets, in the rear.

"I reckon we'll be home in two days," said Charley, attempting to start a conversation.

"Two or three don't matter none ta me," said Roscoe. "Just as long as I can stay here beside Henry Ellis, wrapped in these warm, comfortable blankets."

"There're several other towns we'll pass through on the way. We'll stop in Hondo tonight," Charley told them. "It's still down the road a spell. They got a little boarding-house there where we can stay the night.

They'll feed us and take care of the horses, too." A few drops of rain began to spot the isinglass in front of Charley's eyes.

"Another storm like the one we had last night," said Charley, "could slow us down some. But not enough that we couldn't make up the time once the rain stops."

"What makes ya think it'll ever stop?" said Roscoe.

"Oh," said Charley. "I just got that feeling."

"Yeah," answered Roscoe. "A feelin' like the one you got back in '73, when you said John Wesley Hardin would never come as far west as Del Rio. And then, there he was, plain as day, sittin' in Maria's Cantina that day you, Feather, an' me decided to take our noon meal in that joint."

"When we were stationed in Del Rio, Roscoe, we always took our noon meal at Maria's Cantina."

"Anyway, there we were. Someone mentioned Hardin's name an' you had that feelin' about him not bein' that far west. We made a bet on it, and you had ta go over an' tap him on the shoulder ta see if it really was him."

There was a long pause.

"Well . . . was it John Wesley Hardin, or wasn't it?" asked Henry Ellis, who had just awakened.

Charley glanced over his shoulder with a big grin.

"Oh, it was Hardin all right . . . and thank God he was waiting for someone else, or I'd'a been a dead man for sure that day."

"Wow," said Henry Ellis. "You almost got shot dead by John Wesley Hardin. That's something I'll have to tell all my friends about when I get back to Austin."

"Ol' John Wesley hadn't even drawed his gun," said Roscoe. "He threw his arms around yer grampa an' dern near hugged 'im ta death, is how I saw it. But then he did draw his gun, an' he killed the sheriff who was comin' through the back door to arrest him."

"Using me as a shield," said Charley. "He never knew I was a Ranger, and I didn't tell him. It never hurts to keep your mouth shut when opening it at the wrong time might get you killed."

"Me an' Feather didn't say nothin', either," said Roscoe. "We knew ta foller exactly what Charley was doin'."

"Was John Wesley Hardin fast enough that he could have shot all three of you before any of you could have shot him?" asked the boy.

"Fast, son," said Charley. "John Wesley

55

Hardin was the fastest man alive back in those days. Every lawman in Texas, at that time, couldn't hold a candle to him. That's why we done what we did that day."

"An' no one called us cowards fer not standin' up to him, either," said Roscoe. "It was a known fact that you didn't want ta face ol' John Wesley. That is, unless you wanted ta get yer dang head blowed off."

A train whistle blew from somewhere in back of them. All heads turned to see a continuous rope of black smoke moving up on them from behind. The rain was coming down harder than before, and the engineer had his headlamp on, even though it was still daylight outside.

"Any other time, I'd race that steam-spitting son of a gun into town," said Charley. "But the road is so muddy, I'm afraid these two trotters might get their hooves gummed up and start slipping and sliding."

Henry Ellis had turned all the way around to have a better view of the oncoming train through the isinglass at the rear of the surrey.

His mouth appeared to be locked in a perpetual grin as the locomotive drew up beside them and passed.

For a brief moment, Henry Ellis caught a

glimpse of Ben and Eleanor Campbell sitting at a window in the passenger car. They were both waving at the surrey as the train roared by. The boy waved back, but the foggy weather and the rainwater collected on the isinglass must have prevented them from seeing him.

The train grew smaller as it gained distance, and eventually they were back to the regular slip-slopping of the trotters pulling the rig through the mud.

A sign beside the road said:

HONDO, TEXAS – 4 MI.

"When we get to Hondo," said Charley, "there's a little boardinghouse just the other side of town; it's run by an old friend of mine, Bertie Clyde. She makes the finest blueberry-plumb butter in the state of Texas. That's where we'll stay tonight, if she's got an available room. Just wait until breakfast rolls around tomorrow morning, and you spread that blueberry-plumb butter on a slice of warm bread. Greatest taste since huckleberry pie."

"I hope she keeps a fire goin' all night," said Roscoe. "One thing I need during the winter is a warm room ta sleep in."

"She even puts hot bricks between your sheets so your bed will be nice and warm when you climb in at night," said Charley.

"She's some woman," said Roscoe, pulling the blanket that was covering him up around his neck.

"It all sounds real comfy to me," said Henry Ellis. "I hope we get there soon because I'm getting hungry."

He pulled the dime novel out of his pocket, found his place, then began reading.

"What's that ya got there, Henry Ellis?" asked Roscoe.

"Just an ol' dime novel," said the boy. "I brought it along to help pass the time."

"Bertie Clyde also makes the best pork stew you ever tasted, son," said Charley, continuing his own conversation. "It's even better during spring and summertime when her vegetables are fresh, instead of preserved in glass jars."

About a half hour later, when the rain had turned into a light drizzle, Charley sat up straight in the front seat.

"What's the matter, Grampa?" asked Henry Ellis, closing, then repocketing the book.

"Oh, nothing much, son. I just thought

that train would have cleared Hondo by now and been halfway to Uvalde. Instead, it's sitting right there by the station on a sidetrack, with half the town gathered around her."

Both Henry Ellis and Roscoe leaned forward. They looked across Charley's broad shoulders to see the rear car of the train — the gentlemen's car — stopped dead on the sidetrack, with a little red lantern hanging off the rear railing, glowing in the afternoon gray.

Charley laid the lines to the trotters' rumps, and the horses pulled the surrey over to where the crowd was gathered. The town marshal and two deputies stood talking with the conductor, engineer, fireman, and the baggage car clerk. Two others — obviously high-ranking townsmen — stood nearby. All were somewhat surprised when Charley climbed out of the surrey to join them in their conversation.

"Charles Abner Sunday," said Charley as he shoved his hand into the hand of the marshal. The two men shook. "I'm a retired Ranger from down Juanita way, and it looks to me like something's happened with this train."

"Another robbery, Mr. Sunday," said the conductor.

"It was the Cropper Brothers and their gang," added the clerk. "I know it was them. The one called Dale kept a gun on me the whole time."

"How much did they get?" asked Charley.

"They didn't get nothin'," said the clerk.

"You gotta be kidding me," said Charley. "They got nothing?"

"They got nothin' because we wasn't carryin' nothin'," said the clerk. "But we're pickin' up a big shipment of freshly minted twenty-dollar coins here in Hondo. The government decided to transfer the coins by wagon from San Antonio to our bank here in Hondo. They suspected the Croppers would hit the train between San Antonio and here, and they were right."

The marshal cut in.

"Now we're going to load up them coins inta the baggage car," he said, "where they'll ride safely all the way to El Paso. That's because the government has hired my two deputies to ride along with the shipment, just in case anyone else might want to make a try."

"Well, my partner, my grandson, and me are headed as far as Juanita in that red surrey over there. If they don't go too fast with the train, we should be able to keep up with you and serve as backup if someone else

60

does try to steal those coins."

At the edge of the crowd, Henry Ellis climbed down from the surrey, followed by Roscoe. As Roscoe started off to join Charley and the others, the boy caught a glimpse of Ben and Eleanor Campbell, who were avoiding the drizzle by standing on the depot porch, trying to stay warm. The boy's eyes widened, then he ran over to them.

"Dr. and Mrs. Campbell," he yelled. "It's good to see you."

"It's good to see you, too, Henry Ellis," said Ben as the boy ran up the steps to join them.

"Did you see the robbery?" Henry Ellis asked.

"Not so we'd make good witnesses," said Ben. "We saw them when they rode alongside our train car; they were wearing masks. But most of the robbing was done after they boarded the baggage car and went inside."

"I don't think they got much," said Eleanor. "I heard some townsfolk saying the train wasn't carrying anything of value."

"My grampa will know," said the boy. "He's over there with the marshal and the train crew." He pointed.

"I understand the train will remain here in Hondo overnight," said Ben. "Maybe you, your grandfather, and his friend could take supper with us this evening."

"Well . . . we're supposed to be staying at a friend of my grampa's boardinghouse tonight. But I'll tell him you invited us to join you, anyway."

"The railroad is putting us up in the only hotel in Hondo, the Lawry House," said Ben. "I'm sure there'll be a nice restaurant nearby."

"I'll tell my grampa when I see him. Right now, I better go find him. He could be worrying about where I am."

Bertie Clyde's Boardinghouse was one of the five fully built structures that made up Main Street in Hondo, Texas. The rest of the businesses were tent houses — a wooden floor, built three feet above ground, with three-foot sides. On top of the structures was a frame, covered with canvas — all with hopes of becoming full-fledged buildings as the town continued to grow. The Lawry House Hotel, at the other end of the street, had two stories with four rooms upstairs, and a lobby and small café on the ground floor. Not big, but plenty big for Hondo, Texas.

Bertie's, as the locals called the boardinghouse, was tucked in between Slawson's Saloon, one of the canvas-covered buildings, and the City Marshal's Office and Jail, which had been built from rocks found locally. It was around five o'clock in the evening when Charley pulled up in front of the old wooden building in the surrey. Even though the rain had started to come down harder again, Charley stepped down from the vehicle and went about tying off the trotters. Roscoe and Henry Ellis slid out of the backseat and to the muddy ground, joining Charley as they climbed the steps to the front porch of Bertie's and went inside.

All three of them stood in the vestibule to shed their topcoats. As they turned to go farther on into the boardinghouse, they were met by a short, gray-haired woman, wearing a white apron over her calico housedress.

"Charley Sunday, you old law-dog," said the woman, grinning from ear to ear. "What brings you to Hondo?"

Charley threw a big hug around the woman, kissing her fondly on the cheek.

"Nice to see you, Bertie," said Charley. He stepped back.

"We were just passing through on the way back to Juanita when we saw that the train was stopped here. When we found out there had been an attempted robbery, I offered our assistance to the town marshal . . . We'll be following along with the train from now on, just in case someone else decides to rob her again."

Bertie's eye finally caught sight of Roscoe.

"And, Roscoe," she said much louder. "What are you doin' these days? Still running around with this handsome old charmer?"

"I sure am, Miss Bertie," said Roscoe. "We both retired from Rangerin' around the same time, and we decided ta buy a ranch together."

Charley threw him a distinct frown.

"Well," Roscoe went on. "It was Charley who bought the ranch. I just hang around an' help him fix things. I do all the cookin', too."

"We need a room that'll hold three for the night," said Charley.

Bertie glanced around, squinting.

"Three?" she said. "Where's the other one? Don't tell me you got ol' Feather Martin with ya, too."

"No, Bertie," said Charley. "Feather's back in Juanita, taking care of the ranch and my cattle. We have my grandson, Henry Ellis, with us."

Henry Ellis stepped out from behind the two men, and with his hat in hand, he bowed to Bertie Clyde.

"Name's Henry Ellis Pritchard, ma'am. Charley's my grampa. Nice to meet you."

He held out his hand, and the two of them shook.

"Pleased ta meet you, too, Henry Ellis," said Bertie. "You must be Betty Jean's boy. My, how you've growed up."

"So, can you help us out?" said Charley, changing the subject. "Do you have a room that'll hold us all?"

"Oh, I think I might have a room available that'll hold you three. What about your animals?" she asked.

"We're not on horseback this trip, Bertie," said Charley. "I just bought a new surrey in San Antonio. We got two brand-new trotters pulling it. You wouldn't happen to have a couple of spare stalls and feed for them in your barn out back, would you?"

" 'Course I do," said Bertie. "I got more room in the barn than I do in the house. I've been known ta put people up out there in the barn . . . when the weather's good."

"Just so my trotters don't freeze to death, Bertie," said Charley.

"I got plenty of horse blankets out there in the barn," said Bertie. "Plus some oil lamps that'll help keep the cold out."

"That'll do for one night, I s'pect," said Charley. "I just hope none of the animals kick over one of those lamps."

"These're hangin' lamps, Charley. They're up too high to get kicked."

"Hearing that puts my mind at ease, Bertie," said Charley. "Otherwise I was going to have Roscoe sleep out there with the trotters."

"Me?" said Roscoe. "You was gonna ask me to sleep out in the barn?"

"It woulda been just for the one night, Roscoe," said Charley. "One night sleeping in the barn never hurt no one."

A flash of lightning lit up the vestibule, followed by a loud clap of thunder. Henry Ellis pulled the door closed behind them, as the rain had started to come down harder again.

"I'll show you to yer room, gents," said Bertie. "Then I'll have Juan, my handyman, help you put away the horses. I serve supper around here at five p.m. sharp. No need ta dress up at my table, Charley, but I do get a little touchy if someone shows up with dirty hands. You can wash up out on the back porch. I had a water spigot installed out there to help me with my laundry."

"Oh, Lord-a-mighty," said Henry Ellis, throwing his hands into the air.

Everyone turned to the boy.

"What's the matter, son?" said Charley.

"I promised Dr. and Mrs. Campbell that we'd join them for supper tonight."

"That's all right," said Charley. "They're your friends, so why don't you go on and join them. Roscoe and me got a lot of catching up to do here with Bertie, so we'll take our evening meal with her.

"Just be back here before eight o'clock, son, if you know what's good for you."

Ben and Eleanor Campbell were only a little bit upset when Henry Ellis showed up alone for their supper engagement. Ben told the boy that he'd really been looking forward to talking with his grandfather and his friend, because Ben had never conversed with any real Texas Rangers in person before. So, without Charley and Roscoe, Ben and Eleanor bundled up some more, and the three of them walked up the boardwalk, two buildings from the hotel, where Eleanor had found a little restaurant earlier, and they went inside.

At the same time, Charley and Roscoe joined Bertie and some of her regular boarders at the dining table.

One of the regular diners was Nathan Hambler, the local druggist. Another was Annabelle Troutman, a nurse who worked in the local doctor's office. Plus, a third person, who joined the table a few minutes after five with the excuse that he'd been caught in a downpour on his way home from the office, was one of the two deputy marshals Charley had met at the train station earlier.

"Pleased ta meet you again, Mr. Sunday," he said as he sat down and removed his hat. "Name's Buck Wadell, deputy marshal here in Hondo. We met earlier today."

"Nice to officially meet you, Buck. Anything new on the train robbery?" asked Charley as the local lawman tucked his napkin into his collar, then stuck a fork into a chicken thigh on the large plate in the table's center.

"Just that we've officially identified the robbers as the Cropper Brothers' Gang. Turns out one of the passengers had gone to school with the Croppers. They all grew up together in Eagle Pass . . . the witness, and Sam and Dale."

"We had the pleasure of meeting Sam and Dale Cropper a year or so back, when they tried to rob a train we were on headed for Denver," said Charley. "We ended up getting the drop on the ones who boarded the train, and the last we saw any of 'em, they were being hauled off to jail by some local Colorado badges."

"Well," the deputy went on, "Sam and Dale escaped from prison a few months back, and they've been robbing trains along this San Antonio to El Paso line ever since. They've even become local legends in several counties."

"Any idea where they hole up?" asked Roscoe.

"The marshal thinks they're here in the area somewhere. Close to a town so they can easily get information on shipments and time schedules."

He pulled his handkerchief from a rear pocket and blew his nose again, wadding it up, then returning the soiled cloth to the same pocket he had retrieved it from.

"Damn," he said. "I almost forgot to tell you folks what time the train's pulling out tomorrow morning. Passengers board at five forty-five, train departs at six . . . sharp. I'll be the early bird come tomorrow morning," he added, "because it's my job to make sure all the passengers make it to the train on schedule. I'll get you folks up earlier because I know harnessing and hitching two horses can take some time."

"Thank you, son, but we can wake ourselves up on our own just fine," said Charley. "And Roscoe here is probably the fastest harnesser and hitcher in all of Kinney

County, so we won't be late. That's for sure."

"When'll we eat?" asked Roscoe.

"Since a few of the passengers are staying with Bertie Clyde, just like us, the marshal has made arrangements for your breakfast to be served at four a.m. . . . sharp."

"We'll be here," said Roscoe.

"Then all of us better be thinking about going to bed early, don't you think?" asked Henry Ellis, who had just returned from supper with the Campbells.

Charley winked at the boy before turning back to the deputy.

"I reckon I never told you that I got me a real smart grandson, did I?" He winked again.

CHAPTER FIVE

Henry Ellis lay in his hotel bed thinking, while Roscoe and his grandpa Charley fell asleep immediately. Charley had taken the main bed, while Roscoe grabbed the smaller second. All that was left for the boy to sleep on was a rickety old chesterfield over in the corner.

As Charley and Roscoe began to snore, rattling the windows and doors as if a freight train were passing, the boy closed his eyes and began to think of that time, over a year ago, when he and Grampa Charley, Roscoe, and their friend, Feather Martin, took the northbound train out of Del Rio, with hopes of reaching Denver, Colorado, in time to participate in the longhorn cattle auction. The auction that would eventually terminate in the cross-country cattle drive that would bring the longhorns back to Texas where they belonged. As Henry Ellis began to drift off to sleep, his thoughts turned into a reverie, of sorts, reminding the boy of that particular time in his past.

Inside the train's darkened mail car nothing moved except Charley's dog Buster's hind leg. The dog had begun scratching himself behind his left ear.

"Can't you hush him up?" whispered Charley.

Henry Ellis took hold of Buster's rear paw and the scratching stopped.

The boy's eyes widened considerably as the rear door burst open.

Sam Cropper, followed by his brother, Dale, and three other outlaws, stepped quietly into the darkened mail car.

Their only source of light was the orange glow from the tiny flame inside a lantern's globe on the box that had been used earlier as a card table. Nothing moved — no sound was heard — until a loud snore cut the air.

Five revolvers were cocked in unison. "What was that?" said Dale.

Another snore was heard — all eyes turned in the direction of the obtrusive reverberation.

And there he was in all his glorious splendor — Feather Martin. He was still passed out cold, only now he lay faceup on a pile of empty mail pouches. And right there on the other side of Feather was the iron strongbox containing the mine payroll.

"There it is," said Sam Cropper.

"So far this has been like slicing butter . . . real smooth," said Brother Dale.

"Well, don't just stand there waitin' for it to come to you," said Sam. "Go on over there an' get it."

"Obliged," said Dale, motioning for the three henchmen to follow.

As they all decided at once to step over Feather, instead of going around him, Feather passed some gas and turned over so he was facedown. One of the bandits stopped in his tracks, directly over Feather, where he got a good whiff of the recently expelled vapors.

"Oh, hell," he said, gagging. "That's enough to strangle a boat full a' water rats."

"Don't be wasting time," said Dale. "Get your butt on over here."

Since Feather's spurs were now positioned "rowels up," it didn't take that much for them to hook on to the outlaw's own spur rowels. When the outlaw reached out to regain his balance, he grabbed hold of a large piece of Dale's shirtsleeve. Dale reached out for something to grab himself, and he latched on to the other two bandits' shirt collars, causing all four of them to fall on top of Feather in a mangled pile.

"Jeeezus God!" yelled Feather, and a shot rang out.

A few more bullets were expelled, with their black powder flashes lighting up the mail car with each explosion.

From where he'd hidden himself at the other end of the car, Henry Ellis could barely make out what was happening those few yards in front of him. The one thing he could feel was the long hair of Buster's coat, reminding him that the dog was still at his side.

"Go get 'em, Buster," he urged. "Go help Grampa and Uncle Roscoe."

Buster let out a nasty growl. Then he began barking as loud as he could.

Eventually the confusion and tumult of the sightless fight came to an end.

A match was struck and another lantern's wick was lighted. As the flame was turned up and the glass brought down, the interior grew brighter. It was apparent Roscoe, Feather, and Buster had everything under control.

At first, Henry Ellis grinned in relief, but when the door behind the others swung open to reveal the two marshals with their weapons cocked and ready, his smile faded completely.

"Everyone hold it right there," the first marshal shouted.

"You're all covered," said marshal number two.

Buster hadn't moved an inch. He remained

standing in the same place and continued barking.

Relief was now showing on Sam and Dale Cropper's faces as well as their three henchmen.

Roscoe and Feather raised their hands as soon as they figured out whose side the marshals were really on.

Sam turned to his brother.

"Dale . . . you and those other three open the side loading door and shove that payroll box off the train."

Dale and the men nodded. Dale took care of the door while the others went to the locked iron box and began their struggle to slide the heavy container across the rough floor planks. It wasn't an easy job.

One of the marshals turned to Sam. "You better get someone to go back and tell the rest of your gang what's happened, pronto," he said.

Sam nodded. "I'll have them send a wagon up here for the strongbox."

Buster's barking was incessant. The dog wouldn't stop.

"But before I go, I'm going to shut that dog up once and for all." He raised his revolver and pulled back the hammer, slowly aiming at the defiant canine. Buster stood his ground with Henry Ellis's arms wrapped tightly around him.

"Get away, kid," said Sam Cropper, motioning with his gun's barrel.

Like Buster, Henry Ellis wouldn't budge.

"I said get away!" repeated the gunman. "I'm going to shoot that dog and I don't want to hurt no kid while I'm doing it."

"If you do, it'll be over my dead body."

It was Charley's voice coming from behind a shipping crate. He slowly stood up with his Walker Colt aimed directly at Sam Cropper.

The outlaw realized it was all over. He immediately cocked his gun.

BLAM! BLAM!

Henry Ellis sat up straight on his sofa bed. The gunshots in his dream had become real gunshots.

Both Charley and Roscoe were on their feet in a beat; both had literally jumped out of their beds. Having gone to sleep fully clothed, the two ex-lawmen grabbed their weapons and immediately bolted for the door, disappearing into the hallway.

Henry Ellis swung out of his own bed and raced to the nearest window. He threw open the sash, then peered out onto the main street of Hondo.

Icy crystals on the frozen ground reflected a sparkling glitter throughout the little berg.

Near the marshal's office, Henry Ellis could see three horsemen, still in their saddles, firing their guns into the windows and doors of the marshal's office. The marshal, Henry Ellis could only assume, was firing back whenever he found an opening, as one window shattered after the other.

Within moments, there was a clattering of boots on the boardwalk in front of the boardinghouse below Henry Ellis's perch. Charley, followed by Roscoe and the deputy called Buck Wadell, moved out into the street with all guns blazing.

One of the horsemen was hit, and when his spur hung up in his stirrup as he fell from the saddle, his horse made its getaway, dragging the man across the frozen mud until the stirrup broke, freeing his boot. The frightened animal kept on going, running on past the depot at the eastern entrance to the settlement.

The other two outlaws, who had come for the newly minted coins being stored in the marshal's office, were forced to hang on to their weapons while they mounted their skittish animals. Once they were aboard, they had a brief exchange of gunfire with Roscoe and Charley, before spurring out and nearly running down the two ex-Rangers as they made their getaway, heading out of town in the opposite direction.

Henry Ellis continued to watch from the hotel window as the deputy called Buck dragged the dead outlaw's body, by one boot, over to where Charley and Roscoe were standing in front of the marshal's office.

"Never saw this one before in my whole life," said the deputy. "Did either of you gents get a good look at them other two?"

"Too dark," said Charley. "Otherwise we'd be hauling those two by their boots, just like you're doing with that one."

"It is dark, all right," said the deputy. "I reckon it was just a lucky shot brought this one down, 'cause I ain't no sharpshooter, even in daylight."

About then, the marshal stepped out onto the boardwalk. He took a look at the dead man, then turned to Charley.

"Was it you that nailed him, Mr. Sunday?" he asked.

" 'Fraid not, Marshal," answered Charley. "It was your deputy Buck over there who knocked him outta the saddle. Being dragged along by his horse like he was is probably what killed him."

The marshal crossed over to where his deputy was still standing — gun in one hand, the outlaw's boot in the other.

"Ya think you might wanna turn that body over to the undertaker, Buck? You look pretty silly standin' out here in the cold hangin' on to him by one foot."

Buck gave his boss's words a long thought, then he let go of the man's foot. The boot dropped to the ground from the dead weight inside.

"I'll go notify the undertaker, Marshal," he said.

"You do that, Buck."

As the deputy started moving away, the marshal continued.

"You could be up for a nice promotion, Buck. I'm really serious this time."

The marshal turned to the others. "Better go on back to sleep, gents. Mornin'll be comin' 'round awful early tomorrow."

"We'll be glad to stay with you, Marshal," said Charley. "In case they make another try."

"No," said the marshal. "I don't think they'll hit us again tonight . . . but if they do, Buck and I got it handled."

They all looked up as Henry Ellis slammed the hotel room window across the street.

CHAPTER SIX

Young Buck Wadell, the deputy marshal, was banging on their hotel room door at precisely four a.m. Roscoe went down to see about the trotters, while Charley and Henry Ellis stopped by Bertie's kitchen for a hot mug of coffee for Charley and a glass of juice for the boy.

When they got to Bertie's barn, Roscoe had already harnessed and hitched up the trotters. He was in the process of wiping down the isinglass when he was joined by the others.

Charley pulled out his watch and checked the time.

"We got fifteen minutes to get over to the depot and meet the marshal," he said. "Do you want to start off driving, Roscoe, then we can switch off down the road . . . or do you want me to start off?"

Roscoe, who was now making a final check of all his buckles and couplings, said that he'd be glad to start out driving.

"Why, thank you, Roscoe," said Charley. "I still got me a little shut-eye to catch up on from last night. How about you, Henry Ellis?" he asked the boy. "Do you still have any sleep left in you?"

"If I'm going to go back to sleep," said the boy, "I sure wish I had me something to eat beforehand."

Buck, the deputy, rejoined the three. He carried a large basket, covered with a red-and-white-checkered cloth.

"I heard that, sonny," he said to the boy. "My wife stayed up half the night makin' these burritos." He handed one to Henry Ellis, then passed several more to the others. "Said she didn't want you starting out followin' that train without you havin' somethin' in your bellies."

"Well, that was mighty kind of her, Buck," said Charley. "Will you tell her thanks from us all for thinking of us?"

"Yeah, thanks," said Roscoe, biting into his burrito.

"Me too," added Henry Ellis as he wiped away the dripping salsa from his chin with his coat sleeve.

"The marshal wanted me to tell you that you can take off anytime you want to," said the deputy. "The train's darn near loaded, but there's always one or two that're stragglers."

Charley reached over and picked up his grandson, setting him on the surrey's rear seat. He started to climb in behind the boy as Roscoe pulled himself up and into the front seat. After making sure the isinglass was fastened all around, Roscoe turned to get Charley's permission to go. Then he picked up the lines in both hands and clucked his tongue. The trotters moved out in the direction of the train.

Charley pulled the several blankets that had been left there over himself and Henry Ellis, then they both settled back in the seat.

A second later, Roscoe butt-slapped both trotters, and the surrey was on its way again.

About three-quarters of a mile out of Hondo, Charley told Roscoe to pull over and stop.

"We'll wait here for the train," he told him. "After it passes us, I want you to stay on its tail for the rest of the way."

"Are you sayin' that we gotta follow that train day an' night until it reaches its destination?" said Roscoe.

"If it sounded that way, I'm truly sorry, Roscoe," said Charley. "I talked with the marshal this morning on the way over to the barn, and I told him we'll be bedding down in Uvalde come dusk and he'd be on his own after that. He promised me he'd telephone ahead and make sure there'll be someone to replace us when the train makes its regular stop in that town."

Roscoe shook his head.

"Thank the Lord . . . and thank you, Charley Sunday, fer havin' the courtesy to do that."

"Any time," said Charley as he sank lower in the surrey's rear seat beside the now sleeping boy. "And remember to let me know when you want me to relieve you. But please, let me get a little sleep before you do."

It must have been two hours later — though not one of the three really knew how much time had passed because Roscoe had fallen asleep, too — when Henry Ellis awoke to the slower cadence of the trotters' hoofbeats. He could still see the train's tail lantern up ahead in the gray of the day, but the distance between them had grown immeasurably. The boy was about to wake his grandfather when he saw something in the tall, swaying bushes on the right side of the road. The head and neck of a bay horse had edged itself out several feet onto the road in front of the approaching surrey, before being reined back quickly by its rider.

"Grampa . . . Roscoe," Henry Ellis called out. We need to stop . . . Right now!"

Charley sat up straight, his head bumping Roscoe from behind. That woke Roscoe, too.

"What's goin' on?" said Roscoe, reining in the trotters.

"Pay attention," said Charley.

He turned to the boy.

"What's going on, Henry Ellis?" he asked for himself.

"I just saw a horse stick its nose out of those bushes up ahead. Somebody reined him back."

"Where's the train?" asked Charley.

"We've drifted back some," answered the boy. "Otherwise we would have passed the place where I saw the horse. Grampa," he said, "I think it's those same robbers. I think they're going after the train again."

Charley slowly removed the Walker Colt from his boot, bringing it up where he could use it if he had to.

Roscoe unholstered his old Walker, too, setting it on the seat beside him.

There was more movement coming from the bushes in front of them. Then, five horses and riders broke out of their hiding places in the bushes and raced after the train, which was about three-quarters of a mile in front of them by then.

"Whip 'em up, Roscoe!" shouted Charley. "There they go!"

Roscoe slapped leather, and the trotters took off at a run, headed after the riders who were chasing the train.

Henry Ellis could feel his heart in his throat as he sat beside his grandfather, both of them leaning as far forward as possible, almost into the front seat beside Roscoe.

"I'm going to have to ask you to get down on the floorboards, Henry Ellis," said Charley in his gentle but firm way. "I don't know how I would explain it to your mother if anything happened to you."

"But, Grampa . . ." the boy whined.

"Now, damnit. I said get your butt down on those floorboards, *now*!"

Henry Ellis did what his grandfather said, just as the first bullet fired by the bad men tore a hole in the isinglass, then embedded itself in the back support of the front seat, barely missing Roscoe.

"That was a close one," said Roscoe.

"Well, shoot back at 'em," said Charley. "They know we're here now."

Roscoe reached for his Walker, pulled back the hammer, found the opening in the isinglass for the reins, then sent some lead in the train robbers' direction.

Charley slid all the way over to the opposite side of the vehicle and fired after them with his own Walker Colt.

"Save your lead," said Charley. "We ain't going to hit anything bouncing around like we are."

Just then, the surrey passed the dead body of one of the outlaws in the mud, and his horse could be seen where it wandered off beside the railroad tracks.

"It was either you or me got 'im, Charley," said Roscoe.

"It sure wasn't Henry Ellis," said Charley. "He doesn't have a gun."

The boy popped his head up for a look. Charley immediately shoved it back down.

By then, Roscoe had advanced the surrey up much closer to the band of outlaws. Close enough that small specks of mud were dirtying the isinglass between Roscoe and the trotters.

"Now, pick one and aim good," said Charley. "If we can knock off two more, they'll give up before they get to the train."

Both men picked their targets, then aimed as best they could under the circumstances. When they fired, the two men closest to the rear of the bunch ate mud.

And like Charley had said, the other two riders reined off to the right of the road, then disappeared into the tall bushes for good.

Roscoe reined the trotters to a stop, and the three of them — Henry Ellis had popped up again — watched as the red lantern on the tail end of the train kept getting smaller and smaller, until it disappeared completely.

There was a deadly quiet all around for a brief moment before someone spoke.

"You know," said Charley, "I don't think anyone on the train even knew what was going on back here."

"That's because we never let them robbers get close enough."

"And the money," said Henry Ellis. "Boy, I'll bet those Cropper Brothers are really . . . upset."

CHAPTER SEVEN

They were lucky — real lucky. Even though a cold rain had started to fall again, the train was still waiting at the Uvalde station when the surrey rolled into town. Charley found the conductor and the engineer inside the station manager's office next to the potbelly stove. The two Hondo deputy marshals were there, too. Besides taking the edge off the day with some rotgut whiskey mixed in with some stale coffee dregs, they were filling in the local constable on what they thought might have happened to the men in their backup surrey. That's when the door opened and Charley walked in.

"Just wondering if y'all knew how close you came to getting robbed today," said Charley as he moved on into the office, followed by Roscoe and Henry Ellis.

"We found several bullet holes in the last car, next to the hanging red lamp, and a mirror was shattered inside the very same car. It was Buck's idea to wait for you boys to catch up."

Charley nodded his thank-you to Buck.

"That would have been the gentlemen's car at the rear of the train," said the conductor.

"Well, I figure them bullet holes was as close as they got to the train before you run 'em off, Mr. Sunday," said Buck.

"So you did see what we done."

"Every move you made, Mr. Sunday . . . every shot you fired."

"It was the Croppers again," said Charley. "I'm sure of it."

"Mr. Phelps here, the conductor, got a real good look at 'em this time, Mr. Sunday," said the engineer.

"And I'd bet my last dollar that it was Sam and Dale Cropper leadin' that gang. I know their faces, even when they're covered by masks. Hell, I've come face-ta-face with 'em enough times over the years."

"Have you?" said Charley.

"Six times, for sure," said the conductor. "In the beginning, they used ta only rob the passenger cars. It was just later on that they started going after our shipments . . . our money shipments, mine payrolls, and things like that."

"Where do you suppose they get their

information from, when those shipments are going to be shipped?" asked Charley.

"Oh, we've discussed that," said the conductor. "And we even made up a list of who we thought might have a good reason to be workin' both sides. But we couldn't agree on any one man."

"So the information still gets leaked to the Croppers, and the Croppers continue robbing your trains," said Charley.

The conductor shrugged.

"It's the railroad owners who don't really seem to care about it, Mr. Sunday," said the engineer.

"Now don't you start giving away any company secrets," said the conductor.

"It ain't no company secret that the Cropper Brothers always seem to know when we're gonna be carryin' anything of value."

"Did you have any of the railroad owners on that suspect list of yours?" Charley asked.

"No, sir, we never did," said the engineer. "It was the owners . . . one particular owner . . . who had the idea for the suspect list in the first place."

There was a long moment.

"What do you two think?" Charley asked the two Hondo deputy marshals.

Not thinking that they were going to be brought into the conversation, the two deputies could only hem and haw.

"How about you, Buck?" said Charley to the deputy he knew the best. "What do you think of the suspect list being started by one of the railroad owners?"

"It does sound a little fishy now that you brought it up, Mr. Sunday."

"Does anyone know this owner's name?" asked the constable.

No one said a thing.

The constable continued, "Mr. Sunday has made a very good point, and now I'd like to know the name of the railroad owner who came up with the idea of the suspect list."

"It was Mr. Madison," said the conductor. "Mr. Edwin J. Madison. And he's the only one of the three owners that lives here in Texas. The others make their homes in the East."

"Is there any way I might sit down with this Madison fellow for a talk?" asked Charley.

"He rides in his private car from El Paso to San Antonio on occasion, or the other way around."

"Do these two trains pass somewhere on the line?" said Charley. "What I mean is, when one train leaves San Antone, does the other one leave El Paso at approximately the same time, or thereabouts?"

"I believe so," said the engineer. "Yes, yes they do, Mr. Sunday. When they turn this train around in El Paso, the following day our departure time will be the same as it was in San Antonio. That's right. The other train, with the executive car, should have left El Paso the same day and time we left San Antonio."

"I want to have a little talk with this Mr. Edwin J. Madison, if it's possible. Do you think he'll be in his personal car?"

The conductor answered, "Mr. Madison rides from El Paso to San Antonio, and back, once or twice a week. He's the hands-on partner of the group . . . the one who's directly in charge of all railroad business in the absence of the other two partners."

"I'll still be driving my surrey behind you tomorrow," Charley told the engineer. "If you see that other train coming our way, toot your whistle to let me know, will you?"

"Sure thing, Mr. Sunday," said the engineer. "I'll do 'er."

Charley turned to the constable.

"My friends and I'll need a place to bed down for a few hours, just like we done in Hondo."

"The passengers are all staying at the

Texas House Hotel over on Main Street. Overflow is at the Oriental, two blocks this way. Soon as I get back to my office I'll send a man over there to see if they have any rooms left. Where'll I find you, Mr. Sunday, if there's a room available?"

"Right here by this stove, Constable," said Charley. "Right here beside this beautiful hot, stove. My partner will be here, too . . . and so will my grandson. Oh, is there a livery close by where I can get my horses out of the weather?"

"Right over there," he pointed. "Red Mullins owns that stable across the way. Tell 'im I sent you, an' he should give you a deal on the oats."

Charley, Roscoe, and Henry Ellis were sitting around a table in a small restaurant that was a part of the Oriental Hotel. Those who had joined them for supper were the conductor, the engineer, and the Uvalde constable.

"I sure hope those coins are in a safe place," said the conductor.

"They're sittin' in my most trusted jail cell with those two Hondo deputies," said the constable. "I believe between Buck and Stan, that's the other one, at least one of them should be able ta stay awake through the night."

The waiter had taken their orders twenty minutes earlier and was now serving the main course to his customers.

"And the glass of milk is for . . . let me guess. The milk is for the boy, am I right?" the waiter was asking.

"That's right," said Charley. He watched as the foaming glass was placed directly in front of his grandson.

Henry Ellis's eyes widened. He picked up the glass of milk in both hands and took three giant gulps of the ice-cold liquid from the container.

"Thank you," he said to the waiter. "You better bring me another glass, because I'm sure I'm going to be needing more of it real soon."

The waiter nodded to the boy before he turned to the others.

"Does anyone else need anything while I'm in the kitchen getting the lad's milk?" he added.

"I'll have some more of them buttermilk biscuits, if you still got some," said Roscoe.

Most of the others shook their heads . . . they were satisfied with what was on their plates.

Twenty minutes later when everyone was

busy scraping their supper plates clean, the constable called out.

"Oh, waiter, if you have any of that blueberry pie this restaurant's famous for, I suggest everyone try a slice." The waiter pulled out his pad, writing down the order.

"If you give me a few other extra long minutes, I can crank you up some vanilla iced-cream to top off the blueberry pie. Anyone game?" he said.

"Too cold outside fer iced-cream," said the engineer along with both the conductor and the constable.

"It's never too cold for iced-cream," said Charley. "Give my partner a big scoop on his pie. My grandson, too, if you don't mind."

The conductor went for the iced-cream topping, too.

When he was done writing, the waiter disappeared into the kitchen one more time.

Charley leaned back and began packing his pipe from the pouch he always carried.

The constable took a skinny cigarillo from his inside pocket and bit off the tip.

A couple others did the same.

When Charley finally had his pipe ready for fire, the constable scratched a large Lucifer match somewhere under the table, then brought up the flame. Everyone who had prepared for smoking leaned in close to borrow some of the Lucifer's spitting flame.

With all that puffing going on at one time, that portion of the restaurant's dining room became smoke filled within moments.

Henry Ellis began to cough.

"Why don't you go on out into the hotel's lobby, son," said Charley. "Take Roscoe with you."

Roscoe got to his feet.

"That's right fine by me," he said. "I never much cared fer the smell a' cee-gars anyways."

He nodded to Henry Ellis, then the two of them left the room together.

Henry Ellis called back through the curtain of smoke, "Let us know when the pie and iced-cream gets here."

"Don't you worry, son," answered Charley. "Better yet, when it gets here, I'll bring it out there to you two."

Henry Ellis sat down on a divan in the hotel's foyer. Roscoe took a comfy chair across from the boy.

They both just sat there, eyes darting around the room like anxious animals. Neither of them had stayed in that many fancy hotels before, and now, being in one without Charley by their side — Charley, who always seemed to know his way around

— was making both of them a little nervous.

After a few minutes, the front door opened with a rush of cold air, producing Ben and Eleanor Campbell. They were in quite a bustle, having just walked up the street with the cold wind following them all the way. Lightning crackled behind them — thunder rolled.

"Dr. and Mrs. Campbell," called out Henry Ellis from across the room.

They both turned. And when they recognized the boy, they moved over to where he was sitting across from Roscoe.

"Why, Henry Ellis," said the woman. "We weren't expecting to see you here."

"I wasn't expecting to see you two, either," said the boy. "I figured you'd be staying at the other hotel."

"That's where they put us at first," said the woman. "But when we asked around and learned that the Oriental, even though it's older, was a classier caravansary, we asked if we could make a change."

"Are you just now coming from the other hotel?" asked the boy.

"Heaven's sake, no," said Eleanor. "We found a nice little eating place down the block . . . home cooking, it said."

"But it didn't taste like anything I ever had at home," said Ben. "We were going to

97

take our supper here, but Eleanor thought somewhere quieter would be better . . . considering."

"Considering?" said Roscoe, who had been following the conversation since they had joined them.

"Oh," said Eleanor. "Considering how hectic this whole journey has been from its inception."

"For two nights in a row now, we've been taken off the train and put up in unfamiliar surroundings," said Ben. "And my wife is just getting fed up with it, that's all."

"Well, tomorrow could be more than just another day," said Roscoe. "The boy's grampa is hoping to meet up with one of the owners of this here railroad."

"How's that?" said Ben.

"Oh, you'll see," said Roscoe. "And if everything works out the way we expect it to, those Cropper Brothers may never hit another one of this railroad's trains again in our lifetime."

"That's all well and good about the railroad," said Ben. "But my wife and I were just wondering when we'll get to Juanita. We do have some business to take care of once we arrive, and we'd like to get it out of the way as soon as we can."

"Well, we only got forty miles ta go 'til we

get ta Juanita," said Roscoe. "That ain't countin' Cline. Cline's a little bump in the road by Turkey Creek. The town sits about halfway between Juanita and here. Once we've passed Cline, it'll be clear goin' all the way."

Several gunshots were heard coming from the street outside, with one of the projectiles shattering a pane of glass in the front window of the hotel.

Roscoe grabbed hold of Mrs. Campbell and Henry Ellis at the same time, taking them to the floor.

"You two stay right here," he told them. "I'm going to run outside for a minute to see who's doin' that shootin'."

As Roscoe got to his feet, Charley came running in from the adjoining room, his Walker Colt cocked and ready in his right hand.

"Follow me, Roscoe," he said. "Sounds like someone's shootin' up the town."

The front door of the Oriental Hotel flew open as Roscoe and Charley burst through. They immediately came to a stop at the edge of the boardwalk to avoid the heavy rain, which was now coming down again. Both men backed themselves up against the hotel's facade and scanned the street, up and down, with their highly trained eyes.

Nothing was visible, except for the rain and the ever-present mud.

"Don't look like anyone's out in this weather at all," said Roscoe.

"Sure don't," echoed Charley. "Over there," he pointed. "The constable's office. Do you see it?"

"Sure do," said Roscoe. "There's a lamp alight inside, and there's still some daylight left."

"I was referring to the half-open door, Roscoe. No one leaves their door open when it's this cold outside."

"Maybe we oughta take a look," suggested Roscoe.

"You two need any help out there, remember I'm right behind you," came the constable's voice from just inside the hotel door, where he now stood with his gun in hand.

"So are we," said the conductor's voice seconds later. "Me and the engineer, here, have yer backs covered, so go ahead and do what ya hafta do."

Charley and Roscoe exchanged glances.

"Maybe we're mistaken about where those gunshots came from," said Roscoe.

"No-sir-ee, Roscoe, my friend," said Charley. "Those shots came from over there, sure as I'm Henry Ellis's grandpa."

"Maybe it was the constable's office," said

Roscoe. "Is that where the mint's coins are being kept tonight? Bein' guarded by those two deputy marshals from Hondo."

Charley gave the constable's office one more look, then they both started off across the muddy street, headed for that particular building.

Henry Ellis had found a place in the corner of one of the hotel's front windows, where he was peering out between several other onlookers. He watched anxiously as the two men trudged slowly through the mud and rain while attempting to cross the street.

When they were nearing the building, Charley could see that the door was cracked open a few inches, and a kerosene lamp glowed from within.

Charley held up a hand of caution for Roscoe. Both men continued their move toward the office, but much slower than before. When they got to the porch, they both stopped again.

Charley called out: "You two fellas' inside . . . you Hondo deputy marshals. Buck Wadell? Stan? Is everything all right in there?"

There was a long moment with no answer, then: "Who is that out there? Constable, is that you?" came a voice from inside the partially open door.

"It's me . . . Charley Sunday. I'm the retired Ranger from down Juanita way. My partner's here with me."

"I can hardly hear you, mister, with all that rain out there. Can you step up closer?"

Charley stepped up onto the boardwalk.

"I'm Charley Sunday," he repeated. "I'm the retired Ranger from Juanita. My partner's with me."

"Then c'mon inside . . . slow and easy. I'm armed with a shotgun, so walk easy . . . and keep your hands away from your weapons."

Using all the caution necessary, Charley slipped his Walker Colt back into his boot. He held his hands out in front of him and stepped inside.

What he saw totally confused him. Two bodies lay faceup on the wooden floor. One was the deputy marshal, Stan. Charley had been able to tell that immediately by the man's badge, which was similar in shape to the Texas Ranger badge he'd worn for so many years. The other body on the floor was an outlaw, Charley had to assume.

Behind them both, in the same cell, were the several iron strongboxes containing the newly minted coins. It rested safely beside Buck Wadell, the other deputy marshal. And on the floor, with his neck held firmly beneath Buck Wadell's boot, was Dale Cropper, younger brother to Sam Cropper, who was the co-leader of the Cropper Brothers' Gang.

Within minutes, the constable had joined Charley and Roscoe inside the office. When others tried to follow him, the constable locked all the doors and pulled the shades.

It was only then that the constable confronted the remaining Hondo deputy.

"Damn it, Buck. How'n the hell did Stan get killed? And who's the other dead one? . . . plus who's that you got underfoot?"

"I never let Stan get killed, Constable," said Buck.

He pointed to the dead outlaw.

"That son-of-a-bitch shot 'im dead when he first come through the door . . . the dead one right there. I was the one kilt him. Most likely he's a member of the Cropper Gang, too. And how I know that, is, because this here is one of the Cropper Brothers, Dale hisself, for sure, who I got my boot on, holdin' him down."

Along with the constable, Charley and Roscoe moved closer to the Cropper brother under the deputy's boot.

"You say that's Dale? Dale Cropper?"

The deputy nodded.

"Let that man up offa the floor, Buck," said the constable. "You oughtn't be holdin' him down like he was a snake or somethin' evil such as that. Let 'im up, now. Show the man some decency."

Slowly, the deputy removed his boot from Dale Cropper's throat. Having done that, the local lawman watched as Dale Cropper managed to get to his feet.

"Now, are you one of those folks who've been trying to rob the railroad for the past few days?" asked the constable. "Are you?"

Dale nodded sheepishly.

Upon seeing Dale Cropper's admission of guilt, the constable swung a roundhouse right that caught Dale Cropper directly on the left temple, and the younger Cropper brother hit the floor with a resounding thud.

An hour or so later, some of the other townsfolk had joined them. Everyone was throwing around suggestions, all headed in different directions again.

"I surely can't keep him here," said the constable.

"And if we take him with us on the train," said the conductor, "his brother and the gang will have even more reason to attack us . . . and steal the shipment from the mint, too."

"Don't any one of you suggest that I can fit him into my new surrey," said Charley. "Four's what she was built to carry, and four is all that I mean to haul."

Roscoe cleared his throat, nudging Charley.

"We're only carryin' three, Boss . . . You, me, and Henry Ellis. Remember?"

Charley's complexion appeared to turn red. He was showing his frustration.

"Well," he said. "I don't want my grandson sharing a backseat with a common criminal. What about you folks? Would you like it if you were asked to let one of your children ride alongside a dangerous criminal?"

"Grampa," said Henry Ellis, slipping his nose into the exchange. "Grampa . . . Dr. and Mrs. Campbell have already said that they'd watch me if I rode on the train with them. So you have plenty of room in the surrey to transport Mr. Cropper . . . to anywhere you want to take him."

"All we gotta do is get him to Del Rio," said Roscoe. "It'll be a lot safer for everyone involved if he rides in the backseat of the surrey with me."

As all the people who were standing around in the constable's office began clapping for Roscoe and his idea, Charley turned to his pal, speaking in a whisper.

"Sometimes, my dear friend, Roscoe, you haven't learned when to keep that mouth of yours shut."

"So Dale Cropper will ride in the surrey with Charley Sunday and his partner," said the constable.

"And Henry Ellis will ride on the train with us," said Eleanor Campbell who, along with her husband, had just walked in.

"Good, it's been settled," said the constable. "Now we can all get some sleep around here before it's time for breakfast."

"One last thing," said Charley. "I'd kind of like to have the Hondo deputy, Buck Waddell, riding in the back with the prisoner. He's younger . . . and it'll let Roscoe keep his hands free in case ol' Sam Cropper decides to rescue his kin."

CHAPTER EIGHT

The engineer waited patiently in his open-air compartment behind the boiler, while his fireman stoked the wood fire that heated the water to its boiling point. It was steam that powered these locomotive giants, and it was steam they were now minutes away from producing.

It had not rained since daybreak, but the sky was dark, and the temperature outside was in the low twenties.

At the rear end of the train, the constable, his deputy, the conductor, and Charley stood between the last car of the train and Charley's surrey, which now held the heavily shackled Dale Cropper in the rear seat. He was being guarded by Hondo deputy Buck Waddell.

Roscoe sat on the passenger side of the front seat. He winked at Henry Ellis, who was watching the whole scene through one of the rear windows of the gentlemen's car,

107

which sat on the tracks beside the surrey. Ben and Eleanor Campbell stood directly behind the boy, placing themselves where Charley could see that his grandson was going to be safe for the rest of the journey.

"Well," said Charley, turning his attention to those around him. "It's probably best that we be on our way."

"The engineer knows to watch his speed," said the conductor. "And that he's to keep his eyes out for that train coming from the other direction."

"Why don't someone just telephone, or telegraph ahead to Cline, and have them stop the other train there?" said Charley.

"I can do that," said the constable. "I'll do 'er right after you leave."

Charley nodded. He shook the constable's hand, then he began his climb into the surrey.

The conductor grabbed the handhold beside the iron steps of the rear car, then he waved the lantern so the engineer up front knew it was time to go.

"All aboard," he called out.

At the same time, Charley settled back into his seat and found the lines. He fussed a moment with the isinglass, which still covered the vehicle, then, with a wave to all, he put leather to the trotters and the surrey surged ahead.

The train was already moving when Charley pulled up beside it. Inside, Henry Ellis had moved over to a side window, where he stood waving at his grampa Charley and his uncle Roscoe.

A few more minutes passed, and the wheels of the engine began turning faster.

Charley did what he had to to help the trotters maintain the same speed as the steam-powered monster on the tracks beside him.

Cline was another one of those half-built, one-sided streets that had been called a town for quite a few years. Starting off as a good place to raise local cattle on the south bank of nearby Turkey Creek, it eventually became a stagecoach stop. The barn and living quarters for the stop had been constructed, along with a store and a makeshift saloon. And even when the railroad decided to include Cline as one of their many regular mail pickup stops along the route, the little town of Cline hadn't grown much since then.

Rolling toward Cline, and slowing his speed, the engineer could see in the distance that the eastbound train had been stopped and directed onto a sidetrack. He slowed even more as he drew closer to the town. He could then see a group of men standing beside the eastbound, involved in some sort of conversation. When they saw the westbound approaching, they broke up into smaller groups and waited until the engineer pulled to a stop opposite the other locomotive.

Coming up on the rear of the westbound in the surrey, Charley turned the trotters, then drove them across the tracks at a wagon crossing. He maneuvered the surrey in between both trains before reining to a stop several yards away from the initial small group of men.

The conductor stepped off the train while it was still moving, crossing over to meet up with Charley and Roscoe, who were just climbing down from the surrey.

"Are one of you men Charley Sunday?" asked one of the better dressed men.

Charley raised his gloved hand.

"I am, sir. I see you got our message from Uvalde and stopped the other train."

"That we did, Mr. Sunday," said the man. "And the first thing we have to do is take you to the executive car where Mr. Madison is waiting to talk to you."

"First," said Charley, "I want to check with the deputy in the backseat to make sure my prisoner is still secure."

He threw a look to Buck, sitting beside the heavily chained Cropper brother.

Buck waved. Everything was all right.

"Now, I'd like to pee before I do anything else," said Charley.

"Use that outhouse right over there," said the well-dressed man. "It's for railroad employees, not the public."

The private car containing Edwin J. Madison, one of the railroad's owners, had been coupled to the last car of the eastbound train.

The group of men, which had grown considerably larger since Charley's arrival, took Charley and Roscoe to the steps that led to the door of the executive car. Once there, the men bid the two retired Rangers well.

When they had finally been left alone, Roscoe threw Charley a little grin, which Charley answered with a wink. They removed their hats, and together they knocked on the door.

A well-manicured black man opened the door for them, bowed, then ushered them into what looked like a lavish whorehouse.

When the two ex-Rangers had finally stopped gawking at everything in the ornately decorated car, they saw Edwin J. Madison sitting behind his, just as ornate, desk at the other end of the car.

"Gentlemen," he said, beckoning them both to join him. He indicated two over-stuffed, red-leather chairs opposite the desk.

"You may sit here," he said. "And Blue," he called to the black man, "please bring the two gentlemen a beverage of their choosing."

The two ex-lawmen conferred with the valet before moving to the overstuffed chairs, where they sat.

When they were finally facing one another, Edwin J. Madison spoke again.

"Which one of you is Sunday?" he asked.

"That would be me, sir," answered Charley. "Charles Abner Sunday . . . and this is my friend and partner, Roscoe Baskin."

The three of them shook hands.

"I've been told you might have a solution to all these train robberies my company has been experiencing as of late, Mr. Sunday."

"That's why we're here, Mr. Madison," said Charley. "We figure there's just gotta be someone on the inside getting informa-tion concerning important shipments out to the Cropper Gang."

"Are you suggesting that someone . . . someone working for the railroad . . . *my* railroad . . . may be guilty of leaking private information to the train robbers? Well, it's not true," he said. "Not true at all. And it's also not possible."

"Why do you say that, sir, that it's not possible?"

"It just isn't. I know it's hard for someone like yourself to understand, Mr. Sunday, having had no experience in running a railroad," said Madison, "but I have personally met with and deeply scrutinized each and every employee of this railroad. And I have faith that each and every one of those employees are as honest as the day is long."

Charley raised his eyebrows.

"Mr. Madison, there are a lot of ways any one of your employees could be working with the outlaws, and you wouldn't know about it . . . at all."

The valet returned with the visitors' drinks, setting them on the edge of the railroad owner's desk with doilies underneath.

"I'm afraid our guests won't have time to consume those, Blue. They were just leaving."

Madison stood up.

Charley nudged Roscoe, and the two ex-lawmen got to their feet.

"Well, Mr. Madison," said Charley. "We

thank you for your time."

He nodded and bowed his head. Roscoe did the same. Then the two men turned. And with hats in hand, they walked back to the portal through which they entered. The valet, Blue, already had the door held open for them as they stepped out into the cold.

As the two men descended the iron steps and began walking back toward the group of railroad workers and Cline townsmen, Roscoe turned to Charley.

"I reckon the man didn't like your suggestion," he said.

"No, sir," said Charley. "You're right about that."

"How come you never told him that we got one of the Cropper boys in custody?" Roscoe wanted to know.

Charley shrugged his shoulders.

"I suppose I thought that it just wasn't any of his damn business," said Charley. "Besides, I have plans for Dale Cropper. He might just be the one who can tell us who it is leaking the information about the special shipments."

Later on that same day, as night was closing in, Dale Cropper sat dead center in the single jail cell used by the citizens of Cline, Texas, when it was needed. Deputy Buck

Wadell, from Hondo, was still sitting at his side, guarding him.

Since the tiny berg was a part of Uvalde County, the Uvalde County sheriff had created a special position for the law officer who watched over the little whistle-stop.

His name was Dee Kuper, a dirt farmer on his own time, but a pretty good law officer when working as the county sheriff's assistant — or assistant sheriff, as some called him. He was in his early fifties, partially gray, with a drooping handlebar mustache.

With Dee Kuper in the little office that the county provided him were Charley, Roscoe, and Henry Ellis, who had just eaten his evening meal with his grampa and Roscoe. Dale Cropper, still in chains, was also there, and Buck Wadell was at his side.

Now it was back to business, and Charley had a few things he wanted to talk with Dale Cropper about.

The first item on Charley's list was the same thing he had tried to discuss with the reluctant railroad owner that afternoon. But this time, Charley threw a twist to it.

"We know who it is giving you, your brother, and your gang information about the shipments being carried on the railroad."

"That's hogwash," said Dale Cropper.

"There ain't no one givin' us any secret information. Don't you understand that we're smart enough ta know what's bein' shipped ourselves?"

"Now, I might believe you were capable of figuring out things like that, Dale," said Charley, "but Roscoe here, and Assistant Sheriff Kuper tend to agree with the man who passes the information on to you."

Dale laughed.

"You gotta be out of your minds thinkin' that I'd fall fer an old trick like that one, Mr. Charley Sunday. There ain't nobody on the outside givin' us inside information. And that's the truth."

"You must think I'm the dumbest person to ever come down the pike, Cropper. We know who it is . . . the person who's giving you the information. I was just trying to get you to confirm it for me."

"Well, I ain't no squealer, Mr. Sunday. Even if what you are sayin' is true, you'll never get me to talk."

"So you are admitting that there's an outside man."

"No, sir." Dale shook his head. "I didn't say that. All I ever said was that we done every robbery all by ourselves . . . with no help from anyone else."

"C'mon, Cropper," said Charley. "Quit

your lying to me. I know there's another person mixed up with you and your brother in these robberies . . . a very important man. But even though I know who it is, I haven't been able to figure out why."

One of the two bullets that entered the jail cell hit Dale Cropper where he sat. The projectiles, almost fired in unison, had come through an open barred window at the rear of the building.

Before making sure Henry Ellis was all right, both Charley and Roscoe plastered the barred window with their own lead. After making sure the boy had not been hit, they ran to the back door, giving chase.

Deputy Buck Waddell, from Hondo, sat in a daze beside the wounded Cropper brother.

Henry Ellis could see that there was something just not right about him.

"Is there anything I can do for you, Buck?" asked the boy. "A drink of water . . . ?"

The deputy shook his head. Though he didn't answer outright, his eyes began to widen. In less than another second, Henry Ellis could see the deputy's life gradually ebb away. Buck Waddell slowly fell forward, facedown on the wooden floor of the cell, a pool of blood forming beneath him.

Charley and Roscoe had been hit by a

blast of cold, wet air as they exited the building into the rainy night. Neither one of them had taken the time to grab their jackets, and because of that, they were forced to give up their pursuit before they even had the chance to see who it was they were chasing.

CHAPTER NINE

The rain that had started falling during the shooting of Dale Cropper and Hondo's deputy Buck Waddell grew into a raging storm, which lasted most of the night.

After he'd sent for the town doctor to fix up Dale Cropper's flesh wound, Roscoe took Henry Ellis to their room at Perkins Boardinghouse, which was being paid for by the railroad. Once there, they both got ready for bed.

Charley, on the other hand, spent a few more hours with Assistant Sheriff Dee Kuper, helping him make Dale Cropper comfortable in the cell, then cleaning up the mess that had been left there.

Charley had another idea, too. After he sent a telegram off to the marshal in Hondo, advising him of the loss of his second deputy, Buck Waddell, he approached the conductor of the eastbound train, which, to Charley's surprise, hadn't left the depot yet.

Charley asked him if it would be all right to send Deputy Buck's body back as far as Hondo in his baggage car.

The conductor agreed, and later on he sent a couple of big switchmen over to the undertaker's office to pick up Buck's temporary casket.

Charley watched with Dee Kuper as the eastbound pulled out slowly into the rainy night with Buck's body aboard, headed home for the final time.

Then he joined Roscoe and his grandson in their room at the boardinghouse, where he would try to pick up a few winks before morning.

Charley decided to continue on to Juanita in the surrey before daylight, at least an hour before the train would be leaving. This was to be the last lap of their journey before home. He and the partially awake Roscoe carried the still sleeping Henry Ellis over to the surrey in the rain, depositing him in the rear seat. All three had slept in their clothes, so doing it that way wasn't as difficult as it could have been.

Within twenty minutes they were on the open road. Mrs. Perkins, who ran the boardinghouse, had prepared a breakfast for each of them, and Roscoe had loaded the basket onto the floor at the front of the surrey beside where his feet were peacefully resting. He reached into the basket and withdrew a sliced-bacon and scrambled-egg burrito, handing it to Charley, who was driving beside him. Charley, holding the lines in one hand, took the burrito with the other. A second burrito went to the boy in the backseat, where he was in the process of waking up. The third, Roscoe kept for himself. They ate as the isinglass-covered surrey continued on through the storm, enjoying their breakfast as the world around them began to brighten.

Around eight in the morning, Charley couldn't keep his eyes open anymore, and since both Roscoe and Henry Ellis had gone back to sleep, Roscoe's snoring, plus the comforting noises being made by the boy in the back, finally got the best of him. Charley pulled the trotters over to the side of the road behind some cottonwood trees, where he, too, could catch up on his sleep.

It couldn't have been more than a half an hour before the whistle of the train in the distance woke them up. Charley stirred first. Roscoe followed, with the boy in the back expelling the loudest yawn either one of the two adults had ever heard the likes of.

By then, the train had come abreast of

their hidden position and was just about to pass them, when several shots were fired from the bushes just a little farther on than the cottonwood grove where the surrey occupants had been resting.

The three of them watched in amazement as five riders on horseback lunged from the bushes and moved their galloping horses in beside the locomotive.

One of the riders shot the fireman, and another killed the engineer, before both rode their horses up closer and transferred to the steps on the side of the roaring behemoth. When they both had made it safely into the engineer's compartment, the first man began slowing the train until it hissed to a stop.

That was when the other three riders urged their horses over to the baggage car, reining up just outside the sliding door.

"Prepare to be boarded," yelled one of the men, who interestingly enough, had a voice that sounded a great deal like Dale Cropper.

"That's him," whispered Charley. "Sam Cropper. We need to take him alive if we want to find out just who it is behind this all."

The two old Rangers had already begun to climb down from the surrey. Charley indicated to Henry Ellis that he should hunker down in the backseat, then they both continued on, on foot, moving out onto the road with their Walker Colts drawn.

They came up directly behind the waiting riders without being heard, and when Sam Cropper stuck his upper torso out from behind the sliding door of the baggage car, Charley shot to wound, and wound he did.

Sam took the Walker's conical bullet in the right shoulder. He fell back into the car. The other two train robbers never even got off one shot before they, too, had intercepted several of those handmade lead projectiles.

The other two outlaws in the engine compartment realized that something was amiss. They jumped to the ground and began running away. By then, several railroad employees had made it to the ground. They became the heroes of the day by chasing down the two runaways, and after a brief struggle, subduing them completely.

At the baggage car, Roscoe had his gun out and cocked, just in case the two men on horseback Charley had wounded tried anything else.

Charley moved in closer.

"All right, Sam Cropper," he ordered. "You can come out of there right now. I reckon a dirty coward like you . . . a man who shot his own brother from ambush . . . won't try any more tricky shenanigans."

Slowly, Sam Cropper's face appeared from around the sliding door. His gloved hand covered the bleeding wound in his right shoulder.

"Shot my brother?" he said. "Now, why would I want to shoot Dale, for heaven's sake?"

Charley spent the next hour questioning Sam Cropper, but he just couldn't get the leader of the train robbers to admit that he had shot his own brother to keep him from talking.

In the middle of the questioning reality appeared to set in, and Sam Cropper began to cry like a baby.

"It wasn't me, damn you," he said. "Besides being my brother, Dale was my best friend. He may have been a tad slow, but he was my blood, and we always stuck together."

"Then who shot him?" Charley asked bluntly.

"There's only one other man who could've done it," said Sam. "The person who was giving us confidential information about the railroad's important shipments."

"And just who would that be, Sam," said Charley. "Just give me the name of the man who shot your brother."

"You oughta know his name, Sunday," said Sam Cropper. "When we were spyin' on you back in Cline, you spent some time with him . . . in his big ol' fancy railroad car."

Since it was the very beginning of the twentieth century, and the telephone was replacing the telegraph system, all Charley had to do was telegraph his friend Dee Kuper, the assistant sheriff back in Cline, from the train's telegraph setup in the baggage car. Then Dee, in turn, placed a telephone call to the marshal in Hondo, and Edwin J. Madison, a major, participating partner in the railroad's ownership, was arrested in his own private car by the marshal of Hondo, Texas, before he could reach San Antonio and the safety of his expensive lawyers.

Sam Cropper, along with his brother, Dale, and what remained of the Cropper Gang, was sent on to Del Rio, where a federal marshal was stationed. Once in federal custody, Sam and Dale Cropper would be tried in a federal court of law — just as Edwin J. Madison would be tried back in San Antonio.

After the fuss with the Croppers was over, and the westbound train had been sent along its way, Charley let Roscoe handle the reins for the rest of the trip back to Juanita. He sat in the backseat with his grandson, Henry Ellis, where they allowed themselves to talk about anything but what they had all just been through.

CHAPTER TEN

1961

"I don't think I'll ever get on another train in my entire lifetime, unless someone paid me a million dollars," said Caleb, the middle child.

"Oh, you would, too," said Noel. "What if we won a free trip to Disneyland. I'll bet you'd take a ride on the train they have out there."

"Would not," said Caleb.

"You would, too," said older brother Josh. "Ever since Disneyland opened, you've always said, 'If I ever get the chance to go to Disneyland, I'll ride every ride they've got to ride on there.'"

"Everything but the train," said Caleb.

"Have it your way, son," interrupted Grampa Hank. "But if I ever got the chance to ride that train out at Disneyland, I'd do it in a minute . . . twice. Then I'd run down the street to Knotts Berry Farm and ride their train, too."

"I'm with you, Grampa Hank," said Noel. "I like trains."

"So do I," said Josh.

"Have you ever been on a train, Josh?" asked Hank.

"Just one time, when I was really young. Mom took me to visit Daddy at the base where he was stationed."

"Why didn't you fly?" said Caleb.

"Because it was too expensive to fly in those days," answered Josh. "Besides, you went with us, Twerp. But you were just a little baby back then."

"Don't call me Twerp, Bonehead," said Caleb.

"I won't, unless you stop calling me Bonehead," said Josh.

"Hey, you guys," said Hank. "I'll bet your mother doesn't allow name calling when she's around."

"She doesn't," said Noel, cutting in. "If they'd said what they just said in front of Mommy —"

"You aren't gonna tattle on us again, are you?" said Josh.

"Tattletale, tattletale, tattletale . . ." said Caleb, trying to start something.

"All right," said Hank in a much louder voice. "You keep this up, I'm going to cut my story short right now and send every last one of you to bed . . . That means no TV, no playing, and like I just said, *no more story.*"

"Sorry, Grampa Hank," said Josh.

"I'm sorry, Grampa," echoed Caleb.

"Me too," said Noel.

"All right then. Everyone settle back, because I'm about to continue on with my story."

CHAPTER ELEVEN

1900

Because the threesome had been gone longer than the time Charley had allotted for their trip into San Antonio and back, they skirted the town and drove straight to the ranch.

The sky overhead had grown much darker. A sharp wind had begun to blow.

Feather Martin — the other ex–Texas Ranger who had helped make up the trio of friends that rode the range together for law, order, and justice in the early years of the Republic — had been put in charge of the ranch in Charley and Roscoe's absence. He should have been staying in the main ranch house. But upon their arrival, Feather sat astride his horse at the main gate entrance to the ranch, down by the road. He carried a double-barrel shotgun and looked to those in the approaching surrey like he was guarding the place from an unseen enemy, instead of just caretaking.

As the trotters grew closer to the gate, Roscoe slowed them some before stopping completely beside the little horseback cowboy with the shotgun.

"What's the matter, Feather?" said Charley from the backseat. "We got trouble?"

Feather tipped his hat back. He winked at Henry Ellis, just to acknowledge him, then he gazed at the surrey and team as a whole.

"That's one good-lookin' surrey, Charley," he said. "Makes you look like a gentleman. I can't wait ta see her when you get her all unwrapped."

"She is unwrapped," said Charley. "What you're looking at is the all-weather-repellant isinglass cover we put on her because of the bad weather. What are you doing all the way down here?" Charley wanted to know.

Feather leaned in closer.

"We've had visitors," he said.

"Visitors?" repeated Charley.

"More than once," said Feather.

"Anyone we know?" asked Charley.

Feather shook his head.

"No . . . don't think so," said Feather. "They looked like hired gunnies ta me. An' they left this."

He reached into his saddlebag and pulled out a poster with printing on one side. He held it up for the others to see.

PRIVATE PROPERTY

Until further notice:
<u>This Property is off limits</u>
to any persons without
special permission
from the
LATTIMER LAND COMPANY
Austin, Tex.

"Feather," said Charley. "You know where that big trash pile is that we keep for burning once a month?" asked Charley.

"Sure do, Boss."

"Take that sign over there and set it right on the top of that pile, will you?"

"With pleasure, Boss."

"Then throw some kerosene on it and set fire to it."

Feather reined around and was about to spur out.

"And, Feather," he said. "Meet us up at the house, will you? There're a few more things I'd like to ask you about our . . . visitors."

Within the hour, the three men were gathered around the kitchen table putting a brand-new pot of coffee to good use. A recently made cup of hot chocolate sat on the table in the spot reserved for Henry Ellis.

The men were deep in conversation when the back porch screen door slammed behind Henry Ellis. The boy walked swiftly through the screened-in area, then entered the kitchen. At his feet was the puppy he had acquired in Mexico at the beginning of the year. Because the pup had become a replacement for Charley's old dog, Buster, this one's name was Buster Number Two.

"What'd I tell ya, Charley," said Roscoe. "I said that it wouldn't be more than two minutes after Henry Ellis got here that he'd have that dog in my kitchen."

The boy reached down and picked Buster Two up into his arms, holding the pup for all to see.

The dog appeared to be smiling, with its tongue hanging halfway out of its mouth. But to top things off:

"That dog has mud on its feet," yelled Roscoe. "I don't need him to be tracking up my floors —"

"Hey, pardner," said Charley. "Calm yourself down. I reckon you're just going to have to get used to tracked-up floors. Just like you did with Buster Number One."

"Sorry, Charley . . . Henry Ellis," said Roscoe. "Sometimes I forget not everyone's a perfectionist like me."

"Come on over here, button," said Charley to the boy. "I want you to be in on this talk. You're getting to be old enough now to be involved in family matters, don't you think?"

Henry Ellis, still carrying the pup, moved over to the table and sat down where the hot chocolate was steaming.

"Thank you, Grampa," said the boy. "Thank you for noticing that I'm growing up."

"Just remember, growed up or not growed up, there'll still be no spurs worn at the table."

That caught Feather by surprise, but within seconds, he had pulled his spurs off his boots and was holding them behind his back, trying to muffle the rowels from jingling.

"Now," said Charley, "let's get down to business. Why don't we start off by letting Feather tell us all about the 'visitors' we had while we were off in San Antonio, and the likes."

"Well," began Feather. "I moved my stuff into the downstairs bedroom like you said I should before you left. Then I went about my chores . . . you know, keepin' the back porch swept, milkin' the one cow you have, even paintin' the screen door out back. After a few days, I'd finished with them particular chores and was lookin' fer others ta start on, when three men on horseback rode up from the front gate and served me with some 'Rightful Ownership' papers."

"Rightful Ownership papers?" said Charley. "You still got them, don't you, Feather?"

"Sure I do," said the little cowboy. "I got 'em in my room. Gimme a minute, I'll go get 'em, for ya."

Feather made a beeline to his room, through a door that led to the hallway, and returned with the papers in no time at all. He unfolded them and handed the official-looking documents to Charley.

"Roscoe," Charley called out. "Can you get me my magnifier?"

"You bet," said Roscoe.

Roscoe rummaged through several kitchen drawers, and he finally came up with Charley's old magnifying glass.

Charley held it up so he could read the small print on the papers Feather had produced.

"Why," he said quite loud, "this is an Eviction Notice. Someone's trying to evict me off of my own damn property."

"Let me see that," said Roscoe.

Charley handed him the legal papers. Roscoe took a pair of reading glasses from his pocket and put them on, then he shook the papers to smooth them out. With that done, he began to read.

"Well, I'll be hogtied and butter-greased," he muttered.

"What was that you said?" asked Feather.

"Oh, never mind," answered Roscoe, still reading. He turned to Charley.

"I think you'd better take these papers into town and let Flora Mae Huckabee take a look at 'em, Charley. That's what I'd do."

"Can I see them?" said Henry Ellis. "I've taken a few courses in school on how to deal with legal matters."

Roscoe handed him the papers. Henry Ellis began to read, walking around the room as he did. The boy's face kept changing expression as he got deeper and deeper into the legalese.

The three men found that they could only stare at the boy as he read; none of them had an inkling as to how he could understand any of it.

Finally, Henry Ellis handed the papers back to Charley.

"I think you should definitely talk to Flora Mae about this, Grampa, and hopefully she can direct you to an attorney familiar with these types of cases."

"Cases?" shouted Charley. "The only way I ever handled cases like this was with my Walker Colt and six lead bullets."

"That's right," echoed Roscoe.

Feather nodded.

"Grampa," said the boy. "We are now in the twentieth century. As much as I've always respected the way you three fought for law and order, it's just not that simple anymore. You're going to have to fight this one in a court of law, Grampa. I'll bet on that."

"So you think Flora Mae might be able to help me find a good lawyer, do you?"

"She's a businesswoman, isn't she?" said the boy. "And she runs a corporation to boot. She ought to know who's a good attorney or not."

"I just don't want a flannel-mouth liar," said Charley.

"January B. Ellison," said Flora Mae Huckabee. "He's the most honest lawyer I know."

"But is he the best lawyer you know?" asked Charley.

"I said he was the most honest. Isn't that what you wanted? He's not the best, by far. But I still suggest that you hire him for the situation you've found yourself in."

They were in Flora Mae's Pool Hall & Bar. Charley sat across from the lady hotel owner and entrepreneur, while she advised him about legal representatives. The two of them had known each other since childhood. It had been Flora Mae who financed Charley for the Texas Longhorn auction, and also for the cross-country cattle drive that followed. They both trusted one another absolutely.

"So it's January B. Ellison, is it?" said Charley. "I seem to remember a kid called January that we went to school with. Am I right?" asked Charley.

"He's one and the same, Charley. Only he doesn't go by the name of January anymore. He's just plain J.B. Ellison, Attorney at Law, now. And he has his offices in Del Rio."

"Del Rio's thirty miles away, Flora Mae," said Charley. "That's almost a full day's ride."

"And you're gonna ride it, Charley Sunday, more than one time. I'll lay odds on that . . . that is, if you don't want your ranch stolen out from under you."

"Do you think that could really happen to me, darlin'?"

"If you don't get yourself some legal assistance, you can bet your damn life it could."

"Would you telephone this January fella for me, Flora Mae?" asked Charley.

"Why should I have to spend my money on your telephone call?" said Flora Mae.

"I'll pay for it," said Charley. "Honest I will. It's just that you know him —"

She cut him off. "You went ta school with him, too, Charley Sunday. I can't help it if you've forgotten who he was. But I'll let you use my phone, if you want to, providin' you do all the talkin' . . . and all the payin'."

"Well?" said Charley.

"Well what?" said Flora Mae.

"Where's your telephone?"

"You don't think you're going to call him on the telephone now, do you?" said Flora Mae. "But when you do make that call, you'll need to have that . . . that 'phony' eviction notice with you so he'll know what you're talkin' about."

"Oh, yeah," said Charley. "I forgot about that. Will I need the sign, too?"

"What sign?" said Flora Mae.

"The Do Not Enter sign they posted on my front gate."

Flora Mae drew in a long breath, then she sighed.

"Yes, Charley. You better bring that, too. Any evidence January might need. It's for your own good, you know. Come by around ten o'clock tomorrow morning. I'll be here."

Charley stepped out of the pool hall and bar into the little patio behind Flora Mae's hotel where he would sometimes tie his horse. Dice was there now, and Charley took his slicker from behind the saddle where it was tied and put it on. The clouds were swirling overhead, and he knew the storm would certainly hit before he had the chance to get home.

He aimed for the stirrup with his boot, jumped, then swung over into the saddle just as the first drops of rain began to fall. For the rest of the trip back to his ranch, the rain came down in buckets, making it difficult to see, at times, for both man and animal.

When he reached the front gate to the ranch, he had to stop for a moment to pull down another sign that had been posted. It read the same as the other sign, only this one came with a human warning.

"You can stick that sign right back where you found it, old man," said a rough voice coming from the grove behind him, on the other side of the road.

Charley didn't turn.

"The only place I'll stick this sign, mister, will be where sunlight never shines," Charley answered as his hand slipped slowly down his right leg to his boot.

"Don't you threaten me, *amigo,*" the voice went on, "or I'll drop you right where you are."

Charley whirled around in the rain, pulling the Walker Colt's trigger at the same time.

His bullet spun the man on the horse behind him out of the saddle and into a growing quagmire of mud that had gathered in the side ditch.

The three other men, who had been right behind the man in the mud, went for their guns.

The *click* of the Walker being re-cocked stopped them all cold.

"If you three want to try me," said Charley, "make your choice. But I've got five more pieces of lead in this here Texas hog-leg that says you're all cowards. Do I have that correct?"

No one moved.

"Now, throw those revolvers of yours into the mud puddle your friend is laying in over there, and answer me one question."

The men tossed their weapons into the ditch, one at a time.

"Thank you, boys," said Charley with a

smile. "Now, who is it put you up to all this?"

"It was Ben Campbell and his wife," said one of the men.

"Shaddup, you fool," said another. "No talkin'."

There wasn't another word from the first man.

"All right," said Charley. "I can see you don't want to cooperate, so why don't you pick up your man there . . . not your guns . . . and put him back on his horse. Then, get the hell out of here before I put a bullet through every one of you."

While the rain continued to pound as they were fetching their friend and loading him back onto his horse, Charley had one more thing to add.

"And don't any of you come near this ranch ever again, or you'll get ten times what you got today."

Charley remained where he was until all four of them were mounted, then he watched as they rode off down the muddy road, moving away from Charley and his ranch, until the rain closed in around them like a solid gray curtain.

"We just had some more visitors," said Charley as he entered the kitchen through the back porch, shutting the inside door behind him. He tracked in some mud. His jingling spurs were still attached to his boots.

Roscoe didn't say a word. He could sense the level of Charley's ire.

Henry Ellis sat at the table, sipping some hot chocolate and reading his dog-eared dime novel.

The pup was in his basket nearby, playing with a toy.

"What kind of visitors?" the boy mumbled as he turned a page.

"Some real-time, gun-toting visitors, that's who," Charley answered. "A lot more real than what you're reading about there."

Henry Ellis looked up. He could now see that his grandfather was steaming.

"I'm sorry that something's got your goat, Grampa," he said. "I wasn't paying attention."

"Well, what about you?" he said to the still stoic Roscoe. "Can't you see that we got trouble . . . right here on the ranch? Four gunmen stopped me at my own damn gate . . . *my own gate!*"

Roscoe began to tremble.

"We didn't hear nothin', Charley. It was rainin' so hard outside, you couldn'ta heard a bull pass gas."

"Well, one of 'em drew on me . . . but I got him first."

"Are you all right, Grampa?" said Henry Ellis, getting up from the table and moving toward the old man.

"Oh, I'm all right, son," said Charley. "I reckon I'm just still pretty angry."

The boy could see that his grandfather was starting to cool down.

"Well, Grampa," said Henry Ellis. "As soon as you're calmed down a little more, why don't you sit over here at the table and we can all talk about it?"

Charley turned to Roscoe.

"Where's he learning that stuff? He sounds like a schoolteacher."

"That particular sayin'," said Roscoe, "about sittin' down an' talkin' about it, he got from you."

"You don't say?" said Charley with the hint of a grin on his face.

Charley moved over to the table and sat. The others joined him in his thoughts.

"I had to shoot a man today," he said. "The fella drew down on me when I was trying to enter my own property. So I shot him. Better call the sheriff, Roscoe, before he comes looking for me."

"Don't be too hasty, there, Charley, my *amigo*," said Roscoe. "You did say this man drawed on you first, didn't ya? I doubt there were any witnesses."

"I reckon you weren't paying attention to me when I said 'visitors.' That's 'visitors' with an 'S' at the end. There were three others with him, and they sure aren't going to be witnesses for me. Why, I'll bet they're all four of 'em over at the sheriff's office right now filling out the proper papers to have me put in jail."

"Before you go any further, Grampa," interrupted Henry Ellis, "why don't you let Uncle Roscoe make a telephone call to the sheriff's office? If those men were here for a legal reason, you might just be in some trouble with the law. But if they were here for illegal reasons . . . like trying to force us off this ranch . . . I'll bet they'll never report the incident at all."

"My little lawyer," said Charley with a look of empathy in his eyes. He patted his grandson on the shoulder.

"Why don't you let me make that call to the sheriff?" said Roscoe. "Before you scoff any more at what the boy has ta say."

"Fine," said Charley. "Be my guest. The telephone's right there on the wall. All you have to do is crank it."

Roscoe stood up and went to the phone hanging on the wall, beside the stove. He cranked the handle several times for the operator. "Can you put me through ta Willingham Dubbs's office, Mildred?" he said when she answered.

When he finally got through to the sheriff, he asked point blank if anyone had been in to see him lately about a dispute over the ownership of Charley's ranch. He stood there for a few moments more while the sheriff relayed his answer. Then the lawman asked the expected follow-up questions. There were a few "Yups," from Roscoe, followed by nods of the head, plus just as many, if not more, "Nopes," all said while shaking his head. Finally Roscoe hung up the earpiece and turned back to the others.

"Now wasn't that easy?" he asked Charley.

"What did he say?" Charley asked loudly.

"Yeah, Uncle Roscoe," said the boy. "I was right, wasn't I?"

"You were right, Henry Ellis," said Roscoe. "No one has been there to accuse your grampa, or anyone else, of shootin' anyone. But, boy did Willingham have a lotta questions he wanted ta ask me about why I was callin' him."

"None of his business," said Charley.

"Well," said Roscoe, "it was us that called him, an' got him interested in the first place, wasn't it?"

"That's true," said Charley, rubbing his day's growth of stubble with a callused hand. "I think I'd like to go wash up."

"Supper ain't goin' ta be ready for quite a spell, Charley. No need ta wash up now."

Charley stood up from the kitchen table. He held his hands out in front of him.

"I said I wanted to go wash my hands. It feels like I still got blood on 'em. And I don't care how long it's going to be until you have supper ready," he added.

When he lay himself down to sleep that night, Henry Ellis found he wasn't able to doze off right away, as usually happened. All he could think about was what had happened at the supper table that afternoon when his grampa Charley had returned from town.

It was hard to believe that someone had sent four hired gunmen to the ranch to re-post the Keep Off sign advising readers not to trespass. It was just as hard to believe that, due to the timing, the men were there just as Charley was arriving home for the day. And for one of them to have actually drawn down on his grampa . . . *Well, that was pretty stupid,* Henry Ellis thought. His grampa Charley was no one to tussle with, that was for sure . . . and Charley had drawn himself and outshot the intruder. Then he'd held the others at bay until he'd told them to skedaddle and never show their faces around the ranch again.

But, through all the stories he'd heard over the years about his grampa Charley . . . and all the times he'd seen his grampa in action himself . . . he'd never seen his grampa affected by a confrontation like he'd encountered at the front gate.

Henry Ellis was lying there in his bed thinking, when the bedroom door opened a crack, letting a slice of light leak in from the hallway.

"You still awake, Henry Ellis?" Charley said in a gruff whisper.

"Yes, Grampa," the boy replied. "I'm awake."

"Mind if we talk for a spell?" Charley asked him.

When the boy said "No, c'mon in," Charley moved on into the room, turned the light switch on, then sat himself down on the bed beside his grandson.

At first, no words were spoken between the two. Charley just reached over and began running his sausage-like fingers through the boy's hair.

"Did I make a mistake tonight?" he asked. "I was still pretty riled up when I got to the house. I think I owe you and Roscoe some apologies . . . some amends."

"Well," said Henry Ellis, "you were a little grouchy."

Charley switched from toying with the boy's hair to rubbing his shoulders with both hands.

"Well, I'm sorry, son," he said. "And I'll make my peace with Roscoe in the morning. I had this feeling I was out of line, and I didn't want to go to bed without saying something."

"That's all right, Grampa," said the boy. "I know you have a lot of things on your mind right now, and if your head wasn't so cluttered with —"

Charley put a finger against Henry Ellis's lips. The boy showed some surprise at the action, but he didn't pull back or anything. He just sat there and waited for his grandfather to speak.

"I'm afraid, Henry Ellis," said Charley. "I'm afraid I've gotten myself into something that I don't remember getting into. I've always heard that old folks start doing things like this when we get up in years. And now, someone's claiming that my ranch don't belong to me, and I have no recollection at all why that would be."

"You're not crazy, Grampa, if that's what

you're thinking. I'll bet you could tell me right now what the name of your first horse was."

"Rango," said Charley. "No, it was Ringo," he said, sounding sure of himself. He smiled. "I got it right, but it took me two guesses to answer correctly."

"See what I mean?" said the boy. "It may have taken you two guesses, but you still remembered. I don't think you forgot anything concerning your ranch, Grampa. I think someone has set their sights on stealing it from you."

"That's what Flora Mae thinks, too," he said. "How would you like to ride into town with me tomorrow, Henry Ellis?"

The boy nodded at the opportunity.

"Then rain or shine, the two of us are going into Juanita tomorrow," he said.

Henry Ellis laughed, then he threw his arms around his grampa Charley, and the two of them squeezed each other tight.

CHAPTER TWELVE

The next storm rolled in around midnight and continued on for the rest of the night and into the morning. So when Henry Ellis woke up just before dawn and finally rolled out of bed in his ever-present long underwear, something he'd taken to wearing on a regular basis since the cold weather had begun, he made it a point to glance out the window.

The rain was still pounding the old ranch house, yard, and barn like a band of synchronized blacksmiths.

He pulled on his trousers and a new wool shirt, slipping the suspenders over his shoulders even though he knew he would be soaking wet before noon. He put on a pair of socks before pulling on the pair of boots his grandfather had given him for the trail drive a year earlier. The boots had started to feel tight the last time he had visited his grampa, but when he was with

Charley and Roscoe on the ranch, he wouldn't think of wearing anything else.

He put on a leather vest, which also felt tight, then he tied a yellow neckerchief around his neck. He grabbed his wool jacket out of the closet, and he didn't forget to grab his western-style hat, with the leather strings you tied it on with. Then he ran out the door.

When he got to the kitchen it was getting lighter outside. Not like it did on a normal, sun-shiny day, but a lighter gray than the day had been when he'd looked out the window from upstairs.

The kitchen was empty. At first he thought he might have been the first one up, but when he peeked out the lower-level window, he could see the light from a lantern in the barn, where Grampa Charley and Roscoe were feeding the horses.

There was a pot of coffee going on the stove, so he got himself a cup from the cupboard and poured himself a little sip.

When he brought the cup to his lips, it felt as if he had scalded himself. So he did what his grampa always did and added some cold water to the cup from the tap by the sink.

He was trying to figure out what he could make himself for breakfast when he spotted the old, covered pot on a back burner, simmering. He knew it was Roscoe's mush. And he knew he had better eat some of it if he knew what was good for him, because his grampa always had Roscoe put on a pot of mush when he was in a hurry.

There was a large spoon laid out beside the pot. Henry Ellis found a bowl in the cupboard and a smaller spoon in a drawer, then he scooped out a medium-size portion for himself before sitting down at the table.

The dime novel he'd been reading the night before was still on the counter by the icebox. He picked it up, found his place, then began spooning the mush into his mouth while reading.

It wasn't too long before he heard some boots on the outside steps, and the door to the screened-in porch opening. He kept eating and reading until he heard the kitchen door open behind him and his grampa's voice.

"We sure could've used your help out there, Henry Ellis."

He started getting out of his slicker and jacket before he sat down.

"How many times do I have to tell you that chores come first around here, Henry Ellis . . . then we eat breakfast?"

The boy closed — he almost slammed —

the book. He slowly turned around to face his grandfather.

"I'm sorry, Grampa," he said. "I really am."

"Well, I'll forgive you this one time," said Charley as he went to the stove, found a cup, then poured himself some coffee. As he sat down opposite his grandson, he noticed the coffee cup in front of the boy.

"Since when have you been a user of Arbuckles?" he asked.

"Oh," said the boy. "I just thought that since I was here on the ranch, working with you —"

"First of all," said Charley, "we've already discussed the fact that you aren't working. You aren't doing a thing except reading that New York trash in front of you that spews nothing but baloney about . . . about —"

"About you, Grampa," said Henry Ellis. "This book is all about you, Roscoe, and Feather, and your adventures as Texas Rangers in the middle of the last century. And you're calling that 'baloney'?"

"Where did you get that book?" Charley wanted to know.

"Mother gave it to me," said the boy. "It's not new. It belonged to her. She told me your friend Ned Buntline gave it to her when she was a little girl, when you invited him to the ranch for a visit . . . or don't you remember? Mother said Mr. Buntline wrote it himself as a tribute to you, Roscoe, and Feather. The book is all about you three brave men, Grampa. Heroes. Men I can be proud of. Men who never give up. Men who always stand up for what they believe . . ."

He threw the book on the table, next to Charley, then he began to sob. He rose up from the table and ran down the hallway, up the stairs, and to his room.

"Henry Ellis," said Charley in a soft voice as he entered the boy's bedroom. "I'm sorry, son. I didn't mean to hurt your feelings. I don't ever want to do that to you."

The boy was lying facedown on his bed with his head buried in the pillow. After a moment, he rolled over, revealing red and swollen eyes. He wiped away a tear.

"Can I still go along with you to Flora Mae's this morning?" he asked.

"If you clean up your face and blow your nose, you can," said Charley.

Henry Ellis rolled over completely, then he sat up.

"Give me a minute or two, will you, Grampa? Then I'll be right with you."

The two rode horseback into town. Even

though they faced frequent rain showers, the oil-skin slickers they both wore kept them as dry as their heavycoats underneath kept them warm. The stormy weather was showing no change. If anything, the rain was continuing to fall without as many let-ups between downpours.

"Grampa Charley?" asked the boy.

"What is it, Henry Ellis?"

"Why did Ned Buntline only write one story about you?"

Charley wasn't expecting that particular question, so he cleared his throat several times to give him time to think, then he turned to the boy.

"Buntline did write another story or two about me, Roscoe, and Feather, but the governor of Texas asked him not to publish 'em. Seems he didn't want the world knowing who we were back then."

"Wow," said Henry Ellis. "The three of you musta been working undercover on a big case for him to do that. Am I right?"

"You're wrong," said Charley. "The governor just didn't want the fame books like that brought to people going to our heads. Plus he wanted to set a precedent for the department."

"Why was that?"

"The governor felt that a law officer working as a Texas Ranger had enough on his hands without adding the recognition factor to his job."

"Oh, I get it," said Henry Ellis. "The governor wanted to keep you, Roscoe, and Feather incognito."

"In-cog-what?" said Charley. "Remember, son, I only have an third-grade education. We never got past five-letter words when I was in school."

"Incognito means that the governor wanted to make sure that no one could identify you as a Ranger, if you ever had a case that required you to work undercover."

"That's true," said Charley. "So I had to write Ned Buntline and tell him, no more dime novels." He chuckled to himself. "It really hurt his feelings, because the first one . . . the one you're reading . . . had been one of his best sellers, and he had hopes for the follow-up books."

"But he never published them, did he?" said Henry Ellis.

"No," said Charley. "He never did."

There was a long pause.

"Ned Buntline wasn't like a lot of those dime-novel writers, son," Charley went on. "Ned Buntline kept his word. He understood respect."

They rode along in silence while Henry

157

Ellis let everything Charley told him sink in.

"He even offered to give me one of those 'Buntline Special' Colt revolvers like he gave Wyatt Earp and several others. You know, the barrel on it is about three feet long. I told him, thanks, but I don't need it, Ned, I'm partial to my Walker."

"Too bad," said the boy. "I'd sure like to have seen one of those Buntline Specials."

Charley turned to him with a grin.

"Oh, you'll see one, son," he said. "Buntline had one made and shipped to me, anyway."

A sizzling streak of lightning touched down less than a mile away. It was followed immediately by a deafening crash of thunder.

"Why do you think the Latimer Land Company is trying to force you off your ranch, Grampa?" asked Henry Ellis. "They seemed like such nice people."

"You can never be too sure about a man you've met on a train, son," said Charley. "And that includes women, too."

"Do you think Miss Eleanor is a part of it, too?" asked the boy.

"She's the one who told you it was her cousin that left her a ranch, wasn't it?"

"Yes, sir," said Henry Ellis. "But —"

"Ain't no 'buts' about it, son," said Charley. "They sucked you in. They did whatever they had to to get you on their side, so you'd get me to be on their side. So we wouldn't be suspicious of their intended scheme."

"I liked them, Grampa," said Henry Ellis. "I really did."

"Like I just said, they did whatever they had to do to get you on their side. They needed for you to believe them. It wouldn't have worked any other way."

The surrounding rain began to fall much harder than before, so Charley spurred Dice into a slow gallop and kept the horse at that pace until Henry Ellis had caught up to him.

"If you're not afraid of your horse slipping and sliding," he shouted, "keep up with me all the way into town. The quicker we can get there, the less rain we'll have to put up with."

They tied off their horses in a covered corral that catered to Flora Mae's hotel, then they ran as fast as they could for the door to the pool hall and bar, laughing all the way.

Once inside, Charley hushed the boy by placing a finger to his lips. The room was near empty of customers, and its high walls and ceiling produced resounding echoes

159

throughout the large structure.

Charley saw Flora Mae poke her head out of her office door at the far end of the room, just long enough for her to see the two of them and beckon them both to join her in the private alcove.

When they entered Flora Mae's office, the woman quickly introduced them to a smartly dressed dark-skinned man with his hair parted down the middle and slicked back with a sweet-smelling tonic.

"This is J.B. Ellison, Attorney at Law, Charley," said Flora Mae. "And this is Charles Abner Sunday and his grandson, Henry Ellis, J.B."

Ellison stood only long enough to shake hands before he re-sat himself and began digging into a large briefcase that he kept on the floor at his side.

"Flora Mae tells me that you were in our class at school, Mr. Sunday," said the lawyer. "But, of course, I have no recollection."

Henry Ellis stared at the man as he slid a sheaf of papers out of the briefcase and started flipping through them.

"Sit down, sit down, Mr. Sunday," he began. "And you, too, son. I have the Vacate Property papers filed against you right here in front of me —"

"You have what papers right there in front of you?" asked Charley.

"The Vacate Property papers, Mr. Sunday. I took it upon myself to stop in at the county courthouse, down the street, to find out if anything official regarding ownership of your ranch had recently been filed, and they gave me these papers."

"Who filed 'em?" Charley wanted to know.

"They were filed by a law firm in Fort Worth," said the attorney.

"I mean *who* filed 'em?" said Charley. "Just give me the name of the son-of-a-bitch!"

"These papers were not filed by any one, single person, Mr. Sunday," said Ellison. "They were filed by two people . . . a couple . . . a man and his wife."

"Their names, Mr. Ellison," said Charley. "Give me their names!"

"Oh, all right," said the lawyer as he searched for the names somewhere in the stack of papers he still held. "Campbell," he read, "Dr. and Mrs. Benjamin J. Campbell."

Charley smiled. "Campbell," he said winking at the boy. "Those are your friends, ain't they?" he asked Henry Ellis.

"They told me that Mrs. Campbell had inherited a ranch here in Juanita, from a distant cousin, but nothing about you,

161

Grampa," said the boy. "Something must be terribly wrong, I'm afraid."

"You can bet your boots it is," said Charley. "I'm beginning to get this feeling that Dr. and Mrs. Campbell are nothing but two-bit four-flushers."

"Who are these people?" asked Flora Mae.

"Just a married couple Henry Ellis met on the train coming from Austin," said Charley. "They were on the train to Juanita, too."

He suddenly raised his eyes, looking directly at his grandson.

"And it was Dr. Campbell you saw shoot that gambler fella on the train, wasn't it, Henry Ellis?"

"Yes, sir," said the boy.

"They took that gambler fella's body off the train in some little town south of Austin, didn't they?"

"San Marcos," said Henry Ellis.

Charley turned back to the attorney.

"Then don't you think someone oughta be checking with the authorities in San Marcos to find out if they ever identified the dead man?" said Charley.

"There were two dead men," said Henry Ellis, correcting him.

"We want 'em to check out the one —"

"Who was wearing the blue suit," said

Henry Ellis, interrupting.

"I don't think I understand what you're trying to get at," said Ellison. "How does a dead man in San Marcos tie in to these people trying to steal your ranch here in Juanita, Mr. Sunday? Can you tell me that?"

"You're my lawyer, ain't you?" Charley asked the man.

"Well," said Ellison. "We haven't signed any contracts yet . . . plus, you haven't given me any cash or collateral to seal my intention to work for you —"

Charley looked at Flora Mae.

"Give him —"

"Two hundred dollars —" said Ellison.

"Give the man two hundred dollars, Flora Mae," said Charley, "so he can get started."

Without question, Flora Mae went to her safe, dialed the combination, then took out two hundred dollars in crisp, twenty-dollar bills, handing them over to Charley, who in turn gave them to Ellison.

"Are you working for me now?" asked Charley.

"Do you want me to telegraph the authorities in San Marcos?" said Ellison. "Or use Miss Huckabee's telephone?"

It had stopped raining for their ride back to the ranch. Henry Ellis felt good not having

163

the rainwater dripping down his neck every minute of the journey. And it made him proud of his grampa that this ranch mishap was going to be handled in a court of law, rather than his grampa Charley's usual way of handling a situation that affected him personally.

When they reached the front entrance to Charley's ranch, the gate was wide open. There was another Keep Off This Property sign posted, with a large padlock and coiled chain wrapped around the gateposts.

"This isn't funny anymore," said Charley as he leaned forward for a better look.

"There's only one way to handle this, Henry Ellis," Charley told the boy. He reached down and pulled his Walker Colt from his boot. "Get behind me."

He aimed, cocked, and fired!

The lock spun away with a resounding ricochet, and the chain and sign went flying after it.

"I reckon that'll show 'em," he said.

"You can't be breaking any laws by going through your own gate," said Henry Ellis.

"And onto my own property," added Charley, closing the gate behind them.

As the two started up the road toward the ranch house, they heard two distinct gunshots coming from that direction.

Charley pulled his Walker again, then he turned to Henry Ellis.

"You stay here," he said. "Find yourself some cover . . . and don't stick your head out, no matter what happens."

"Yes, sir," said the boy.

And Charley was gone. Slapping leather to old Dice, man and horse were off at a run, heading toward the ranch house at the far end of the access road.

Henry Ellis watched after his grampa for a few more moments. Then he turned and spurred his mount over to a small cottonwood grove by a stream. He dismounted, then tried to blend into his surroundings as best as he could.

As Charley rode into the ranch yard at a full gallop, he could see Roscoe behind a broken window in the kitchen as he raised his rifle and fired toward the barn.

Charley reined up quick, setting Dice down on his rump. He sprang out of the saddle, keeping his eyes on the area by the barn where Roscoe had been returning fire. Then he ran up the steps, across the narrow porch, and through the screen door, disappearing inside.

"Roscoe, don't shoot," he yelled from the screened-in porch. "It's me, Charley. I'm coming in."

Charley ran to the kitchen door and burst through.

Once he was in the kitchen, he could see Roscoe across the room by the broken window. He was reloading his rifle from an open box of shells on the table.

Roscoe turned and threw his partner a grin.

Charley winked back.

"What's going on, pardner?" asked Charley as another bullet clipped some broken glass by Roscoe's head, causing him to duck away.

"Two men . . . rode into the ranch yard . . . they ordered me, and whoever else was in the house, to vacate the premises pronto. I was here alone, and I didn't want them knowing that. So I answered them with a bullet from my rifle. They took off for the barn, and we've been tradin' lead fer close to an hour now. I sure am glad you're back."

"I'm going to leave again, Roscoe," said Charley.

"Now why would you want to do that when yer pretty safe right here?" said Roscoe as he triggered off another round in the direction of the barn.

"I'm going to go out the front door," he said, "then see if I can get around in back of them. You stay here and keep on drawing their attention."

"Will do," said Roscoe, ducking back as another bullet flew past his head.

He moved closer to the window to return some fire. When he turned back, Charley was gone.

From the eastern corner of the front porch, Charley had a view of the barn's right side. The attackers were located at the front of the barn, and from what Charley had observed when he rode in, one was firing through the unlatched barn doors, while the other had worked his way up to the loft above.

It won't be difficult to beeline it for the barn without being seen, thought Charley. *But getting around behind them might present a different set of problems.*

He stopped right there. *No reason to defeat my purpose before I've even tried,* he thought.

So he stepped off the front porch, took a few steps toward the barn, edged around a flock of chickens, then ran like hell.

He slid to a stop. That was to keep his body from slamming into the side of the barn. Then he crept along toward the rear and slipped around the corner with caution.

Once he was on the far end of the barn, he checked the large double doors only to find that they'd been latched from the inside. The only other conceivable way inside was through the smaller hayloft doors, ten feet above his head.

There was a hook and combined pulley system attached to the center beam that stuck out over and beyond those doors, which he and Roscoe used to load hay bales into the loft. Now, all Charley had to do was climb that series of ropes to the top, then swing into the loft.

To do so he had to put the Walker back in his boot, because when performing such a feat, one needed to use both hands.

He found an old crate they sometimes used to carry oats into the barn for feeding. He used it as a makeshift stool so he could reach the hook at the bottom of the pulley that hung down just above his head. He took a slight jump up and grabbed on to the hook at the bottom of the combined pulley system. That sent him to spinning, and he had to wait a few moments longer until his body had stopped rotating before he was able to start climbing.

Hand over hand he went, until he was at

the top. He swung into the loft, stood up straight, then carefully released the rope and pulley so it wouldn't bang against the back of the barn and draw attention to him.

When that was done, he again drew his Walker Colt and began moving silently toward the front.

All the while he was gaining entrance to the loft, he could hear the aggressors as they kept up their rifle barrage against Roscoe in the house.

By the time he had gone about a third of the way to the front, he had come to the open space between the front and rear lofts. From that position, he could look down and see one of the aggressors firing his rifle out the barn doors at Roscoe. He glanced toward the front of the loft, on his level, and spotted the second shooter hiding behind some hay bales, using them as cover as he fired down at Roscoe from that hidden perch.

In the middle of the barn, hanging from the center beam, was another combined pulley system. This one was used for lifting the bales of hay down from the loft to the first level, where they fed the livestock.

Charley drew in a long breath of air, then he began walking toward the back of the man in the loft who was shooting from behind the hay bales.

When he was close enough, Charley brought the barrel of the Walker Colt down hard on the man's head, knocking him unconscious.

He turned abruptly, then moved back to his previous position, pivoting again so he could see the second man below.

The man still had his back to Charley, and he was firing on the house every time Roscoe returned a shot in his direction.

Charley looked around him, trying to figure out the best way to approach this particular problem.

That's when he remembered the steps that led from the lower level to the loft. In his haste, he had nearly forgotten about the steps. He thanked God under his breath, then turned slowly and started down.

There were subtle creaks with every step taken. But he had to assume that the shooter would think the noises were being made by his partner in the loft above.

When Charley finally reached the dirt floor of the barn, and stepped cautiously out of the crude stairwell, he had an almost perfect angle between himself and the rifleman.

He did not want to kill the man, only subdue him. So he could not call him out at that distance. What he did instead was to move slowly over to the hook and pulley in the center of the barn, where he started increasing the length of the ropes used by the combined pulley system, until he figured it was long enough to accomplish what he had in mind.

He took hold of the hook at the bottom of the lower pulley and backed up several paces. He guessed it to weigh around seven pounds. When he had figured he was far enough away from the gunman to make his plan work, he swung the large hook and pulley directly at the man. At the same time he opened his mouth and let out just one word:

"Hey!"

The gunman, his rifle at the ready, turned at the sound of Charley's voice, and he was hit dead center in the face with the swinging hook and pulley.

He dropped as if he were made of lead, his rifle discharging as it fell to the side.

Charley immediately rushed to the slightly parted barn doors. He stuck his face out cautiously, calling to his partner inside the house.

"Roscoe," he yelled. "You can come out now. There's no more threat."

Inside the house, Roscoe backed away from the shattered glass and headed for the screen door.

He stepped out onto the small landing, then moved down the steps to the muddy ranch yard. He could make out Charley's form as he dragged one of the aggressors out of the barn. Then he went back inside to get the other.

By the time Roscoe got to the barn and peeked inside, Charley had the second man hooked to the combined pulley system by his gunbelt, and was lowering the still unconscious shooter to the floor below.

Roscoe gave Charley a hand dragging the man outside, where they left him beside his partner.

Charley then excused himself and went back to the house to call the sheriff. On his way, he turned to the entrance road and waved a couple of times.

It wasn't more than a few seconds before Henry Ellis was urging his horse toward the house at a full gallop.

Charley grinned. He shook his head, then muttered to himself, "I knew that boy wouldn't be able to keep his head down."

CHAPTER THIRTEEN

Kinney County sheriff, Willingham Dubbs, had ridden out to the ranch shortly after he'd received the telephone call from Charley. He had been asked to please come out and pick up two intruder-trespassers Charley had caught on the property, taking potshots at the ranch house.

Sheriff Dubbs had brought two of his deputies with him to handle the lawbreakers, and he'd already sent them back to town with the two men so they could process, then put the two behind bars where they belonged.

Before he'd sent them on, he had interviewed each man separately, receiving no information at all from either one of them.

A cold wind had begun to blow, and now that the two trespassers were on their way to jail, the sheriff suggested to Charley and Roscoe that they go inside where it was warmer, because he wanted to have a few words with the two ex-Rangers.

"This dispute you claim you're havin' with a man named Campbell," the sheriff began. "Have you made any attempt to settle this, uh, land claim, in a court of law?"

"Of course I have, Willingham," said Charley. "I met with my lawye . . ." he corrected himself, "my attorney, just this morning, and there were a few things he was supposed to be taking care of."

"Just make sure you show up in court," said Dubbs.

"You know me better than that, Willingham," said Charley. "We mighta had our differences in the past, but what's going on right now I had nothing to do with. They're trying to steal my ranch right out from under me, Willingham. Except I've owned this ranch for too many years, and God help those who try to take it away from me."

"Don't be makin' threats, Charley. Especially in front of the law," warned the sheriff. "Because if something happens to Dr. or Mrs. Campbell, you'll be my first suspect."

"You know me better than that, Willingham, to be pressuring me for something I ain't even thought of yet. I wouldn't hurt either one of those city slickers . . . unless, of course, one of them tried to kill me. But that don't go for their hired guns. If one of those fellas ever steps in the way of one of my bullets, he probably needs killing."

"I was meaning to ask you that, Charley," said the sheriff. "You didn't even use your gun against those two we just hauled away. That don't seem like the Charley Sunday I know. If I'd been called out here any other day but today, at least one of those men, if not both of 'em, woulda had more blood on 'em, for sure."

"Can I make a suggestion?" asked Roscoe.

Both Charley and the sheriff gave him their attention while Roscoe continued.

"Can you, Sheriff, and your deputies, keep an eye out for all of us out here at the ranch? . . . Go a little out of yer way, maybe, if you happen to be in the area, and check in on us? We got Charley's grandson visiting with us for the holiday, and I wouldn't want to see anything bad happen to him."

"I suppose we can do that, Roscoe," said the sheriff. "And if it looks like there might be another confrontation about to happen out here . . . use your telephone. I found out today that I can be here in under a half an hour."

"Lotta good that'll do," mumbled Charley.

"What's that you say?" asked the sheriff.

"I said," Charley began, "a lot of good that

will do . . . you taking a half hour to get here. In a half hour, they could kill every last one of us, then set the ranch ablaze. How would you feel if that happened, Willingham?"

"All right, Charley. Have it your way. By law, a man is allowed to protect what's his, so go ahead and protect your ranch, if you feel you have to. But mind me, Charley Sunday, if it turns out that these folks who are challenging you for rightful ownership win this case in court, I may have to look at any protecting you've done out here in a different way."

"Willingham," said Charley. "You go ahead thinking like that. But I *am* the rightful owner. And I really shouldn't have to be going to no courthouse to prove that what's mine is mine."

"As long as you remember that this is damn near the twentieth century, and not some ol' Wild West town you're living in, I'll go along with you, Charley."

He stood to go, then he turned for one last word.

"As long as you keep doing what you've been doing," said the sheriff, "you and I have no need to butt horns again."

Charley and Roscoe both began to stand.

"No need to escort me to the door, gentlemen," the sheriff said. "I know the way out."

As the screen door on the porch slammed behind him, Henry Ellis came rushing into the room from the same direction.

"There's some really big gray clouds moving in around us, Grampa. Would you like me to feed the livestock, put our horses away, then lock up the barn for you?"

Charley smiled. He reached over and ruffled the boy's hair.

"If that's what you'd like to do," said Charley. "Then do it. No one's stopping you."

The following morning, after Roscoe and Henry Ellis had hitched the trotters to the new surrey, the two of them helped Charley wrap the vehicle in the isinglass covering. The weather had not changed that much from the day before.

Their intentions were to drive into Juanita so Charley could meet with his attorney again. He was able to do that because his lawyer, January B. Ellison, was staying at Flora Mae's hotel as a guest and would be there for the rest of the week, the lawyer had told Charley.

As the surrey entered town, traveling down Main Street in the direction of Flora Mae's hotel, it passed the other hotel in town, a smaller but pricier place called the

Emporium.

Stepping out onto the porch as the surrey passed by was Dr. and Mrs. Campbell, on their way to a late breakfast, Henry Ellis assumed.

Charley stared straight ahead and continued driving.

"Don't either one of you look at them," he advised the two. "You do, and you're dog meat in my book."

Roscoe, in the passenger seat, kept his eyes straight ahead.

But Henry Ellis, in the back, was able to look over for a brief moment.

Dr. Campbell avoided looking at the surrey at all as the vehicle moved past them.

It was Eleanor who threw the boy a surreptitious wave when she saw his curious face staring from the backseat.

Inside the surrey, Henry Ellis turned his attention back to what was going on around him.

Charley had begun to slow the team. They were approaching Flora Mae's hotel.

The doorman stood waiting as Charley reined in beside him. As soon as the threesome had been helped out of the surrey, the doorman whistled for a hotel teamster, and a roughly dressed man climbed into the surrey and drove it away.

"C'mon," said Charley to the others. "Follow me."

He led them around behind the hotel's facade to where the pool hall and bar were located. They stepped up onto the porch, where they took turns scraping the mud off of their boots before they entered.

Flora Mae had been expecting them. She met them halfway to the door, where she offered to take their coats before they joined her, and January P. Ellison, at a roundtable that had been set up special near the back of the room.

When they had all been seated, including Henry Ellis, no one said a word. It seemed to the boy as if they were waiting for someone else to join them, and the three remaining empty chairs across the large table bore proof to that assumption.

"Oh, Mr. Sunday?" said the lawyer in a low whisper.

Charley cut him off.

"Did you get the information on those two dead gamblers back in San Marcos, like I asked you to do?"

Ellison nodded.

"Only, there's only one body there in San Marcos now. The one wearing the blue suit."

"What happened to the other one?"

"The one wearing the black cutaway coat

179

with the red piping," said Henry Ellis, who had been listening in on their conversation.

"The information I got," said Ellison, "was that the man in the black coat somehow wasn't injured that bad. They think he just woke up in the middle of the night and took off."

Charley shook his head. He turned to Flora Mae.

"Can we get started?" he asked the woman. "I'm the one paying for Mr. Ellison's services around here, so the quicker we can get something worked out, the better."

At that moment, something blocked the light from outside from entering the room. Everyone looked over.

Dr. and Mrs. Campbell were entering the establishment, accompanied by another well-dressed man.

"Over here," called out Flora Mae. "We're all over here."

Ben Campbell led the way, followed by his wife and the other gentleman.

Right off, Henry Ellis felt funny about the stranger who was with the Campbells. He didn't know why the man seemed so familiar to him, but he did. And then he saw it — the man was wearing a black cutaway coat with red piping. He was the same man, the other gambler, who Henry Ellis had watched being shot dead on the Austin train.

At the roundtable, introductions were being made. And when they got around to the man in the cutaway coat with the red piping, Eleanor Campbell introduced him to the others, who were already sitting.

"This is our legal representative, Mr. Aaron Dundee, from Fort Worth," she said.

Henry Ellis had been trying to get his grandfather's attention, but to no avail.

Charley reached past the boy and shook the opposing attorney's hand.

"Charley Sunday," he said. "Pleased to meet you."

Roscoe followed suit.

"And this is my grandson, Henry Ellis Pritchard," said Charley, introducing the boy.

"It's nice to meet you, son," said Aaron Dundee, holding out his hand.

Henry Ellis refused the man's hand. His eyes had found the repaired bullet hole below the attorney's right shoulder, and he couldn't take his eyes off of it.

"Henry Ellis," said Charley.

"Uh . . . Yes, sir," answered the boy.

"Mr. Dundee would like to shake your hand," Charley told him.

"Grampa," said Henry Ellis. "Can I speak with you . . . Alone?" asked the boy.

Before Charley could refuse, or ask him to wait for later, Henry Ellis got out of his chair and moved quickly to the door.

Charley excused himself from the others, and when he got to the door, he took the boy firmly by the shoulder and marched him outside.

"What's the meaning of this, Henry Ellis?" he wanted to know.

The boy stepped back a few paces and looked Charley directly in the eye.

"Did you notice how that Dundee fellow is dressed?" the boy asked him.

"That's a silly question, son. Now get to the point before I —"

"He's wearing a black cutaway coat with red piping," said Henry Ellis. "The same outfit the other gambler on the train was wearing. *And* . . . there's a patched bullet hole in that coat, if you look closely. I saw it."

Charley said nothing.

"He's the same man who was in the gunfight on the train, Grampa," said Henry Ellis. "I know he is."

The boy's got something there, Charley thought to himself. *It's no coincidence that one of those gamblers turned out to be alive.*

And that he up and disappeared before any investigation could begin.

"Thank you, Henry Ellis," said Charley. "I believe you. Now, let's get back inside before they get suspicious."

He took his grandson by the elbow and led him back inside, where they crossed over to the table and took their seats.

Charley showed the others an embarrassed smile.

"The boy wanted to tell me something he forgot to say to me last night," Charley said to the others. "Now that he's got it off his mind, I reckon we can get started."

Henry Ellis noticed that since he and Charley had been away from the table, the two attorneys had laid out several stacks of paper in front of them and were thumbing through the clutter as if the mishmash of papers actually meant something.

The boy glanced over to Dr. and Mrs. Campbell, sitting between their lawyer, Dundee, and Flora Mae. They were busy whispering under their breath to one another until they became aware that the boy was watching them. Then they hushed themselves and sat for the next few minutes in silence.

The boy took a look at his grampa. Charley sat to Henry Ellis's right, with Roscoe on his other side.

The attorneys sat across from one another, continuing to shuffle the papers.

"Why don't we call this meeting to order," said Flora Mae. "Just maybe we can get somethin' settled for once."

"All we want is what's rightfully ours," said Eleanor Campbell.

"Rightfully yours," echoed Charley. "Why, that ranch has been rightfully mine since before you were born, young lady."

"Hush, Charley. Mrs. Campbell," said Flora Mae. "You're both payin' someone else to do your talkin' for you, so why don't you let them talk?"

Everyone threw glances to everyone else around the table.

"So," Flora Mae continued, "Mr. Dundee . . . why don't you begin?"

The tension had been broken. There was a collective sigh around the table as all those present sat back in their chairs, ready for this long-awaited discussion to get under way.

"Firstly," said Dundee, "I would like to submit the letter my client . . . Mrs. Campbell . . . received from Carter, Carter, and Rudner, Attorneys at Law, practicing in Fort Worth, Texas."

He shuffled through the stack in front of

him, eventually pulling out a very official-looking document. He handed it to January B. Ellison, who was sitting across the table.

"I'd be happy to —" Charley began to say.

"No . . . No . . . I refuse to compromise on something that is rightfully mine."

Those were the words of Eleanor Campbell as she jumped up from the table and ran toward the exit. She burst through the swinging doors of the pool hall and bar, then onto the porch outside.

Her husband, Ben, followed her out, moving to her, putting his arms around her for comfort.

Charley was the next one through, followed by Roscoe and Henry Ellis.

"I was only saying, ma'am, that I would be willing to pay you a little something, just to make up for the expense of your having to come all the way down here to Juanita."

The woman pulled away from her husband and faced Charley, her red eyes and tear-stained face now seething with anger.

"If you're going to buy me out, Mr. Sunday," she said, "at least make me a decent offer."

"Mrs. Campbell," said Charley. "I was only suggesting that you and your husband might be the victims of some kind of tomfoolery. That it appears that someone's gone to a lotta trouble to convince you that what is mine is yours."

She turned again to her husband.

"Ben," she said, "I will not give in. Even though our letter in evidence cancels Mr. Sunday's property deed, I will not be satisfied until I see the actual signatures of both Mr. Sunday and the person from which he purchased the property."

She turned to her husband.

"Ben, would you take me back to our hotel? . . . Now."

"Yes, sweetheart, in one moment."

Ben Campbell turned to face Charley, just as Flora Mae and the two attorneys stepped out onto the porch behind them.

"You, sir, are a cad. My wife is a very delicate flower in the first place, and she is often prone to fainting spells. Now you have upset her, and I'm afraid that any business we had planned to discuss for today will have to be put off until another time."

"Can't you just have someone else take her to your hotel?" said Charley. "And you come on back inside for a while? I'll bet you pennies to a dog's tail the two of us can have this whole matter ironed out before you know it."

"I'm sorry, Mr. Sunday," said Campbell.

"But I never do business without my wife being present . . . and that works the other way around, too. The answer to your question, then, is no. I will definitely not be discussing anything further with you, or your adversary, concerning the ownership of the ranch in question until my wife has fully recovered."

"I must agree with you, Dr. Campbell," said Charley. "But while your wife is recovering, I'd like to ask you one more favor."

"Go ahead, Mr. Sunday. Ask your question."

"While your wife is recovering," said Charley, "would you be kind enough to call off your hired guns? It's getting to be old hat for us out at the ranch by now."

"Hired guns?" said Campbell. "I'm afraid I don't know what you're talking about."

"Sure you do, Mr. Campbell. Since you and Mrs. Campbell have been staying in Juanita, either my ranch, or my person, has been attacked daily by your bunch of hired gunmen."

"Wait a minute, Sunday," said Campbell. "I don't do business that way. So help me, it's just my wife and I who you are up against."

"These men seem to know an awful lot about me," said Charley.

"Well, they never got any information from me."

"You hired them, didn't you, Campbell?"

"I most certainly did not. And neither did Eleanor. You are mistaken."

"Well," said Charley, "I can see this is only going to lead to another argument. What is it you city fellas say to one another? 'Why don't you have your attorney get in touch with my attorney.' That is, when you and your wife feel like talking again, let me know."

A gut-rattling clap of thunder exploded barely seconds after a blinding flash of lightning had brightened up the surrounding area like a sunny, spring day.

The surrey was headed back to the ranch with Charley at the reins. Roscoe sat beside him while Henry Ellis napped in the rear seat.

As they approached the main entrance to the ranch, Charley was pleasantly surprised that there had been no new Keep Out signs posted. As far as he could see, there had been no new tampering with the front gate at all. Even so, he made sure his Walker Colt was within reach, plus he advised Roscoe to be on the ready, just in case.

When they reached the ranch yard, Henry

Ellis woke up. As he sat up behind his grandfather and Roscoe, wiping his eyes, he could sense the tension they were both feeling inside.

"Is everything all right, Grampa?" he asked Charley.

"Everything is just fine, son," was Charley's answer. He turned to Roscoe, just as the clouds opened up and the rain began to fall again. "Roscoe," he said. "Henry Ellis and me are going to get out here by the house. You take the horses and surrey to the barn and make sure the trotters get some feed."

He reined in the trotters, handing the lines to Roscoe. Then he worked his way out of the surrey, squeezing his way through a small gap in the isinglass. He helped Henry Ellis out of the backseat and signaled Roscoe to go ahead.

Charley drew his Walker, then put the other arm around the boy to shield him from the rain, then both of them ran for the back steps and up to the small landing before entering through the screen door.

Once they were inside, Charley put his gun back into his boot, turned on the porch light for Roscoe, then shook the water from his hat and coat. The boy did the same.

"Were you afraid those men might have

come back, Grampa?" asked Henry Ellis.

"For a minute or two, yes . . . maybe," Charley answered. "But it looks like the Campbells have called 'em off."

By then, the two were moving into the kitchen. Charley managed to turn on the light before he sat in one of the chairs by the table.

Henry Ellis moved around, sitting opposite.

"You still think there's a connection between those men and Ben and Eleanor Campbell, don't you, Grampa?" said the boy.

"Yes I do, son," said Charley. "Yes I do."

He leaned closer to the boy.

"Listen to me, Henry Ellis," he said. "I know those two are your friends, but I still have my suspicions. It ain't a coincidence that they showed up in Juanita claiming they just inherited my ranch, while at the same time, a bunch of gunnies start terrorizing us on the property itself."

"I know it looks strange, Grampa," said the boy, "but they just seemed like such nice people to me."

"Well, what about that Dundee fella, their lawyer? It's pretty fishy that he's the same one that got shot on the train you were riding. And why did your friend, Ben Camp-

190

bell, have to shoot the other fella when he'd already been shot by that lawyer fella?"

"I know, Grampa," said the boy. "It doesn't look good for the Campbells all the way around, but —"

Roscoe came in through the kitchen door, closing it behind him. He was soaked through to the bone.

"I get the feelin' this storm ain't gonna let up fer a while yet," he said. "When it does, I'll go finish puttin' the new rig away. Will anyone drink any coffee and hot chocolate if I make some?" he added.

"Me," said Henry Ellis. "Make mine hot chocolate. I don't think I'm quite ready for any more coffee."

"And I'll have some coffee, Roscoe," said Charley. "What's for supper?"

Roscoe was already stoking the stove with some torn newspaper, wood scraps, and chips.

"Soup," he said. "Tomato soup. Nothin' better'n soup on a cold, rainy night."

"You got any meat to go along with that, Roscoe? I always like meat with my meal."

"I can fry up some of that leftover chicken I got in the icebox, Charley, if that'll make ya happy."

"That's fine, Roscoe," said Charley. "That'll do."

"It'll be ready in two shakes of a lamb's tail."

"I'll go wash up," said Henry Ellis.

"Me too," said Charley.

They both walked down the hallway to the water closet, another new addition Charley had added on, using his new wealth to pay for it.

The two of them crowded into the room, with Charley getting to the sink first. He turned in the water faucet for a second, wet his hands, then turned it off. He soaped up his hands and washed then, turning on the water again for the rinse. Henry Ellis did the same.

"Make sure to turn off the water while you soap up," said Charley. "Even though it comes from one of my wells, they still charge me for using it."

"Why is that?" Henry Ellis wanted to know.

"Something about where the water comes from under the ground. The county claims they own it."

"No, Grampa," said the boy. "That's not right. Unless you don't own the mineral rights to this property."

"I own everything about this property, son. Makes no difference whether it's above or below the ground."

"And that's all on paper?"

"I got the original deed out in my desk drawer," he said. "I'll show it to you, if you want to see it."

"I *will* want to see it, Grampa. If you don't mind."

They finished drying their hands, then moved down the hall toward the kitchen.

"How many water wells do you have on the ranch, Grampa?" asked Henry Ellis.

"I reckon about five," said Charley. "One for the house. One for the corral yard and barn, and three out in the pastures, for the grazing livestock. Except . . . Except we only use two for the livestock. There's one that don't put out clear water at all. That happens around here sometimes, you know . . . you spend a fortune on digging a water well, and you don't strike any water that's potable."

"One bad water well outta five being nonproductive isn't that bad," said Henry Ellis.

"A man has to live with the cards he's dealt in life," Charley added.

By then, they were back in the kitchen.

"Whoeee, does that smell good," said Charley, changing the subject as he sniffed the soup that had just begun to boil. "You got any bread, close to fresh, Roscoe, that we can use for dipping?"

"Almost a full loaf in the bread box," said Roscoe. "Feather musta brung it when he was here watchin' the place and milkin' the cow. It ain't that fresh, but it'll do fer dippin'."

It wasn't but fifteen minutes later, and the three of them were gathered at the table. They all held hands as Charley said his usual suppertime prayer.

"O Lord, when hunger pinches sore,
Do thou stand us in stead,
And send us, from thy bounteous store,
A tup or wether head!
Amen."

Charley was the first to pick up his spoon and begin sipping some soup. This was the signal for the others to follow.

For approximately five minutes the threesome broke bread, then dipped it into their soup dishes, devouring what had been set before them in record time.

When they were finished, Roscoe got up and brought the pot to the table, ladling up more for everyone.

Roscoe sat down again. Nothing had been said throughout.

Finally, Henry Ellis couldn't stand the silence.

"Is that how you two and Feather used to eat, when you were out on the range chasing outlaws?" he asked.

"That's right," said Charley. "Plus, we had to keep our ears open during a meal, in case someone decided to sneak up on us."

"We were really lucky that ya found Feather when ya did, Charley," said Roscoe. "He's added a lot to our team over the years."

"That does remind me of a story," said Charley. "Did you know, Henry Ellis, that me and Roscoe were a two-man team for a few years before Feather came along? Did you know that?"

"No, sir," he said. "You never told me."

"Me and Roscoe were following some Mexican cattle thieves who were headed for the border. We'd stopped in Alpine to grub up and decided Roscoe had better stay behind, just in case those rustlers got around behind me and headed back north. I went on alone."

Charley got to Terlingua in the late afternoon two days after he'd left Alpine. He was leading the blood-soaked bodies of two Mexican rustlers lashed to both of their horses, much in the same way local hunters tied down the deer they had killed to their own pack animals. Those that had them.

The unlucky rustlers' trappings — sombreros, boots, weapons, and concho-studded holsters — were hanging on the saddles beside the bodies. No one made much of anything about dead Mexicans in Terlingua, except maybe the Mexican mine workers. The few who had gathered — quickly and in silence — between the adobe buildings peered off toward the stiffening corpses, both draped unceremoniously across their own hand-carved saddles, hopeful that the dead men, with fingers and boots almost dangling in the dirt, were not relatives or friends of theirs from across the river.

Charley, with disobedient tufts of hair poking out from under his sweat-stained Stetson, slowed his own horse in front of the Terlingua Mining Company's main structure: a large stone building with a corrugated steel roof and a long, covered porch attached. He stopped his horse and climbed off, glancing over to the lifeless bodies he had been leading for the last fifteen miles in the hot desert sun. Both bodies were now beginning to stiffen and bloat and had begun to draw flies. Charley wrinkled his brow, then spit some tobacco juice before he climbed the twelve steps to the porch, moving through the heavy, double wooden doors and on into the coolness of the building's interior.

"Ranger Sunday, you old bastard," echoed a voice from the rear of the deeply shadowed room. "I haven't seen you since I moved the family down here from Spofford. What are you doin' all the way down here? I thought you was stationed up near Marathon these days."

W.P. Martin, a stocky, large-bellied man in his late sixties sporting an almost white handlebar mustache, twisted with wax into near-perfect points on both ends, stepped into the slant of a late afternoon sunbeam that slid from a side window, carving into the room's soft darkness like a sparkling butter knife. He had his hand outstretched.

"Put 'er there, Charley," he chortled.

The two men shook. "Now, tell me for serious, will ya? What're you doin' all the way down here in the Bend?"

"Oh," Charley began. "I reckon you might say I'm working." He moved slowly past Martin, stopping at a wooden table piled high with papers that served the other man as a combination desk and napping area.

"Mind if I write out a telegram for my partner back in Alpine? You can send it tomorrow, if you'd like."

"Go right ahead, Charley. Want me to send

the bill to Ranger Headquarters?"

Charley grinned. "The Rangers'll return whatever the telegram costs you, W.P. . . . just so I remember when I'm doing the proper paperwork later on, that's all."

He found a stub of a pencil on the desk, along with a piece of paper. He looked up. "Would you mind leaving me alone for a minute or so, W.P.? This here's supposed to be confidential."

Martin chuckled. "I'm going to be sending that confidential message on the telegraph, ain't I? What difference does it make whether I see it now or later?"

Charley nodded back. "I s'pose you're right."

"I was on my way to see a man about a horse, anyway," said Martin. "I won't be long."

Charley waited until the older man had left the room, then he started writing:

Dear Roscoe,

I just got to Terlingua, and I wanted to report in and tell you I had me a run-in with a couple of those border rustlers on my way down here. There were two of them waiting for me, all right, part of the cattle-rustling gang we're after. I got both of them first. I'll have the bodies sent on up to Alpine with the next mineral shipment in a day or two. They're gonna stink

some by then, I'll wager, but not enough
to sicken no one seriously.

As he wrote, he spotted a jar of cigarillos on
a countertop near the wall down from the
desk, where Martin had placed a bunch of
trinkets for sale. He stretched to reach the
counter, moving as far as he could until the
chair in which he sat restrained him. Then,
stretching even farther, he managed to snatch
one of the cheroots from the glass jar that
contained the slim cigars. He put it between
his lips and continued writing.

As soon as I can hire me a pack mule,
get me some more grub and a blanket or
two, then I'll be crossing on over.

The preoccupied Ranger reached over
again to the jar, extracting a few more cigars
and sliding them into his shirt pocket.

I'll be eating chili peppers and cactus
balls for the next few weeks, I suspect.
And I'll do my best to let you know where I
am, any way I can, along the way.

Charley found a box of matches on the desk
— the kind made with yellow phosphorous
and sulfur, commonly called Lucifers. He put
a handful in his front pocket, beside the cigars

he had pilfered. He struck the match he had selected on the rough underside of the desk. The Lucifer ignited with a series of small explosions and pops, scattering bits of fire onto the floor around him. Charley slapped out the glowing embers that had landed on his lap, before putting the flame to the cigarillo's tip. He puffed clouds of blue smoke, savoring the flavor, wincing at the foul smell the burning match had left in the air around him.

"You can c'mon back in here now, W.P.," he said loudly. "And why in the hell don't they invent a safer match than these old Lucifers, I'll never know," he added. "I damn near set your building afire."

"Been usin' them ol' Lucifers for years now," Martin called out from wherever he had gone. "Ain't partial to changin' any time soon."

When Martin eventually meandered back into the room, Charley was puffing on the thin cigar.

"Where can a man get a good pack mule around here?" Charley asked. "It's been a long time since I been out huntin' cattle rustlers; I just hope I ain't forgot how to shoot."

"Might try my boy, Melwood," said W.P. "He's been running my stable down at Lajitas for a good part of the year now. He'll be in charge there for the next few months or so, too,

Charley. The young fool says he's enlisting in the United States Army. Says he expects Uncle Sam'll be in another war soon, and he wants to be ready for it proper-like. He doesn't mind that it's the Yankee Army now, since the Confederate Army don't exist no more. We're all Yankees, now, he says, though I'll never think that way. He'll be glad to see you, I guarantee that, Charley. He's always talkin' about you."

"Is that a fact?" said Charley, taking another puff from the cigar.

The only son of W.P. Martin, and his late wife, Madeline, was Melwood G. Martin, also known as Feather to his friends. At forty-five years of age, Melwood, or Feather, if you like, had been a pleasant-looking, short and skinny, freckle-faced country boy, with deeply tanned skin, plus a shock of greased-down, yellow hair. His ears were as big as buttermilk pancakes, and his feet were even larger than that, when Charley knew him in Spofford. Now, he was starting to gray around the edges, deep wrinkles complemented his still tanned face, and that graying yellow hair was long enough to cover most of his ears. He was still skinny, and if it were possible, Charley thought, he seemed even shorter than before.

Feather was closing the Lajitas Livery Stable's double doors for the night when Charley Sunday approached on horseback.

Feather squinted into the near dark of the early-evening twilight, trying to figure out just what it was the rider had flopped over the two horses he was leading. When the rider slowed, then turned the animals sideways, Feather almost retched. It was a couple of dead men — Mexican carcasses. The lifeless bodies, one tied on the front horse, the other on the one in back, had stiffened completely. They appeared to Feather as misshapen, abstract statuary, carved by some deranged lunatic.

Charley Sunday stepped down from his horse, placing his boots on the hard ground.

Feather smiled. Then he made his way over to greet the lawman. Not that much older than Feather, Charley Sunday was a man whom Feather had secretly worshiped as his hero ever since the Ranger had taught him how to track and shoot in the days Charley had worked his first Ranger assignment in the Spofford area, which had also included Juanita, Eagle Pass, and Del Rio. That had been some time ago, before he had been upped in rank and transferred to the Marathon office.

"Hell's bells," said Feather as he moved closer, grinning from ear to ear. "It's good to see ya, Charley. It's me, Feather Martin. How

202

in the hell are ya?"

"Feather," said the Ranger as they met between the two hanging lanterns that brightened the front of the barn. They shook hands.

"Good to see you, too," said Charley.

"What're ya doin' way down here, Charley?" Feather went on. "I thought —"

"Oh, I'm on a hunting trip," said Charley. "Following some Mes'can rustlers, Feather." He winked. "Already got me two of those bastards."

He indicated the dead bodies on the extra horses.

"Goin' huntin', are you?" asked Feather, winking back. "I can show you a whole bunch a' good places to find the kinda game you're lookin' for around here. Take me along, will ya? I'm a damn good guide. I scouted fer ol' Jeb Stewart during the recent altercation . . . but you already knew that."

"I know all about your wartime record, son," said the Ranger. "But I plan on doing my hunting down Mexico way this trip."

Feather's eyes fell again to the bodies tied to the horses. "Looks like you're expectin' to add a few more to these trophies, right, Charley?"

Charley laughed. "Yup," he replied. "Only these two were tracking me."

203

"Huntin' Texians in Texas, were they?" said Feather.

"That's right," Charley answered softly. "Hunting Texians . . . in Texas."

"Ya know, huntin' cattle thieves in Mexico ain't gonna be no vacation, Charley," said Feather. "Ye're here alone ta do a two-Ranger job."

Charley nodded. "They told me at headquarters it was a one-Ranger job, son."

"Then all the more reason ta take me with ya," said Feather. "I'm a grown-up man . . . have been fer a few years now. Gonna be a Yankee soldier boy in a couple a' weeks, when I enlist. Take me along, Charley. I can shoot damn good. You know that. You taught me. Why, I can even —"

Charley cut him off.

"I'll do right fine by myself, Feather. I just rode over here because I need to hire me a good pack mule, that's all."

"Mules I got . . . good-mannered ones. C'mon around back and take a look-see."

Charley set off following the younger man until they got to the corner of the barn and were in shadow. That was when Charley stopped, raised his nose to the air, and took in a couple of good whiffs.

Feather had stopped when Charley did. He turned and was now studying Charley closely, trying to figure out what was going on.

"You all right, Charley?" he said.

The Ranger held up one finger, meaning stop talking.

Feather did.

"You got any *mojados* working for you, Feather?" asked Charley, now whispering.

Feather shook his head.

"My daddy don't like ta hire wetbacks, Charley. He's had some bad experiences with 'em, stealin' him blind."

"Are any living nearby?"

"None," whispered Feather.

"What would you say if I told you there's about five or six of those Mes'can cattle rustlers I've been following right close by to where we're standing."

"How do ya know that, Charley?" asked Feather.

" 'Cause they're all in need of a good bath, you might say."

"You can smell Mes'cans, can ya?" said Feather.

"Only when they ain't bathed in a while, I can. Right now," Charley continued in a low voice, "I'd bet that gang of cattle thieves I've been following have set up some kind of ambush for me, right here beside your livery stable, Feather. Got a gun?" he asked.

"Just this thirty-six-caliber Navy Colt I always

carry on me."

He started to reach toward his belt, but Charley physically pushed his hand down to his side.

"Don't be showing your weapon to the whole damn, wide world, Feather. You never know who's watching you."

"Sorry," whispered Feather.

"Now, let's you and me turn around and march ourselves right back to the front of this barn, then on inside."

"What fer, Charley?" asked Feather. "Ain't we better off out here where we can meet 'em head on?"

"Being inside'll give us cover," said Charley. "Those rustlers'll still be outside here, where the lanterns got it all lit up. It's to our advantage to be inside."

Feather nodded.

"Then, let's go on in. There's a couple a' old Winchesters in there, too, if I'm rememberin' correctly."

"All right," said Charley. "Let's go."

The two of them moved off toward the front of the barn.

When they had reached a spot opposite the double doors, a shot rang out from the surrounding darkness.

Charley had his own pistol out of his holster, and he fired toward where he'd seen the flash.

They both heard a man cry out as they turned and raced for the double doors.

Crashing through into the interior of the barn, both men were grateful that Feather hadn't taken the time to latch the doors, making their entrance much easier than if he had.

As they turned to look out the doors they had just come through, they saw a Mexican bandit stumble out of the darkness and into the pools of light made by the two lanterns. He grasped his bleeding stomach before crumbling to the ground.

"There's one down," said Charley, grabbing Feather and moving in behind some hay bales for cover.

Several more muzzle flashes exploded in the darkness outside.

Charley returned fire, shot for shot. In moments, two more cattle rustlers hit the ground in the lighted area.

"Don't expect the rest of 'em to be that easy, Feather," said Charley. "Do you remember where those Winchesters might be?"

"I'll go get 'em," said Feather.

He moved away, using the natural shadows of the barn's interior as cover. He retrieved the two rifles and a box of cartridges, loaded a few bullets into each rifle, then started back to join Charley.

As he passed a small window in the side of

the barn, another muzzle flash caused him to duck back, while glass shattered.

A quick return of fire by Feather, directed through the window, took out another rustler. Like the others, this one also stumbled out of the shadows before he fell face forward.

"That's number four, Charley," Feather yelled across to the Ranger.

Feather eventually made it back to where Charley was waiting. There had been no shots fired from outside in several minutes. Feather handed Charley a rifle and a handful of ammunition. Both of them began loading more ammo.

They noticed a deadly silence that now surrounded them.

"I know there's more," said Charley. "One . . . if not two, out there, thinking just like we are."

"An' it's our job ta start thinkin' like them, if we wanna come outta this alive," said Feather.

"You're sounding more like a Ranger all the time," said Charley. "Ever thought about becoming a Ranger?"

"Like you, Charley?" he asked. "All the time."

"Well, maybe, when this little confrontation is all over, I'll have a little talk with my captain — find out if he could use another good man."

"Gee, Charley," said Feather. "Then I'd hafta quit the Army before I even started."

"You haven't signed anything yet," said

Charley. "If you have, then I'm afraid —"

A loud creaking sound came from the loft above.

Charley ducked back. He raised his eyes to the loft. "Tell me what you think they're gonna do, Feather?"

"Well," Feather began, "if I was them, I'd move around to the other side of the stable and find a way ta go high . . ."

BLAM, BLAM!

It was Feather's Winchester. A moment later, two bodies fell past them, dropping from the loft above, to the floor at their feet.

Feather continued. "Oh, I ain't dumb enough ta sign anything, unless I've made up my mind on my own. And besides, that recruiter fella was kinda pushy about me signin' up right then."

"So you're still free to walk away. Is that right?"

"S'pose so, Charley," said Feather, " 'specially if somethin' different opens up fer me. The recruiter fella I talked to told me I should forget about the Army and keep my job here at the livery. But then he also told me if I'd really made up my mind ta be a soldier boy, ta come back next month. But I'd like it a lot better if I was workin' alongside you an'

Roscoe for the —"

BLAM, BLAM, BLAM!

Charley's Winchester this time. Three more bodies dropped from the overhead loft.

". . . for the Texas Rangers," Feather continued, completing his sentence.

"So," said Charley, "I talked to Feather's old man that night, and by the next day he was ridin' back up to Alpine with me, a week away from filling out the papers that would make him a Texas Ranger for good."

"And he rode together with us two until we all retired."

"I'll bet that wasn't easy getting your captain to let Feather ride with you two, without any training," said Henry Ellis.

"In the history of the Texas Rangers, there are more than a few good men who only had on-the-job training. And Feather was one of 'em."

"Still turned inta a mighty fine lawman," said Roscoe.

"Feather Martin was what we call in the Rangers, a Natural," added Charley.

When Charley and Roscoe went down to the barn the next morning to feed the livestock and milk the cow, they had to fight another raging thunderstorm along the way. They both wore their slickers, with hats pulled down over their ears to keep the sharp wind from blowing them off.

Henry Ellis watched their advance on the barn from his bedroom window, upstairs in the ranch house. The rain was coming down at such a slant, it beat against the window-pane with the staccato of a military drum-mer.

As the two men entered the barn, the boy's eyes were pulled to the opposite end of the entrance road, where several silhou-etted figures on horseback were making their way toward the house.

By the time the riders reined their mounts to a stop in the ranch yard, Henry Ellis had gotten dressed and run downstairs to greet whoever it was come a calling.

Charley and Roscoe had seen them, too. They interrupted the feeding and milking and stepped out into the storm, crossing through the mud to the house. Their guns were drawn and hidden in the folds of their slickers.

As Charley and Roscoe approached the new arrivals from the side, Henry Ellis bolted out the screen door wearing his slicker and hat against the rain.

The boy held his right hand over his eyes, as if he were saluting, to keep the rain away so he could identify the newcomers, who were now all facing the back porch.

Charley and Roscoe arrived, coming up on their right side.

The four riders, still sitting their saddles, all wrapped from top to bottom in their shiny, wet slickers, with hats pulled down to ward off the weather, were suddenly exposed when a bright flash of lightning illuminated their faces for all to see.

A roll of thunder followed, and fluttering hearts were put at ease, when the riders were identified as Rod and Kelly Lightfoot, Feather Martin, and Plunker Holliday.

"Anyone mind if we get offa' our horses and come inside, before we drown out here?" said Holliday. "Feather told us you was havin' some trouble up here, so we thought we'd pay you a visit."

Henry Ellis backed up to the back porch screen door and opened it wide.

"C'mon in," he said. "You, too, Grampa and Roscoe. I'll make sure their horses are put away and rubbed good."

"Can ya finish up feedin' the livestock and doing the milkin', too, Henry Ellis?" asked Roscoe.

"You bet," said the boy. "I'll be with you

all in a little while."

He took the horses' reins in two hands and began pulling them toward the barn.

By the time Henry Ellis made it back to the house, Charley and Roscoe had finished filling the others in on the whole situation with Dr. and Mrs. Campbell. They had also been advised of the several encounters Charley and Roscoe had experienced with the gang of ruffians who had used force in their several attempts to discourage them from living on Charley's property.

"Did I understand you to say," said Rod, "that these Campbell people say they are not connected in any way to this gang of thugs?"

"That's what they say," said Charley. "But they weren't in any court of law when they said that . . . not under any oath."

"I'd sure like to talk to these people," said Rod, "so I can see it all from a lawyer's point of view."

"Flora Mae hired me a lawyer, Rod," said Charley. "I knew you were still going to law school, and I needed someone real fast to meet with my opponent's lawyer. I saw no reason to bother you, son."

"Well, you're right about my still being in law school," said Rod, "but I probably could have answered any questions you might have had since I'm taking my classes by mail."

"Believe it or not, Rod," said Charley, "but Henry Ellis was able to help me with the legal questions I had. He's been studying certain aspects of the law in that private school he goes to up in Austin."

"Well," said Holliday, cutting in. "I ain't been schooled in the law, in any way, shape, nor form. But it still seems awful fishy that someone can make claim to land that's been in your name for so many years."

"Problem is," said Charley, "I am not in possession of the document that legally says I'm the owner. Oh, I got the deed, all right, and some other papers that say I'm the rightful owner, but Mrs. Campbell wants to see the actual transaction signatures . . . and they are filed in the capitol building in Austin."

"Why don't ya send someone from both sides up to the capitol ta look at the ledger?" said Holliday. "I'll go, if ya want me to."

"That's all right, Holliday," said Charley. "If anyone goes, it'll be me."

"Why don't you call them on your telephone?" asked Henry Ellis.

"The telephone lines are down between here and there," said Holliday. "I saw them myself when I was ridin' down here."

"We got a telegraph office right here in Juanita," said Roscoe.

"Well," said Kelly, "Charley can ride into town and send a telegram to the state capitol. Have someone up there find the ledger in question and witness the signatures. Then they can wire us back with their answer."

"Sounds good to me," said Charley. "Roscoe?"

Roscoe crossed over to where Charley was standing.

"You wanna ride into town with me tomorrow morning and send that telegram?"

Roscoe nodded that he would.

"Me too," said Henry Ellis. "I want to go with you, Grampa. Can I?"

Charley reached over and tousled the boy's hair.

"Of course you can come along," he said. "You can be our scout if you'd like."

"We're goin' along with ya, too," said Feather. "Me, Rod, and Holliday wanna ride with ya in case there's any trouble."

Charley chuckled.

"There won't be no trouble at a telegraph office, fellas."

"But there could be goin' and comin',"

said Rod. "Kelly'll stay here with Roscoe in case those riders decide to come this way."

CHAPTER FOURTEEN

Wind-blown sleet was now stinging the horses' velvet-like noses, as well as their riders'. Clumps of the wet, frosty material were stuck to bib-fronted wool shirts and cowhide jackets. Holliday's hat appeared to be white instead of its usual faded black, but these old members of Charley Sunday's original Texas Outfit were on their way to town, and nothing was going to prevent them from getting there, whether it be the elements or man.

Feather spurred out from behind and joined Charley and his grandson, who were in the lead. His horse was kicking and swatting at the sleet, as if it were flies in the summertime.

"If this weather gets any worse," he said, "we'll be slidin' inta town, instead a' ridin'."

"We'll get there all right," said Charley. "It just surprises me that we haven't been attacked by that gang."

217

"Don't be too sure of that, Grampa," said Henry Ellis. "Look up there."

He pointed off to what appeared to be silhouettes of seven men on horseback, fading quickly into gray outlines because of the heavy sleet.

"That could mean trouble," added the boy.

Charley tightened the knitted neck scarf he was wearing around his neck. Then he reached into his boot top and removed his Walker Colt.

"All right, men," he called out. "Get your weapons ready; it looks like we may be having us some visitors."

The rest of the outfit unholstered either their pistols or their rifles, making sure the hardware was loaded to capacity.

In the near whiteout conditions, both parties of men continued to advance toward the other.

Revolvers were cocked. Bullets levered into Winchesters.

Horses' hooves from either side didn't break cadence, they just kept on advancing. Closer and closer.

Almost at the moment of contact, there was recognition.

"Charley Sunday, is that you?" a voice called out from the whiteness.

"It's Sheriff Dubbs," said Charley, turning to those around him. "Hold your fire."

The sheriff shouted the same words to his group of riders.

Both factions reined up their horses, as they were now close enough to recognize the faces of their friends.

"What in the hell are you doing out in weather like this?" said the sheriff as he faced Charley.

"We're headed into town," said the ex-Ranger. "What's it look like?"

"Well, we were on our way out to your place to tell you that Sam and Dale Cropper escaped from custody while they were transferrin' them from train to train in San Antonio. Because of this weather we're havin', they got clean away."

"Sheriff figured since you had a part in puttin' them both away," said a deputy, "they just may be headed back your way."

Charley threw a look to the sky.

"That's all we need," he mumbled.

"Anyway," said the sheriff, "consider yourself warned. Now, I hope you won't mind if we ride along with ya back to Juanita. I've been dreamin' of a hot bath ever since this sleet started flyin', and now that you've been made aware of the threat to your life, I intend to go home and take one."

He reined around, followed by his men, and the two groups joined up for the rest of the ride into town.

The outfit waited outside the telegraph office while Charley and Henry Ellis went inside to send Charley's telegram to the state capitol. Because of the weather, they had all dismounted and were standing on the porch of the tiny Western Union office. The rain continued to fall — light at times, heavy at others — and the incessant wind, with its added chill, didn't help anyone to stay warm.

Charley and the boy stepped outside for a moment, just to let them know that the message had been sent and an answer would be forthcoming. Then he went back inside, followed by the boy.

A half hour had passed when the telegraph key started rattling. Five minutes later, Charley and Henry Ellis stepped out onto the porch again. Both carried bewildered looks on their faces.

"It ain't there," said Charley.

"What ain't there?" asked Holliday.

"The signature page," answered Charley. "Someone's ripped it out of the ledger."

"You gotta be joking," said Feather. "Now, who woulda done that?"

"Who do you think?" Charley asked.

With Charley's huge fist still wrapped around his necktie, Ben Campbell was slammed into the wall of his hotel room. Charley pulled back his other fist so he could solidly punch the man in the face but was held back by Campbell's words.

"Can you please tell me what this is all about, man?" he said.

"I think you know the answer to that question as well as I do," said Charley. "You either did it yourself, or you had someone else pull the signature page out of the official ledger on property sales up in Austin," said Charley.

"I did no such thing," sputtered the good doctor. "We changed trains in Austin, but there was no time for me to get from the depot to the state capitol."

"Then it must have been that sleazy lawyer of yours."

"Dundee?" said Ben Campbell. "He was on the train with us. Remember?"

"He was on the train with you is right," Charley repeated. "He was one of those two gamblers that shot each other . . . and in order that the other gambler didn't shoot

221

him a second time, you killed that man to save your lawyer's life."

"Where did you come up with a story like that?" Campbell wanted to know.

"I have a witness . . . but I'm not telling you just who saw you pull the trigger. I'll wait to disclose that in court."

He grabbed Campbell by his coat collar, pulling him closer.

"Who is the Lattimer Land Company, Dr. Campbell? That's what I'd like to know."

"I'm the Lattimer Land Company," said a woman's voice coming from behind.

Charley whirled around.

Eleanor Campbell was standing directly behind him with a small pocket gun pointed at his heart.

"Drop your gun, Mr. Sunday, drop it now, and step away from my husband."

Charley did just that.

"I'm taking you two to court," said Charley. "I've figured out your little game."

"You've figured out nothing, Mr. Sunday," said Ben Campbell. "We've taken over your ranch while you were away, Mr. Sunday. We own that property now, including right of possession."

"I don't think that'll stand up in court," said Charley.

"Oh, it will," said Eleanor. "Because we

have all your papers . . . including your deed . . . out at the ranch right now."

"You abducted my lawyer."

"That we did, Mr. Sunday."

"And what's going to keep me from going to the sheriff with all you're telling me?"

"Nothing," said Ben. "Except you aren't going anywhere until my lovely wife and I are with our friends out at your . . . I mean, out at *our* ranch."

He took the pocket gun from his wife and pushed Charley toward a closet door.

"You see, you'll be in here, while we're on our way to meet our friends. Once we're there, there'll be no way *legally* to get rid of us."

He opened the closet door and pushed Charley inside, shutting, then locking it behind him.

CHAPTER FIFTEEN

1961

"This story is starting to confuse me, Grampa Hank," said Josh, the oldest Pritchard child. "How did Henry Ellis know so much about the law, especially when he was only Caleb's age?"

"Yeah," Caleb cut in. "I'm in the sixth grade, and we've never talked about law at all in my class."

"Well, things were a little different at the turn of the century, I'm afraid," said Hank. "And remember, Henry Ellis was going to a private academy."

"So, does that make Henry Ellis smarter than Caleb?" Noel wanted to know as she got up and went into the kitchen.

"In a way, I suspect," said their great-grandfather. "Back in those days, private schools were way ahead of public schools. And they taught little pieces of some college-age subjects, every so often, just to make sure their students were well rounded."

"Do you think my school will ever teach me anything about the law?" asked Caleb.

"Frankly," said Hank, "I would have to say, no."

"Why not?" asked Josh. "Don't most schools today want to produce students who are well rounded?"

"I'm sure they do, Josh," answered Hank. "But it's not the same. Maybe they still do talk about the law in some private schools."

"Is anyone hungry?" came Noel's voice from the kitchen.

"I am," said her two male siblings in unison.

Noel moved into the living room carrying a tray of tunafish sandwiches, setting them on the coffee table.

"I reckon I forgot about lunch," said Hank. "Mind if I have one, too?"

Noel picked up the tray before the boys could get to it, and she swung around to Hank.

"Here you go, Grampa Hank," she said. "You're the one doing all the work, so it should be you that gets first pick."

Hank took one off the plate the sandwiches were sitting on, and he took a bite.

"Ummm, is that tasty," he said.

The boys then lined up in front of their sister and picked out their own.

When everyone was seated again, Noel set the tray down and found a comfortable place for herself.

"You can continue, now, Grampa Hank," she said. "I think everyone's ready for you to go on with your story."

CHAPTER SIXTEEN

1900

When Henry Ellis and the outfit couldn't find Charley anywhere in town, they stopped in at Flora Mae's Pool Hall & Bar to see if the old rancher might have drifted down that way.

"No," said Bud Rawlins, the bartender, when they asked him. "I ain't seen ol' Charley in here all day. I got no idea where he might be."

"Oh, I do," said Flora Mae, coming out of her office. "I seen him go inta that other hotel we got here in town . . . and he looked like he was ready to tangle with five grizzly bears."

"Campbell," said Rod. "Where else would he have gone except to confront Ben Campbell?"

They all turned, clearing the room, before Flora Mae knew what had happened.

■ ■ ■ ■

They were told by the hotel clerk that Dr. and Mrs. Campbell had checked out earlier, but if they wanted to take a look around in what had been their room, it was fine with him.

He held out a key.

They could hear Charley's subdued yelling as they came up the stairs. As soon as Rod unlocked the door and opened it, they all crowded through the opening and into the seemingly unoccupied hotel room.

Everyone stopped to listen.

Charley's muffled voice was coming from behind the closet door. But before Rod could insert the key, the door was knocked off its hinges from inside by Charley, who burst through at that precise moment with shattered wood flying everywhere.

"Where's my gun?" were his first words. "Anyone see my Walker?"

Henry Ellis had discovered the large weapon on the floor where Charley had dropped it.

"It's right here, Grampa," he offered.

"Thanks, Henry Ellis," said Charley. He slipped it into his boot, then he turned to the others.

"We gotta get out to my place as fast as we can," he said. "Those swindlers are stealing my ranch!"

They stopped by Flora Mae's place just long enough to drop the boy off with her, then they hightailed it out of Juanita faster than a cat with its tail on fire.

CHAPTER SEVENTEEN

Before the outfit even got to the entrance gate, they knew something was amiss. Coming around a bend in the road, about a quarter of a mile south of the gate, they could see two figures mulling around at the side of the road. Charley raised a hand and they all came to a stop.

The grayness of the sky didn't help them to recognize the people who stood by the gate. Even when Charley squinted his eyes, it was no better.

Charley's plan had them splitting up into two groups — the first would contain Feather and Holliday, the second, Rod and Charley. Feather and Holliday were to ride wide around the front of the entrance gate, staying out of sight until they reached the road again about the same distance from the gate that they were now, only farther north.

Charley and Rod would stay right where

they were, giving the others time to get around to the other side of the gate and settle into place, then they were to move out themselves, staying just parallel to the road, using the spindly trees, yucca plants, and scrub brush to keep them from being seen.

When Feather and Holliday were finally in place, Feather puckered up his mouth and made a perfect imitation of a mourning dove. Just the right length and pitch to blend with the other sounds of nature that surrounded them.

Upon hearing Feather's bird call, Charley nodded to Rod, and the two men gently urged their horses on toward the gate.

Feather and Holliday did the same, spurring their mounts gently until they came abreast of the gate. They were joined by Rod and Charley.

The two people who they had seen standing in the road beside the gate were not part of the Campbell's hired bunch, at all. When they finally did turn around some, Charley was the first to see beyond the heavy clothing and turned-down hat brims that they wore, to recognize them as:

"Roscoe . . . Kelly," Charley called out. "Stay right where you are. It's me, Charley . . . I got Rod, Feather, and Holliday with me."

He urged Dice over to where they stood, then dismounted.

Rod, Feather, and Holliday also dismounted, then they walked over to the others.

"What's going on?" asked Charley. "What are you two doing down here by the gate, instead of up at the house?"

Roscoe hemmed and hawed, clearing his throat.

"Those . . . those gunmen forced us to leave," said Kelly.

"The same ones we had trouble with before?" asked Charley.

"Same ones," said Roscoe. "Only this time they told us that Holly Birdwell would be joining them in the near future."

"Holly Birdwell?" said Rod. "Isn't he the fellow who gunned down old Sheriff Tate in Eagle Pass last year?"

"One and the same," said Roscoe.

"He's someone I sure wouldn't wanna tangle with," said Feather. "He's one bad actor."

"Well, whoever this Holly Birdwell is, we *are* going to have to tangle with him," said Charley. "We should all know that."

Ben Campbell sat in a hired rig beside the

train depot, watching as the Eastbound Express pulled to a stop, releasing steam into the frigid air and sending clouds of vapor rising around the engine that pulled the several passenger cars.

His eyes were drawn to the second car, where a man had just stepped out into the chill, pulling on a sheepskin coat.

He wore a double-buscadero rig that held two nickel-plated Colts — both appeared to sparkle at his sides.

As the man descended the three steps to the platform next to the train, besides his eyes, which were as gray as the sky overhead, Campbell couldn't help but notice the scar that ran from the man's cheek to his chin, making his mouth look as if it were off center by a few millimeters. He had made an attempt at disguising this flaw by wearing a heavy mustache over his upper lip, but still, the remnants of the scar, still visible at the top and bottom of his mouth, worked as double arrows, pointing out to those who faced him that he was a man to be reckoned with.

"Holly Birdwell, I presume," said Ben Campbell as the man was about to pass him by on his way to the depot's door.

Hands moved to the guns before the man turned to face Campbell.

"I'm Holly Birdwell," said the man. "You must be Ben Campbell."

"That I am," said Campbell. "I've reserved the best hotel room in Juanita for you, Holly, and I —"

"Don't ever call me by that name again," warned the gunman. "Mr. Birdwell is what I prefer my business associates to call me."

"Yes, sir, Mr. Birdwell," said Campbell. "I was just saying, I've reserved the best hotel room in Juanita for your stay."

"My short stay," said Birdwell. "As short as possible. Now, what again is the name of this old rancher you want eliminated?"

Large drops of rain had begun to fall as Charley, Rod, and Holliday urged their horses back in the direction of town. Kelly and Roscoe rode double, behind Rod and Holliday.

"Like I told you, Roscoe," said Charley, "now is not the time for us to attack our own ranch house."

"Well," answered Roscoe, "it looks like we'll have to fight them hired gunmen one of these days. There ain't no other way we can get 'em out of there. God," he added. "Please don't let them break any of my good china."

"I know how you feel, Roscoe," said Kelly.

"I wouldn't want any strangers in my kitchen, either."

"Where're we goin' ta stay now?" asked Roscoe.

"If Flora Mae has a few rooms available, I suppose we'll bunk there. If she's full up, I know she'll let us sleep in her stable, out back."

"I'm dyin' of the chilblains just thinkin' about sleepin' in that stable, Bossman," said Feather.

"I don't really care where I hafta sleep," said Holliday. "Just as long as I can help out my friend Charley Sunday."

"Well, the first thing we'll do is check in with Flora Mae, and hopefully get us some rooms," said Charley. "Secondly, we'll pick up Henry Ellis, then find us a place that serves a hearty noon meal."

On a brushy hilltop overlooking the main road into Juanita, Holly Birdwell sat in the hired rig beside Campbell. Squinting into a collapsible telescope, the hired gunman watched as Charley led the outfit toward town.

"So that's the great Charley Sunday," said Birdwell. "He don't look that tough. But he sure looks a lot different than you described him. Is it true that he was a Texas Ranger at one time?"

"Charley Sunday, and his two friends, Roscoe Baskin and Feather Martin, rode together as Rangers for a good many years," said Campbell. "Their record for stopping lawbreakers, before and after a crime was committed, led to over a thousand official arrests over the years, I've been told."

"So, what was it made you pick Sunday's ranch as your target?" asked Birdwell. "An old feud between the two of you? Did he send you to prison, Dr. Campbell? Or did he steal a woman's love? Those are the usual reasons I'm hired to kill a man."

"It's for another reason altogether, Mr. Birdwell. One that I'd prefer not to discuss."

"It doesn't bother me if you want to keep secrets, Campbell. I do my killing for cash money . . . it doesn't matter to me what the reason is."

"Then, perhaps you'd like to continue on out to the ranch. My men have secured the ranch house for our use, to plan any further moves against Sunday."

"And you, Campbell, may assist me in figuring out where the proper location will be for Charley Sunday to die."

CHAPTER EIGHTEEN

Flora Mae was able to accommodate Charley and his friends. She offered them three of her best rooms. Charley, Roscoe, and Henry Ellis were in one room together. Holliday and Feather doubled up in another. And finally, Rod and Kelly took the third.

Flora Mae had to apologize, though. Her finest room was already taken. Booked by Ben Campbell and his wife, Eleanor, for a third party who had just checked in about an hour earlier.

Flora Mae told Charley who the special guest was — Holly Birdwell — and immediately Charley wanted to know the room number.

"He's in Room Two Twenty-two," Flora Mae told him. "But it ain't gonna do ya no good."

"Why's that?" asked Charley.

" 'Cause he left town with Ben Campbell

as soon as he got his room key," said Flora Mae.

"Any idea where they were headed?" asked Charley.

"More'n likely," said Flora Mae, "they were headed out ta yer ranch. I did overhear Campbell say that your ranch is where the rest of his hired guns are holed up."

"They come ridin' in with guns blazin'," said Roscoe. "It didn't take Kelly and me long ta think it over, once we were asked ta vacate the property."

Flora Mae turned back to Charley, a worried look on her face.

"What'd ya plan on doin' about that, Charley?" she said. "Are you really goin' ta let 'em just walk in and steal your ranch? Just like that?"

"Of course not, darlin'," he said. "I just got to do me a little thinking on what the Campbells are up to. That's all."

"Well, right now they've stolen your ranch out from under your nose. So, you better get ta thinkin' soon."

He moved past Rod and Kelly, and over to the bar, where Roscoe, Holliday, and Feather were squabbling over who should buy the first round. He tossed two bits in change on the countertop, in exchange for a shot of whiskey.

He leaned on the bar, then studied the drink in front of him.

"Give him a bottle, on me," Flora Mae yelled over to the Bud, the bartender. "The man has some serious thinkin' ta do . . . may as well be tyin' one on at the same time, because it's all a waste a' time anyway, if you ask me."

Henry Ellis sat at a table near Flora Mae's office. After a moment of thought, he got up and walked over to where his grandfather stood at the bar.

"Please don't let her talk to you that way, Grampa," said the boy. "I know you can get us out of this mess. You always have before."

Charley continued to stare at his whiskey glass.

"I don't rightly know about this time, Henry Ellis," he said softly. "It seems the more I want to start thinking, the more that thinking doesn't come to me."

"Well, maybe if we all put our heads together, and thought on the same subject, we'd come up with a solution."

"That might work, Boss," said Feather.

"I'd be willin' ta give it a try," added Holliday.

"Why, putting all of our heads together, we're bound to come up with something," said Kelly. "Thank you, Henry Ellis."

She motioned for the others to gather around Charley, and they did.

"All right, now," she went on. "Let's all put our heads together and see what we can come up with."

"What's our next move, Dr. Campbell?" Wolf McGrath wanted to know. McGrath had been the leader of the Campbells' henchmen since their first visit to Charley Sunday's ranch, a week, or so, earlier.

"After Mr. Birdwell disposes of Charley Sunday tomorrow," said Campbell, "all that's left will be to move my, and Mrs. Campbell's, personal belongings out here permanently. Plus, I'd like to keep a few of you boys on as my regular employees, if that's possible. After all, there is a small herd of longhorns, and a few horses, that need regular care here on the ranch."

"Plus this young dog," said Eleanor Campbell, who had just entered the room carrying Henry Ellis's pup.

"Cute little feller, ain't he?" said Wolf McGrath, moving over closer so he could pet the animal.

"Not so rough, Mr. McGrath," said Eleanor. "Right now, this pooch needs something to eat." She turned to her husband. "Ben, why don't you send Mr. McGrath out to the barn to look for something for the dog to eat."

"You heard Mrs. Campbell, Wolf. Go see what you can find," said Campbell.

McGrath nodded. Then he headed for the screen door, out on the back porch, where he stepped out into the rain.

"Speaking of food," said Holly Birdwell. "I ain't had a bite to eat since I was on that train."

"Well, I found the larder," said Eleanor. "It's on the north side of the house, with a wire grid on it to let in the cool air from outside."

"See what you can find, Eleanor, and fix us all up with something nourishing," said Ben.

Charley Sunday, Roscoe Baskin, and Feather Martin rode along together beside the gently flowing Rio Bravo. It was one of those lazy Texas days, and the first time their captain had allowed Feather Martin to go along with them. They were pursuing some renegade Comanche Indians, who the governor thought might be hiding in the Chisos Mountains, located in the Texas Big Bend.

The three Rangers had ridden away from the town of Marathon, where all three were stationed, and arrived in Alpine the following day.

In Alpine, they'd picked up a scout — a middle-aged Mexican *vaquero* called Esteban Ortega. He had lived in the Big Bend for all of his life. Ortega could still remember the first few years of his life as a boy, when literally hundreds of Comanche warriors would use the Big Bend as an unobstructed passage into Mexico, where they would raid and steal cattle — plus abduct women and children — from the Mexican villages and *haciendas.*

With the expansion of white settlement into the West, plus the killing and dying off of the Comanche, mostly attributed to disease, the U.S. Army, and the Texas Rangers, the Indians ceased using the Big Bend as their access into Mexico.

There had been one exception — a small band of outlaw Comanches who had remained in the Big Bend. They raided the local settlements and outlying ranches in the area, and they continued to ride into Mexico on occasion, to bring back provisions for their survival, plus Mexican women for their personal pleasure.

Their Ranger captain had told the threesome that the band of Comanches numbered no more than twenty-five, or so — some of them women and children. So, before they

242

left Marathon behind, Charley knew their opponents would be few, but still, the Comanche were one of the most intelligent, yet brutal, forces he'd ever had to contend with.

The captain had recently learned that this dwindling tribe made their home in the Chisos Mountains. A small area in the usually flat land that had been pushed up by underground seismic activity thousands and thousands of years earlier, when most of the present-day desert had been a vast swampland.

"Are we gonna make Terlingua our base?" asked Feather. "Or are we goin' ta be stayin' in Lajitas? You know, my father still has some business interests down there."

"How could I forget, Feather?" said Charley. "That's where I found you, isn't it?"

"Yes, sir, Boss," said the newest Ranger. "An' remember, I still know this country like the back of my hand."

"How much do you know about the Chisos?" asked Charley.

"I used ta do a lot of huntin' up in them mountains," said the little man.

"Any roads into those mountains?" asked Charley.

"No," said Feather. "Just deer trails, plus some passageways left there by the ancients."

"Ancients?" said Charley.

"The ancients were human beings who lived

here way before Jesus ever set foot on this earth," said Ortega. "Some say their spirits still haunt those mountains."

"I been up there a whole bunch a' times," said Feather, "and I ain't never seen any ol' spirits, anywhere."

"So you won't mind sleeping on the ground up there," said Charley, nodding in the direction of the mountain range.

"Ahhh, Boss," said Feather. "And here I was lookin' forward to a nice featherbed every night while we tracked them cold-blooded, killer Comanches durin' the day."

"We need ta be up in the mountains with 'em, mule-face," said Roscoe, cutting in, "so they can't get away from us once we spot 'em."

"And I suppose your back never hurts from sleepin' on the ground, either?" said Feather.

"I got me one of the best backs ever made fer ground sleepin', my friend," said Roscoe. "My back is just like my feet . . . flat. Makes ground sleepin' feel like I'm floatin' in one of them featherbeds you was talkin' about a minute or so ago."

Charley reined Dice away from the road, setting a new course toward the mountain range now directly ahead. The Chisos were partially blocking their view of the Mexican cliffs on the southern horizon.

"I figure for sure that if we can keep on moving now, the way we have been," said Charley, "we can be close to halfway up that mountain by nightfall."

"Can you lead us to a good place to camp, Señor Ortega," Charley asked the Mexican scout.

"*Sí,*" said Ortega. "I will take you to a safe place where I have personally made my camp many times before. The Comanches do not know of this place."

The three Rangers followed Ortega into the mountains. They continued to ride over small rises, passing deep gullies and grotesque rock formations, until the inclines they traversed grew steeper and steeper, leveling off, every so often, to produce a flat, verdant meadow. At times, they would find free-flowing water in these small grassy areas, which attracted many forms of wildlife that scattered as the four men spurred their horses upward.

It was during the crossing of one of these meadows that Feather saw something move in the grass, about a hundred feet away.

"Don't nobody stop what yer doin'," said Feather, continuing to look straight ahead. "But I got a hunch we got company."

The other men stiffened, then they relaxed and continued to ride on, as if nothing had been said.

"Where?" Charley whispered, wanting to know.

"About forty yards to the west," said Feather as the horses continued to plod along.

"What do you think we should do about it?" said Charley.

"Well, I'm goin' ta get off my horse like he's havin' trouble with a shoe," said Feather. "Just maybe, my bein' alone'll bring 'em out in the open."

"Good idea," said Charley. "We'll keep on going and try to keep an eye on you. Yell out if you need us."

"Will do," said the little cowboy. Then he reined up and stepped down from his saddle.

The others continued on, moving away from Feather and his horse. The little man knelt down and picked up one of Chigger's hooves to check it.

It wasn't long until Feather's hunch was proving to be correct. The pint-size cowboy sensed something moving through the high grass, coming toward him. So all he did was draw his Walker Colt, cock the hammer, then lie back in wait.

"It's been a while," said Roscoe to the others. "Do you think Feather's all right?"

"Feather knows what he's doing," answered

Charley. "Feather's going to handle this just fine."

KA-BOOM!

Feather's Colt could be heard discharging behind them. They turned to see a cloud of black-powder smoke drifting up from the position they had last seen their little partner. About then, there was another loud retort from Feather's gun, and even more smoke rose toward the sky.

Charley turned to his left just in time to see a running, knife-wielding Comanche brave, who had just taken Feather's bullet, knocked backward into the grass.

Charley called out a warning to the others.

"There's more of 'em out there! Be careful."

Ortega drew his rifle, then he spurred his mount toward another attacking Comanche.

One shot from his Winchester stopped that one in his tracks, then he moved out after another one.

Roscoe had still another Indian in his sights. A quick pull of the trigger sent that man tumbling until he stopped rolling at Roscoe's horse's hooves.

Charley spotted two remaining members of the scouting party, who had seen their brothers die, and were now running away. He stuck the spurs to Dice's underbelly and took off after them.

Within moments, Charley had ridden the two Comanches down. He drew Dice up to one side of them and dove off the horse, just like he had always done to a runaway steer that needed stopping.

When all three of them hit the ground, he unwrapped his arms from around their necks and drew the Walker quickly.

KA-BOOM . . . KA-BOOM!

Charley's bullets hit their marks almost at the same time. That was a good thing for Charley, as one man carried a feathered tomahawk and the other was brandishing an old Navy Colt.

Charley watched as the second Comanche he'd shot ceased to breathe. The other one had died from the first bullet's impact.

Charley stood up and saw that Feather and Roscoe were waving in his direction, kind of an all-clear signal, meaning that they had gotten them all.

In the near distance, Charley could see Ortega riding toward them. The Mexican scout had taken off toward the end of the skirmish, following another Comanche who was trying to get away.

Now he was returning. He carried a bloody machete in one hand. The other held, by the hair, the head of the Comanche he'd been chasing. Blood dripped from where it had been severed from the body.

"Do not worry, *mi amigos,*" said Ortega. "This was just a small hunting party. We will pray that they are not expected back for another few days. Their lack of any freshly killed game tells me that they had only just begun their hunt."

He pulled his horse up to Charley, then dropped the head beside the other Comanches' bodies.

Roscoe and Feather dragged over the bodies of the other dead Indians, then left them with the others.

"It is probably not such a good idea to stay around here too long," said Ortega. "That special campsite I was telling you about is not that far from here. I suggest we go there as soon as possible."

The campsite Ortega took them to was located off the main trails, set back away behind a large rock formation, with a strangely shaped monolith on its top that Ortega called Alsate's face — a name the Comanches themselves had given the gargantuan boulder.

"It was more than likely named after one of

the early Comanche chiefs," said Ortega, answering a question from Feather.

"He sure must have been ugly," said the little man. " 'Lessen I'm lookin' at him all wrong, ol' Alsate looks more like the ass-end of a sick Mes'can burro than a respected Indian leader."

"Well, that's the story going around, Feather," said Charley, "that the rock was named after an old chief."

Charley then changed the subject. "If nobody minds, I'd kind of like to throw out my blanket and get a little shut-eye."

"Thank the Lord somebody said it," said Roscoe. "Because hittin' my blankets is probably all I have left in me today."

He tore his bedroll from his saddle and threw it on the ground at his feet, then he gently melted into the blankets with his entire body.

Feather and Ortega spread their bedrolls out near the others. Only, the two of them stayed awake, smoking and telling each other old tales until the wee hours of the night.

Chapter Nineteen

Feather woke up with a start. He was still standing upright — on his feet. He had drifted off to sleep when they'd all put their heads together to think. He was now coming out of his slumber after a vibrant dream had appeared to him during his extended catnap.

The others were breaking up the circle — unaware that Feather had not been with them during their group think, that had lasted close to twenty minutes.

"Anyone come up with any solutions?" asked Charley.

Heads shook all around. There was a general feeling of despair, until Feather slowly held up his hand.

"Feather Martin?" said Charley. "What is it that you thought of that might save my ranch?"

Feather cleared his throat. It was apparent that he was hemming and hawing.

"Uh," he began, "I had me a dream. An' it was all about that time we run them Comanches outta the Big Bend together . . . Remember?"

"Sure, I remember," said Roscoe.

"Tell us about your dream, will you, Feather?" said Charley. "And how you think it relates to the trouble I'm in right now."

Feather took a few minutes to describe his dream to the others. And only when he had finished did he speak.

"We ignore 'em," he said. "We ignore the fact that they've taken over Charley's ranch. An' we jest keep usin' Flora Mae's place as our headquarters. Their lack a' knowin' what we're up to should bring 'em out into the open before we know it . . . Just like them Comanches in my dream, their curiosity'll get the better of 'em, and they'll come out ta see what we're doin'. Just like them Indians done when I stopped ta check my horse's hoof," he added.

"Sounds logical to me," said Charley. "How 'bout you others. Do any of you have a better suggestion?"

There was some additional thought given to the problem, but in the end, no one had spoken out.

"I think Feather's idea just might have a chance of workin'," said Roscoe.

"I do, too," said Henry Ellis.

"Oh, you do, do you?" said Charley, tousling the boy's hair. "And just why do you think it will?"

" 'Cause Feather got the idea from a dream," said the boy. "And the Bible says you should put a lot of faith in your dreams."

"Where exactly does the Bible say that?" asked Roscoe.

"Somewhere," said the boy. "It's in there somewhere."

"All right, then," said Charley. "We'll do it like Feather's dream. We'll just lay low at Flora Mae's for a while. Don't show ourselves anywhere except town . . . and by all means, we won't go anywhere near my ranch."

"They'll hafta come lookin' fer us," said Feather, grinning.

"What about Holly Birdwell?" said Kelly. "He's staying in Flora Mae's hotel, too . . . just like we are."

"We'll just have to keep an eye on him and not show ourselves until he's gone off to the ranch to join the others every day," said Charley. "Then, we can hang out in Flora Mae's pool hall or bar all day until he comes back at night. We just have to be careful not to let him see us . . . not any

253

one of us, at any time."

"What about the Campbells?" asked Rod. "What if they come back to town every night, too?"

"My gut feeling says that those two will stay at the ranch, now that they have possession of it," said Charley. "After all, they're using their custody of the property to keep the law away, right now, so I expect they'll be living out there twenty-four hours a day."

"Does anyone have any idea where their lawyer is staying?" asked Charley.

"I seen 'im eatin' breakfast over at the other hotel yesterday," said Feather.

"Good," said Charley. "He's staying close to the Campbells like I thought he would. Feather, I'm appointing you to keep watch on him from now on. Let me know if he makes any move to go out to the ranch . . . or if he tries to leave town."

"Will do, Boss," said Feather.

"But don't let him see you. That's an order."

"Yessir," said the pee-wee cowpoke.

"And, Rod," said Charley. "I want you to find a place near the south end of town, and keep an eye out for whoever leaves and comes into town. I want to know where every single member of that Campbell gang is, morning, noon, and night."

"What about me?" asked Kelly.

"You stick with your husband, Mrs. Light-foot," he said. "I'm sure he can use your help."

"Roscoe, Holliday, and Henry Ellis. You three stay here with me . . . just in case Holly Birdwell finds out we're rooming here, too. It ain't that I'm afraid to go up against Birdwell, it's just that I like to hedge my bets. It makes me feel a lot safer with Holliday around."

"So, those'll be our positions every day, from now on," he continued. "We'll be watching them, but they won't know we're watching them. That way, we'll keep one step ahead of 'em, no matter what they're up to. And if any trouble does start, we'll be right on top of it before they know what hit 'em."

"So, do y'all know where you're supposed to be?"

"Yeah . . . Yes . . . You bet," they all said.

"Then get a going," said Charley. "We'll meet back here tonight."

As rain from the third storm of the day rolled down the kitchen's windowpanes, casting eerie reflections everywhere, the Campbells, Ben and Eleanor, sat beside each other at Roscoe's table. They were sipping coffee and reading a week-old San Antonio newspaper.

Ben studied the front page — with all its big city stories, plus a few that passed for world news — while Eleanor flipped through the pages of the lady's section, stopping every so often when something of interest caught her eye.

Wolf McGrath sat across from Ben, cleaning his gun, while two of the other hired guns played a game of two-man poker on what space was left for them on the tabletop.

From outside, the sounds of riders approaching could be heard over the constant rainfall.

Wolf McGrath got up from his chair and went to a window, pulling back the curtain.

"It's Birdwell, with Acey and Bear," said McGrath. "They don't look no worse fer wear. I still don't know why you had ta send two of our best guns inta town ta escort Birdwell out here. Holly Birdwell don't need no protectin' that I'm aware of."

"Right now, Holly Birdwell is my greatest asset," said Campbell. "I got Charley Sunday, and his outfit, right where I want him because of Birdwell."

He chuckled.

"I actually think old man Sunday is afraid

of him. At least I know Birdwell will keep Sunday guessing for a while. Keep him and his friends outta my hair."

The screen door opened and Birdwell came in, followed by the other two. They removed their slickers, dropping them to the floor in puddles, before they all tramped their way into the kitchen.

McGrath was waiting for them with three cups of steaming coffee. He moved his chair around and made room for the new arrivals, setting their coffee cups in front of them.

"We stopped out on the back pasture, Mr. Campbell," said Birdwell. "I think I found what you thought might be there."

"Thank you, Mr. Birdwell," said Campbell. "We can talk about this when we're alone."

Birdwell got the message and stopped talking. He picked up his coffee and took a sip.

"Now that's good coffee," he said. "Takes the chill off a man's aches and pains."

The others went on about their business. None of them noticed the exchange of glances between Birdwell and Ben Campbell except for Eleanor, who just smiled softly to herself.

Henry Ellis saw them riding back into town,

led by Ben and Eleanor Campbell in their hired buggy. Their hired gunmen, the ones that stayed in town, trod solemnly along behind them.

"Hey, Grampa," said the boy. "Come over here, will you? The Campbells are back."

Charley left the pool table, where he was beating Rod, handed his cue stick to Kelly, then joined Henry Ellis at the window.

"They're dropping off Holly Birdwell here, at the front of Flora Mae's place," said Henry Ellis. "The Campbells are headed down the street to their own hotel."

"Meanwhile," said Charley, "as soon as everyone gets back, we have things to do. Rod, Holliday," he called out. "I want you two to go with me tonight . . ."

CHAPTER TWENTY

If the moon was out you couldn't tell, because the clouds still hung low over the countryside. Charley, Holliday, and Rod rode their mounts silently until they came to the gate to Charley's ranch. After making sure that the access wasn't being guarded, they moved in closer, while Rod dismounted and began working at the lock with a special piece of metal he'd taken out of his saddle-bags.

Once the lock was opened, Rod removed it from the hasp, then swung the gate open, just wide enough to let Charley and Dice through. Holliday and his horse followed, and Rod brought up the rear, closing the gate behind him.

"We only got between now and an hour before sunup to get what we came for," said Charley. "We have to be off this ranch on time, or we're really pushing it."

The others nodded.

"All right," Charley went on, "we'll have to take a roundabout way to the ranch house, in case they have someone watching the road. C'mon," he said.

Charley quietly spurred Dice away from the gate, sliding his Winchester from the scabbard as he moved off into the darkness.

Rod and Holliday also pulled their rifles, then they took off after Charley just as a crackling bolt of lightning lit up the ground around them.

By the time the thunder exploded, seconds later, the three intruders had disappeared into the night.

"Uncle Roscoe," Henry Ellis called out as he stepped back into the darkened room after using the water closet down the hall. "Uncle Roscoe, are you awake?"

Henry Ellis crossed over to Roscoe's bed in search of his grandfather's partner, but he found the bed to be empty.

"I'm over here," came Roscoe's voice from the shadows. "Over here by the window."

The boy made his way through the pitch-dark room until he found Roscoe sitting in a chair beside a partially open window, with his Winchester in his lap.

It was raining outside, so the gentle sound of the steady drops drifted into the room, along with some of the coldest air the boy had ever felt.

"Do you hafta keep that window open, Uncle Roscoe?" asked the boy.

"Gotta have a place ta stick my rifle barrel through in case I need ta shoot someone," said the older man.

"Who do you think you'll have to shoot tonight?" said Henry Ellis.

"Yer grampa asked me before he left ta make sure no one left this hotel after nine o'clock," said Roscoe. "That way he won't have ta be worryin' that Holly Birdwell might be lurkin' outside the ranch house when yer grampa pays it a little visit tonight."

"Grampa went out to the ranch?" said the boy. "That's awful dangerous, isn't it?"

"A whole lot less dangerous than it could be if Holly Birdwell up and decided to ride out and join his friends tonight."

"But, if Birdwell does leave the hotel, what are you supposed to do . . . shoot him?"

"Naw," said Roscoe. "Feather's waitin' with Chigger across the street in the livery stable. If I see Birdwell leavin', I'll signal him, and he's supposed ta ride out there before Birdwell to let yer grampa know it's time ta get outta there fast."

"What's Grampa doing out at the ranch?"

asked Henry Ellis.

"I sure dislike doing this to my own property," said Charley. "But it seems like it's the only way to get into the house."

Both Charley and Rod were inside Charley's toolshed, while Holliday stood by the door, guarding the others.

There were a few moments more while Charley and Rod stood at the small window and watched the house across the ranch yard. Charley took out a Lucifer and struck it on the workbench. The phosphorus tip exploded with a flare, causing tiny sparks to dance around the popping flame as the match began to burn. Next, Charley set a pile of rags afire, followed by several stacks of old newspapers near the wood storage bin. At each point of combustion, flames began to grow larger and larger.

"C'mon, you two," said Charley. "Let's get outta here."

The threesome stepped out into the chilly night, took a look back at Charley's handiwork, then moved off toward the front of the ranch house.

It was between rainstorms, so the fire had no trouble spreading through the tiny structure.

Charley, Rod, and Holliday ducked behind

some bushes at the front of the house. They were still able to see the toolshed in the ranch yard, which was now burning brightly, lighting up the barn on one side and the house on the other.

Cries of "Fire" . . . "There's a fire out back in one of the out buildings," came from the ranch house. Several figures of men buckling on their gunbelts raced across the yard to the well, where a bucket brigade was set up.

It was during all the confusion that Charley and the others made their way to the front porch.

Charley had his house key out and was turning the lock before the other two realized what was happening. Within moments, they had all entered the house.

"Follow me," said Charley.

The others did as they were asked, following Charley into a hallway. He led them to a door, which he opened, revealing the wood-paneled ranch office.

"This is my office," he told them. "I just hope the Campbells are using it for the same purpose as I do."

"What are we looking for, Charley?" asked Rod, whispering.

"Anything that looks like a page from the county records office," Charley replied.

"The one that's missing from the county records office in Austin."

Charley went over to several cupboards and started checking through them, being careful not to misplace any of the papers being kept there.

Rod took the other side of the room, checking desk drawers and the several other cupboards on that side.

Holliday placed himself by a window where he could keep tabs on what was going on out back.

"They're all out there, Charley," he said in a loud whisper. "They got a bucket brigade goin'."

"Are you sure of that, Holliday . . . that all of 'em are out there?"

"Well," said the tent-show gunfighter, "it looks like all of 'em are there. And they're startin' ta get the best of the flames."

Charley took that as a chance for him to run into the kitchen.

Once there, Charley meticulously went through every cupboard while light from the fire outside danced on the walls around him.

Just when he was about to give up, something on the table caught his eye. He leaned forward and picked up a piece of paper from a pile that was spread across the tabletop's surface.

A quick look told him he'd hit the jackpot. He folded, then tucked, the paper into his pocket and hurried back to join the others.

"I found it," said Charley, for Rod and Holliday to hear. "Let's get outta here."

The two other men followed Charley, both coming out of the office down the hall, and through the parlor, until they were out of the building.

Charley checked on the fire one more time, just to be sure all of the men were still involved in extinguishing the dwindling flames. Then he led Rod and Holliday back the way they had come.

They found their horses behind the barn where they'd left them, then they walked them way around the house and yard to avoid detection.

When they arrived back at the gate, they mounted up. Rod stayed on foot for a few moments so he could relock the lock and make it look as if it'd never been tampered with. Then he swung into his saddle, and with the others at his side, he galloped away, back toward town.

CHAPTER TWENTY-ONE

Charley, followed by Rod and Holliday, barged their way through the batwing doors that opened into Flora Mae's pool hall and bar.

"Flora Mae," Charley called out before he realized it wasn't that late, and before he observed several customers still drinking and shooting pool in the room.

Flora Mae broke away from the bar where she'd been having a conversation with her bartender, Bud, and rushed toward the overly loud threesome. She indicated to Charley with her facial expression to shut his mouth.

He did. And when the woman got close to him, she indicated with her eyes that someone was over by the end of the bar.

"Charley Sunday," she said out loud, "I wasn't expectin' ta see you in here tonight."

She was still busy using her eyes to point out the man at the end of the bar.

But that wasn't necessary, any longer, when Holly Birdwell left the bar and crossed over to where Charley stood with Flora Mae.

"So, ye're the great Charley Sunday I bin hearin' so much about since I got ta this little flytrap of a town."

"That's me," said Charley, who was still smiling. "And you're Holly Birdwell, I suppose."

The two men were sizing one another up.

"Bigger'n life," said Birdwell. "You were a Ranger some years back, am I correct?"

"I was," said Charley. "But I don't remember ever running into you."

"That's probably because I wasn't even a spark in my old man's eye when you was Rangerin'."

"You can stop with the insults any time, Birdwell," said Charley. "I may be long in years, but I ain't dead. Besides," he added, "years have only made me better . . . in everything I do."

"Is that so," said the hired gunman. "Can ya still hold yer whiskey?"

"Drink for drink with the likes of you," said Charley.

"Ha!" said Birdwell. "I haven't met the man yet who can drink as much as I can . . . ever."

"Meet Charley Sunday," said Charley. "Flora Mae," Charley called out. "This gentleman and myself . . . are going to have us a little drinking contest."

"Set 'em up," said Birdwell. "I'll buy, since I don't think there's any chance you can keep up with me, old man."

Flora Mae got the go-ahead wink from Charley. Then both she and her bartender, Bud, set up a few bottles on the bar top, along with two, normal-size shot glasses.

"We got rules for this game here in Juanita," said Flora Mae. "It's shot for shot, not the amount of liquor consumed. That's the way we do it, mister. If ya don't like it, go have yer contest in another town."

"No, ma'am," said Birdwell. "Shot fer shot works fer me. Let's get this thing goin'," he said. "Start pourin'."

Bud uncorked the first bottle, pouring equal amounts of the brown liquid into each sparkling shot glass.

When he had finished, both Charley and his challenger stepped up to the bar. Each man reached out and took a glass in their hand. Then, after a long wait, as they looked one another in the eye, Charley winked, then downed his glass.

Birdwell threw back his first one just as fast as Charley had. That drew a small reaction from what was becoming a crowd.

The glasses were refilled, then both men downed their second.

Refilled for a third time, the men tossed down that one, too.

A half hour later, the two men were still drinking — playing the game, but at a slower pace. The first and second bottles had both been emptied, and now they were on the third.

"How ya feelin', Sunday?" said Birdwell between drinks.

"Doing better than you are, Birdwell," said Charley. "Hell, you're starting to slur your words. I can hear you."

"That's bullshit, Sunday," said Birdwell as both sloshed down another shot. "I'll make you eat them words, too."

Bud continued to pour.

"Belly up, Mr. Birdwell," said Charley. "Time's a wasting."

They both threw back another shot.

"Are you feeling any of the effects of this alcohol, Sunday?" asked the gunman.

"I've been going drink for drink with you, Birdwell. What do you think?"

"I think ye're cheatin' somehow," said Birdwell.

Charley lifted his next shot and tipped it back.

"That ain't cheating," said Charley. "It's your turn now, Birdwell."

Birdwell picked up the glass, then swallowed its contents in a single gulp. When he looked up, Charley was reaching for his next shot.

Birdwell reached for his glass but had to wait until Bud had finished pouring. Then he threw back his shot.

Charley drank his next.

Birdwell followed suit, only this time, his hand seemed to be a bit unsteady.

"I think it's about time I call you," said Charley.

"Call me?" said Birdwell. "We ain't playing a game a' poker here, Sunday," said Birdwell, "and if we were, I ain't about ta throw in my hand."

"No," said Charley. "I'm just calling on you to stop drinking. Neither one of us is going to drink the other one under the table tonight, so why don't you go for your gun right now? That's what you wanted in the first place, isn't it?"

The expression on Birdwell's face turned ugly.

"You think I'm too drunk ta draw, don't ya? Well, I'm not."

Birdwell went for his pistol in the holster at his side, and when he pulled the gun, he lost his grip on the weapon.

Charley stepped forward and easily took the gun out of Birdwell's hand, and without as much as the blink of an eye, he had the hired gunman's own weapon pointed back at the man. Charley's own Colt was still in his boot.

"H-how in the hell did you do that?" said Birdwell.

"Let's just say it had something to do with how you hold your liquor," said Charley, twirling the gun around and handing it back to the gunman.

Holly Birdwell was astounded.

"First ya take my gun away, then ya give it back ta me."

"That's so there ain't no hard feelings," said Charley. "Can I buy you a drink?"

"You gotta be outta yer mind, Sunday," said Birdwell. "I just wanna get outta here."

He stopped directly in front of Charley, putting a drunken finger in his face.

"You just made a fool outta me, Sunday . . . and no one does that to Holly Birdwell and gets away with it. Now, I'm goin' up ta my room fer a little shut-eye. Just don't let me catch ya out in the open, ya hear? 'Cause if ya do, it'll be all over for you, Mr. Charley Sunday. All over."

Birdwell began to back away. And when he felt the batwing doors at his back, he quickly slipped through them. Then he stumbled over to the hotel proper where his bed was waiting.

Flora Mae turned to Charley.

"I never knowed you to be able to hold that much whiskey," said the woman.

"I never knew I could hold that much, either," said Charley. "But I reckon I found out I can hold more than he could."

"Would you like ta know just how much ya put away between the two of ya?"

"I reckon it was a lot," said Charley, who was beginning to get a little wobbly now himself.

"Between both you and that fancy-pants gun shark," said Flora Mae, "I'm gonna hafta get in touch with my supplier a week earlier than usual, so I won't run outta my best-selling stock."

Charley chuckled.

"What was Birdwell's bar tab, anyway?" asked Charley.

"When he sobers up and comes in to pay it," said Flora Mae, "he jest might want ta go on another drunk ta help him forget it."

When Charley got back to the room he was

sharing with Roscoe and Henry Ellis, he was so out of it that he stumbled straight to his bed and passed out on the top of the covers.

"What's the matter with him?" Roscoe wanted to know.

Rod and Kelly, who had walked the old Ranger to his room and were still standing outside the door, provided Roscoe with the answer.

"He got into a drinking match with Holly Birdwell, down in Flora Mae's bar tonight."

"I never seen 'im this drunk before," said Roscoe. "I hope he won."

"He did," said Rod. "But I'm afraid that next time he won't get off this easy."

The voices in the room woke Henry Ellis. He glanced over to where his grampa Charley was laid out on the bed, snoring like a lumberjack.

A terrible feeling ran through the young boy's body for a brief moment, as he thought: *What if Grampa's not so lucky next time. What if he has to go up against Holly Birdwell with his gun and he gets killed. What will I do if that happens?*

When Roscoe woke up the following morning, neither Charley nor Henry Ellis were in their beds. He was alone in the room, and another storm had just moved in. He began to get dressed.

It was about to open up into a downpour when Roscoe stepped outside, making a beeline for the little Mexican café, where he knew Charley would be taking his breakfast.

As Roscoe entered the little adobe restaurant, the sky opened up with the beginnings of a heavy rain that wouldn't let up for an hour.

He spotted Charley and the boy at a table near the kitchen door and started moving toward them.

As Roscoe was nearing, Charley spotted his partner and waved him over.

"Hey, Roscoe," he called out. "We're over here."

Roscoe continued to walk toward them, and when he arrived, he took a chair between the two.

"Why didn't ya wake me up?" he asked Charley.

"Henry Ellis wanted to let you sleep some more," said Charley. "He thinks you work too hard for a man of your years."

"A man of my years?" repeated Roscoe.

He turned to the boy, who was nonchalantly sipping on his glass of buttermilk.

"Hasn't your grandfather ever told you that I'm younger than he is?" said Roscoe.

274

"Um, well," said Henry Ellis. "I suppose I made that assumption because you look older, Uncle Roscoe," said the boy.

"Well, I'll be darned," said Roscoe, shaking his head in disbelief. "What is it about me that makes you think I'm older?"

"Oh," said the boy. "Maybe it's the way you walk. And you do talk slower than Grampa. You'll have to agree on that."

"It's no use," said Roscoe, burying his head in his hands. "Next thing I know you'll be sayin' that he's better lookin' than I am."

There was a long moment of silence. Nobody spoke.

"Ahh, ta heck with it," said Roscoe. "What's a man gotta do ta get some breakfast around here?"

"I knew you'd be showing up, Roscoe," said Charley, "so I ordered you the same as me . . . four eggs, sunny-side up, with a double order of bacon on the side, four pieces of toast . . . with the right amount of jelly and butter. Coffee . . . black, and a medium-size cinnamon roll, made for dunking. Plus a lot of hot salsa."

"Why, that was mighty nice of ya, C.A.," said Roscoe. "I couldn't've chose a better breakfast if I'd a' been here myself."

"I ordered a stack of dollar-size pancakes for myself," said Henry Ellis. "With butter and syrup. Maple syrup."

Something about the mention of dollar-size pancakes set off a memory from Roscoe Baskin's past, as the image of an old dirt road began growing in his mind.

"What would ya like me ta fix ya fer breakfast?" said a much younger Roscoe to his Texas Ranger partner, Charley Sunday.

It was some years after the War Between the States, and shortly before Feather Martin would be joining up with the two as a third partner.

They had camped alongside the road the night before, so they wouldn't be riding into the town of San Angelo in the dark.

The two Texas Rangers had been following a couple of renegade bank robbers who had robbed a bank in Del Rio at gunpoint. Then they'd headed north. The two men were either very smart, because they were dressed in U.S. Army uniforms, or they were plain stupid, for the very same reason.

It hadn't taken the Rangers long to figure out that these robbers were just a little more than downright stupid. They had not used the Army uniforms to throw any pursuers off their trail. Instead, they were just a couple of stray soldiers who had been reported AWOL from Fort Concho, near San Angelo, seventeen days earlier.

The soldiers had been easy to follow, even though traveling from Del Rio to San Angelo was a pretty long way.

Charley figured the two soldiers must have been drinking for a while when they planned their departure from the fort. They had more than likely stayed drunk from the time they escaped from Fort Concho, all the way to Del Rio. Once there, more liquor gave them the courage to rob the bank. Then, a few days after the robbery, when they had both sobered up, they had decided to travel north, back to Fort Concho, where they had decided to go on another drinking spree, then turn themselves in.

"How about you make some of those dollar-size flapjacks, like we had in that little café back in Sonora last year?" said Charley. "I've kinda had a hankering for some more of those little nuggets, ever since I realized we may never go through Sonora again in our lifetime."

"If it's dollar-size flapjacks you want, my friend, it's dollar-size flapjacks you'll get," said Roscoe, searching through his possibles sack for the bag of flour he would need. "We got some bacon left. Would ya like me ta slice some off an' fry that up, too?"

"You bet," said Charley.

"An' I got both sorghum syrup an' blackstrap molasses . . . choose yer poison," Roscoe continued.

"Sorghum," answered Charley.

"All right then," said Roscoe. "Soon as I whip up the batter, an' slice the bacon, I'll have yer breakfast cookin'. In the meantime, could you go fetch me some more wood fer the fire?"

"That I will," said Charley as he stood up and stretched. Then he moved over to the edge of a small wooded area and disappeared into the underbrush.

Charley could smell the bacon frying as soon as it touched the skillet and began to sizzle. He drew in a deep breath, then moved deeper into the tangle of bare branches and trees.

Charley hadn't taken three steps before a gun exploded nearby, with the bullet clipping twigs and branches from its path, and just missing Charley, before it slammed into the hulk of a dead tree trunk, four feet away.

Charley dove to the ground, pulling his Walker Colt on the way down. He raised himself up on his elbows and did a quick search of the area.

All he saw was the flash of a human form, dressed in blue clothing, as it was swallowed up by the twisted trees of the leafless thicket.

He fired one shot. And even though the target was no longer there, he heard a faint yelp.

"Sounds like ya hit somethin' that was breathin'," said Roscoe, who was coming up behind him with his rifle at the ready.

"It was just a wild shot, but I think I hit him, too," said Charley.

"Did ya see the other one?" asked Roscoe.

"Only the one that shot at me," said Charley. "Even then, it was just a quick glimpse. All I really saw was a blue Army pant leg."

"The one that did the shootin' mighta laid back some ta throw us off their trail," said Roscoe. "Or else, the second one was right there with him, only he kept outta sight."

"It doesn't really matter now, Roscoe," said Charley. "I nicked one of 'em, so there'll be a blood trail until they find someone to work on that wound."

"What's the nearest town ta here?" asked Roscoe. "They might decide ta go lookin' fer a doctor."

"San Angelo," said Charley. "But they'll be taking one hell of a chance, because San Angelo backs up to Fort Concho. And the U.S. Army is probably looking to hang those two for desertion."

Not wanting to attract too much attention to themselves, they entered San Angelo from a back road. The section of town they found themselves in catered mostly to customers of brothels, saloons, and gambling halls — there were enough of those sinful businesses in one square block to handle every adult man in town, plus twice that many soldiers from the fort.

Charley was quick to note that nearly all of the enlisted men in San Angelo were Negroes — as Fort Concho was the headquarters for the Buffalo Soldiers. Therefore, the two men they were looking for would be a cinch to spot if they ever decided to hang out with some of their dark-skinned buddies.

Their plan was to frequent the local taverns and card halls every day for a week or so. Just to let themselves be seen. After nearly five weeks on somebody's trail, Charley was certain that the two bank robbers would know what he and Roscoe looked like by then. As for the Rangers recognizing the bank robbers, even though they had never gotten a good look at them, Roscoe said they would stand out in a crowd of Buffalo Soldiers like two lighted matches in a darkened room.

Well, it didn't take long. On their second day sitting in a bar called Horace's Tavern, two Caucasion soldiers walked in for a drink around five in the afternoon. The soldiers bellied up to the bar and ordered their beers, while at the same time, the two Texas Rangers bellied up to the white soldiers, putting the barrels of their Walker Colts against the men's backs.

"We'll be needing you two to turn around slowly and walk out of this place ahead of us," whispered Charley. "No suspicious moves. We don't want your fellow soldiers to think we're harrassing you, or anything like that."

The two backed away from the bar, turning slowly until they were facing the door. Then, with a smile and a nudge, Charley and Roscoe walked them toward the exit.

Just when the foursome were about to move through the batwing doors, two black soldiers came in from the outside. One of them got a good look at Charley's face as they passed, and his eyes widened. He turned to his partner, right beside him.

"It's them two Texas Rangers that's been followin' us since Del Rio," he said, and the two went for their guns.

KA-BOOM . . . KA-BOOM!

went the Rangers' Walkers.

Both black soldiers were spun away into the street outside. The two white soldiers dropped to the ground for cover, as every member of the Buffalo Soldiers inside the saloon drew a weapon of some kind.

Charley and Roscoe stepped out onto the

boardwalk, ducking quickly to either side of the door frame, while bullet after bullet chipped away at the batwings, until both swinging doors fell off their hinges with a double thud.

"I thought you said the men we were chasing were white," said Charley.

"Looks like I was wrong," answered Roscoe.

"Texas Rangers!" yelled Charley, reaching to unpin his badge from under his vest, so he could show the aggressors they were officers of the law. Roscoe already had his badge in his hand and was holding it up so the soldiers could see it.

The shooting stopped.

Then Charley stuck his face through the opening where the doors used to be.

"Just give me a minute or two, fellas, and I'll try to explain it all."

Chapter Twenty-Two

By the time the remnants of the story had left his head, Roscoe was finishing up his meal, scraping his plate with a fork for any leftover syrup and bits of bacon.

The waitress had already cleared away the dirty dishes from in front of Charley and the boy. So when Roscoe's dishes were taken away, Charley laid a few coins on the table and got to his feet.

The others followed suit, then the trio stepped out into another gray day, with a heavy drizzle falling all around.

"Just what do you have in mind for the day?" asked Roscoe as the threesome walked along the boardwalk, headed toward Flora Mae's pool hall at the rear of the hotel.

"Why don't we go on into Flora Mae's place and find out what she's got on her mind?" said Charley. "Then, maybe if we're lucky, there'll be a table open, and Henry Ellis can beat you in a game of billiards, Roscoe."

Holliday, Rod, and Kelly entered through Flora Mae's batwings, followed by Feather, who looked like he might have had a few too many the night before. They crossed over and joined Charley, Roscoe, and the boy at a poker table near the bar.

Flora Mae took a seat nearby. She glanced around the table at the stoic expressions, then she narrowed her concentration on Charley.

"Have you taken that new piece of evidence you found out at the ranch to the judge yet?" she asked.

"I intend to do that," said Charley, "when the courthouse opens its door at ten o'clock this morning."

"I just hope you're keeping it in a safe place," said the woman.

"I got me a safe place for it, woman," said Charley. "So safe I might just forget where it is, if you keep hounding me about it."

"I ain't houndin' ya, Charley," said Flora Mae. "I just wanna make sure ya don't lose it."

"I told you, I ain't gonna lose it, Flora Mae."

"Do ya want me ta run over to our room an' get it?" asked Roscoe.

"Yes," said Charley. "And take Holliday with you. If it'll shut her up to know that we have it in our possession. By all means."

Roscoe and Holliday excused themselves and left the room.

Once they were outside, they began walking around to the front of the hotel. Suddenly, Holliday stopped. He restrained Roscoe with an open hand against his arm.

"What are ya doin' that fer?" said Roscoe.

"Can't you see them horses tied up out front?" said Holliday. "They's the same ones I saw out at Charley's ranch . . . the same horses that those low-down sidewinders that are workin' fer the Campbells ride. They must be in the hotel. Is there another way to get inside besides the front entrance?" he added.

"There's a worker's entrance over there by the buggy barn," said Roscoe. "We could probably sneak in through there, one at a time."

"Well," said Holliday. "What are we waitin' fer? Just make sure your gun is loaded and ready fer bear."

In Flora Mae's place, Charley stood up from the table. He drew the Walker Colt from his boot and checked the chambers.

"What's the matter with you?" asked Kelly.

"That's right," echoed Flora Mae. "Where do you think you're going?"

"I just got me this feeling," answered the ex-Ranger. "Rod," he said softly. "Why don't you and Feather come along with me?"

The other two men stood, checked their guns, then followed Charley out the door.

Once outside, they, too, were surprised to see the hired gunmen's horses tied up in front of the hotel.

"Maybe we oughta go in behind them," said Rod.

"No," said Charley. "I'm betting that Roscoe and Holliday are doing that right now. We, my friends, are going in through the front."

Inside Charley, Roscoe, and Henry Ellis's room, Wolf McGrath and the other hired gunmen were going through the threesome's belongings. They were pulling extra pairs of trousers, shirts, and undergarments out of saddlebags and flinging them everywhere. The torn-out page was yet to be found.

"Check under the mattresses," said McGrath. "Check between the mattresses, if there're two."

The gunmen turned to the beds and began ripping them apart.

It was about that time that Charley, Rod, Roscoe, Feather, and Holliday appeared. They were all coming up the stairs from the floor below, where their paths had crossed. When they saw the commotion going on in Charley's room, they cocked their weapons and moved in closer.

Charley stepped into the room and fired a shot through the ceiling.

The gunmen stopped what they were doing and turned to the door.

Roscoe stood in the doorway with his legs spread and his Walker Colt pointed at the intruders.

Rod Lightfoot stood right beside the onetime lawman, his .45 being used for backup.

"Throw down your guns, you miserable bunch a' polecats," ordered Charley. "Or my friend here just might put you outta your misery."

"Don't shoot, mister," howled Wolf McGrath.

The other gunnies echoed McGrath's words, and their weapons were dropped to the floor instantly.

Holliday began lining them up, while at the same time kicking their guns into a large pile near a stand that held the washbasin.

"I want those guns to equal the men in this room," said Charley. "Because if they don't . . ."

Two more revolving pistols were dropped on the pile. No one saw where they had come from.

"That's better," said Charley. "Now, all of you take off your neck bandannas, hold 'em in your left hand, and face the wall."

The trespassers did as they were told.

Charley, Roscoe, and Feather moved around the room, using the neckerchiefs to tie the men's hands behind them.

When Charley got to Wolf McGrath, the gang leader warned him softly.

"You're goin' to regret what you're doing, Sunday," he said. "As soon as Dr. Campbell finds out that you have that document, he's not going to protect your life anymore."

"And what's that supposed to mean?" questioned Charley.

"Up until now," said McGrath, "we've had orders not to kill or injure you or any of your friends. But now, unless you're prepared to give me that page you took from the kitchen table last night, Campbell's going to hear about your little visit to the ranch yesterday evening."

"And who, may I ask, is going to tell

him?" said Charley. "Because it sure isn't going to be you, or these other boys. We have a special place where you're going."

"You can't keep us hidden for that long," said McGrath. "One of us'll find a way to escape."

"Oh?" said Charley. "I think not. Holliday," he called out.

Holliday moved over to where Charley was standing by McGrath.

"What can I do for ya, Mr. Sunday?" he asked.

"I want you, Roscoe, and Feather to take these fellas out for a ride. Out to that place we talked about this morning. Put 'em all in there, and lock it up tight."

"Yes, sir, Mr. Sunday," said Holliday.

"Or, just take 'em to jail. That's better. In the meantime, I'm going over to that other hotel and have me a face-to-face conversation with Dr. and Mrs. Campbell."

Charley burst into the Campbells' hotel lobby, nearly missing the couple, who were finishing up their morning meal in the area off the lobby that served as the hotel's restaurant.

"Oh, Mr. Sunday," Mrs. Campbell called out, stopping Charley in his tracks.

He turned and saw the two at the table,

both of them acting as if nothing had happened. He crossed over to where they were sitting.

"Just to let you folks know," he began. "I am now in possession of a certain page of the official documentation of land sale records, regarding my ranch, that you so unceremoniously cut or tore out of the state's book of records of such transactions. And as soon as the judge has seen it, I'd be obliged if you and your men would vacate my property, before I have the sheriff and his deputies throw you off."

He turned to walk away, then turned back again to face them, one more time.

"And don't be thinking that you can sic your dogs on me again, Campbell, because Wolf McGrath, and the rest of your hired guns, are over in the Juanita jail waiting to see the judge, too."

"I think you may have overstepped your boundaries, Mr. Sunday," said Campbell. "I will still deny that my wife and I have done anything unlawful."

"The court don't need any words from you two in defense of your actions," said Charley. "I have witnesses now who'll testify that you gave them the order to remove that page from a government book of documents, and that, Dr. and Mrs. Campbell, is a felony, right off the top."

"You're not going to take the word of those . . . those gunslingers . . . are you, Sunday?" said Campbell.

"It ain't me that's gotta believe them 'gunslingers,' as you call them . . . it's the judge."

Campbell began to get to his feet, helping his wife to do the same.

"I don't have to stay around here, and neither does my wife, while you slander us both with your false accusations. We're leaving now, if you don't mind."

"Oh, Mr. Sunday does mind," came the voice of Willingham Dubbs, sheriff of Kinney County, who stood to the right of the couple, blocking their exit. He had his gun out and pointed at the couple. Two of his deputies were at his side, and they were the ones who put the cuffs on them.

"Why, I've never been so humiliated in all my life," said Eleanor Campbell as the steel restraints were tightened around her wrists.

"You'll be sorry for this, Sunday," said Ben Campbell as the deputy started to lead him away.

The second deputy, who was taking Mrs. Campbell into custody, could only chuckle to himself.

"Ya know, Sheriff," he said to his superior.

291

"I'd sure like two cents fer every time I've heard that one before."

The Campbells were ushered toward the front door of the hotel. Charley followed, with a wink at the other customers.

"Sorry we disturbed your meal, folks. But it was very important that I did."

He turned and continued following the others, until they were all out the door.

On the street, where the sky was just misting, the sheriff bid Charley good luck, then, with both of his deputies, he marched the Campbells across the street to his office, which also housed the Kinney County jail.

Charley watched as they followed the sheriff up the few steps and entered the building. As the doors closed behind them, the street seemed to be a quieter place.

Charley stood there for a moment, thinking to himself.

Lord in Heaven, his prayer began. *Thank You for all You've done to help me get my ranch back. I was able to do it with the help of my friends,* and, *no one had to get killed.*

"Charley Sunday!"

The voice had interrupted Charley's prayer. He knew who it was, and he immediately rescinded a portion of the words he had just prayed.

Sorry, Lord, if I said no one had got killed. I reckon I just forgot about . . .

"Holly Birdwell," he said out loud, slowly turning in the direction of the voice.

Birdwell stood in front of the Juanita livery, with both legs spread. His gun was tied down and his hand hovered over his pistol like a hawk waiting to strike a rattler.

"It's all over, Birdwell," said Charley. "The people who hired your services have been arrested, and they're being locked up at this very moment. The rest of their hired guns are already behind bars. So, you can go home, Birdwell. You haven't broken any laws."

"And I ain't gonna be breakin' any laws in the future, Charley Sunday. Because I'm gonna kill you in a fair fight. I just need me some witnesses, that's all."

He drew his gun slowly, then fired into the sky.

Doors opened all around as people stuck their heads out to see what was going on.

Even the sheriff appeared, stepping through the courthouse doors. He was stopped cold when he saw Birdwell and Charley facing off in the center of the street.

Roscoe, Feather, Rod, and Holliday came running from the direction of Flora Mae's hotel, followed by Kelly, Flora Mae, and

Henry Ellis. They all slid to a stop when Charley and Birdwell came into view.

"Now I ain't wearing a slick-draw holster like you are, Mr. Birdwell," said Charley. "I carry my weapon in my boot."

"I can see that, Sunday," said Birdwell.

"So, don't you think it'd be a fairer fight if I had the same advantage as you do?"

"Someone give the man a holster."

Feather unbuckled his rig, removed his gun, then tossed it toward Charley. It landed at his feet.

"Now, I'm gonna give you just fifteen seconds to buckle on that belt and move your gun from your boot to the holster. Starting now," the gunman added.

Charley did what the man said. He retrieved Feather's gunbelt and buckled it around his waist. Then he bent forward and reached toward his boot . . .

"Time's up," said Birdwell.

Charley glanced up from his precarious position to see Birdwell was beginning to draw his gun.

KA-BOOM!

Drawing from his boot, Charley beat the man, hands down, sinking a conical piece of lead from the Walker Colt several inches into the hired killer's heart.

The blood didn't even have time to reach the surface of the gunslinger's skin before he fell facedown in the dirt — dead.

Henry Ellis broke away from the two women and ran to his grandfather.

Charley threw his arms around the boy, picking him up into his arms.

"Uh," said the boy, who appeared to be getting squeezed to death. "I think I'm a little too big for this anymore, Grampa."

"You will never be that big, Henry Ellis," said Charley. "And you will never be too old for me to hug you. The day comes when I can't lift you up . . ."

CHAPTER TWENTY-THREE

A ranch wagon, piled high with fresh-cut pine trees, was stopped in the Sunday ranch yard. Roscoe and Feather were helping the driver unload a pretty hefty specimen from the top of the pile.

When they got the tree down to the ground, Roscoe held it by its trunk, mid-tree, then he bounced it on the ground several times to open up the boughs. Doing that also helped the tree to dispel the rainwater that had collected in its branches. Roscoe got himself wet all over.

"It sure is pretty," said Henry Ellis, who had been standing nearby with his grandfather, watching the others work.

"We better get it in the house as soon as we can, before it starts ta rain again," said Roscoe. "Otherwise, it'll make one fine mess for me ta clean up."

"Feather," said Charley. "Why don't you give Roscoe a hand taking it into the house, while I pay the man for our tree?"

Feather nodded, then he moved to the other side of the tree and took hold of it. The two men started off toward the back steps, carrying the tree between them.

"Hold it right there, you two," called out Charley. "Don't you think it'd be better to take it around through the front door . . . ? That's where the parlor is. It'd be a shame to drag it all the way through the house, wet like it is, and with them damn needles falling off in every direction."

"We'll do 'er, Boss," said Feather.

"Thanks fer thinkin' of me, C.A.," echoed Roscoe.

As they stared off around the house, Henry Ellis called after them.

"Wait for me, fellas," he said. "I want to be there when you pick the spot for the tree."

He looked up for Charley's permission to go and got an immediate nod.

He took off running after the others.

Charley paid the driver for the tree, then he stepped back as the man climbed up to the seat, took the lines, and slapped the mules into a slow trot.

As the wagon rolled down the muddy entrance road toward the front gate, two riders passed him coming from the other direction.

As the riders got closer, Charley recognized the horses as belonging to Rod and Kelly Lightfoot.

When the couple entered the ranch yard, reining up in front of Charley, the old rancher removed his hat.

"Welcome, you two," he said. "You got here just in time to help set up the Yule tree. Roscoe, Feather, and Henry Ellis just took it around to the parlor."

"We've brought two saddlebags full of trinkets to hang on the branches," said Kelly. "Plus we brought a couple of boxes of candles."

"I don't rightly know if I still have any of Willadean's Christmas tree candleholders," said Charley. "But if we do, Roscoe'll know where they are. C'mon," he added, "c'mon inside. Now that I know you're staying for a while, you can help us with the tree trimming . . . and Roscoe's going to whip up something special for our midday meal. I sure hope you'll break some bread with us."

"Thank you, Charley," said Kelly. She removed the saddlebags from both horses and climbed up the steps to the screen door. She opened the screen.

"I won't forget to wipe the mud off my boots," she said. "I know how it bothers

Roscoe when someone forgets."

"Go on in, darlin'," said Charley. "I'll make sure your horses get tied up under some shelter so's your saddles don't get too wet if it rains again. Tell Roscoe I'll be there by and by," he added. When she had disappeared into the house, Rod turned back to Charley.

"Mind if I tag along with you, Charley?" he asked.

"Come right along, son. I ain't going far," Charley answered.

With Rod following along, Charley led the two horses over to the side of the creek house, where he tied them off to a metal ring that was embedded into the stonework beneath the roof's extended eaves.

"That oughta keep 'em dry if we have another one of those storms come through," said Charley.

Then, standing side-by-side, the two of them began loosening the cinches on the horses' saddles.

"Charley," said the young Indian. "I didn't want to talk in front of Kelly, but I overheard from an old acquaintance of mine that the little town of Langtry . . . out west of Del Rio . . . is in some big trouble, if someone doesn't do something to help the old judge who owns the property."

"Why, that's Roy Bean you're talking about," said Charley. "What is it that's going on out at his place?"

"Mind you," said Rod, "this is only hearsay, but my source is reliable. He told me that a band of desperados, who some are calling the *New Comancheros*, have taken over Bean's Jersey Lilly saloon and are using it as their headquarters while they transport stolen United States horses across the border into Mexico. Once there, they're sold to the highest bidder."

"Roy's a pretty tough old man," said Charley. "He's also the Justice of the Peace down there."

"Not anymore," said Rod. "It seems that these fellas, the New Comancheros, rode in to Langtry one day last week posing as a bunch of cowboys going home after a drive. They moved into Bean's saloon, and within minutes a shooting match broke out."

"Judge Bean is used to that kind of behavior," said Charley. "He usually has some of his hangers-on stop the ruckus, then he opens court and fines the offenders."

"It didn't happen that way this time, Charley," said Rod. "This gang was ready for Bean's men and stopped 'em cold before anything could be done. My friend says that the old judge marched out of his back room with his law book in his hand, all ready to convene his court, and he ran right into the leader's gun barrel. In one weekend, two days, the gang had set up shop in the Jersey Lilly. Not just that, Charley, but they took over the Langtry Hotel, up the street, kicking out anyone who was lodging there, then they started using it as a place for the gang to sleep."

"Any idea how their operation works?" asked Charley.

"Only that the first thing they did was to build a few corrals to pen the stolen horses, until they have enough to cross over into Mexico."

Charley scratched his chin. He was thinking.

"How many days left until Christmas day?" he asked.

Rod did the calculation in his head.

"Nine days," he said.

"If we left tomorrow morning, could we be in Langtry in two days?"

"If we were to push it hard," said Rod.

"Well, let's go on inside and see what the others have to say. And I promise that I won't let on to Kelly that it was you who told me about all this."

As the two men walked back toward the house, Charley added, "I'd sure like to meet this 'friend' of yours one of these days. Any man that Kelly doesn't approve of you being around must be somebody special."

Hearing all about a friend in need perked everyone's interest. Especially when Charley reminded them that it was the judge who helped them get the Colorado to Texas cattle drive moving again after they'd come face-to-face with a train when trying to take a shortcut across a railroad bridge that spanned the Pecos River. "So, you're all up to helping out old Roy?" Charley asked.

"I can stay here and watch over Henry Ellis," said Kelly.

The boy, standing behind Kelly, made an awful face. He wasn't happy hearing that he would have to stay behind.

"I mean it, Charley," Kelly went on. "The two of us'll be just fine staying here at your ranch."

"No, darlin'," said Charley. "I'm pretty sure I'd like you to go with us on this one. I want to take Henry Ellis, too."

Henry Ellis's face brightened considerably.

"Gee, Grampa," he said. "Do you really mean that?"

"I think you're getting to be old enough

now to ride with us. Especially when I need you to."

The boy and Kelly couldn't keep from throwing their arms around him and covering him with kisses.

"Not so fast, you two," said Charley, pulling away. "This ain't going to be a vacation. You're both going to approach the Jersey Lilly as a mother and son who've been traveling and just lost your way. All you'll be asking for is the road to El Paso. Hopefully, they'll give you directions and you can leave. That's when Feather and Holliday will . . ."

The Texas Outfit rode along at a good pace, paralleling the railroad tracks. Like they had done so many times before, Charley took the lead, with Roscoe, Feather, Holliday, and Rod spread out behind them.

Henry Ellis, who usually rode beside his grampa Charley, was riding this time in the old chuckwagon — which had once been Charley's two-seat buckboard.

Charley and the others had removed the chuck box from the rear end, plus any other additions that had helped it to function as a working chuckwagon. And finally, after replacing the old canvas covering with relatively newer material, the old two-seat buckboard had begun to resemble a small covered wagon.

That would serve as a mode of transportation for Kelly and Henry Ellis. Charley told them what he wanted them to say and made them both memorize those words.

Charley also filled them all in on the rest of his plan when they made camp alongside the Rio Grande. As with Kelly and the boy, he made sure everyone else knew their part, too.

CHAPTER TWENTY-FOUR

Judge Roy Bean must have liked signs. The front of his tiny saloon in Langtry, Texas, had at least five of them nailed to its facade. The sign on the roof read: JUDGE ROY BEAN NOTARY PUBLIC, another beneath that proclaimed: JUSTICE OF THE PEACE, and a larger one beside that one stated: LAW WEST OF THE PECOS. There was still another, below that, displaying the saloon's name, THE JERSEY LILLY (named after the Judge's favorite singer, Lilly Langtree), plus an advertisement that simply offered: *Ice Beer.*

Another building had been added to the original structure since Charley had visited before. It had been attached to the right-hand side of the saloon, and had another sign tacked above its door that said: BIL-LIARDS.

When Charley saw the place from a distance through his old Army field glasses, he was surprised by how much the landscape around the tiny building had changed since he was last there.

As Rod had told him, the horse rustlers had constructed several sturdy corrals near the saloon, one of which was only half filled with horses. And the old two-story hotel, up the street behind it all, now had quite a few saddle horses tied in front of it, as opposed to the scattered number Charley had remembered from before.

They were waiting. Waiting for Feather to get back. Charley had sent the little cowboy on ahead so he could check the layout inside, then bring the information back to Charley and the others.

Charley lifted the Army binoculars to his eyes once again, and after several jerky, searching movements, he found the under-size ex-Ranger, riding along slowly through the desert fauna, still a few hundred yards or so away from the saloon.

Charley moved his look forward, down the road in front of Feather, to frame the Jersey Lilly. Several men slept in chairs on the front porch with their hats pulled over their eyes, while others worked lazily around the corrals.

One of those men spotted Feather as he got closer and closer to the saloon. Other members of the horse-rustling band gathered together in front of the building, while one of their number climbed the steps, then entered the building.

Sticking his head inside, the man called out from the door.

"Tell the *Jefé* someone's comin'. So far, he don't look like he'll be any problem. Barkley, Guterrez. You two go out back, now. Cover the front, just in case there's more comin' behind him."

"Whatever you say, Fernando," someone yelled back to him.

The door to the back room opened, and the white-bearded face of Judge Phantly Roy Bean Jr. appeared. He had been beaten — puffy eyes, red stains in his white beard, and several black and blue bruises around his nose and left ear told the story.

He was only there for a few moments before someone shoved him violently from behind, causing him to stumble forward into the arms of one of the gang members. Immediately, the judge was shoved to the floor.

Bean lay there on the floor, breathing hard, unable to move. Blood dripped from his nose onto the floor in front of him. Stepping through the same door the judge had just passed through came a bull of a man dressed in an all-leather outfit. His clothing was not the usual backwoods hunting garb seen on many men of the day. Instead, it was a hand-sewn, tailor-made getup — one that helped show off his muscular build. He also wore a black eye patch over his left eye, and topped it all off with an old beaver-skin top hat that he'd probably taken from the judge when they had first met.

"Whoever it is comin' our way," said the man, who was obviously their *Jefé,* their chief, "just leave him alone 'til he gets inside. When we figure out just who he is, then I'll tell ya what ta do with him. Fernando," he said in a louder voice, "tell the men out front what I just said. I wouldn't want whoever this person is comin' ta see us ta get killed before I even get ta meet him. Now, you others, take the judge in the back room again, where he was, and watch him good."

The two nearest men took hold of Bean by his boots and started to drag him away. The one called Fernando headed for the front door, tipping his hat to the large man in the leather outfit as he passed.

From his vantage down the road, where he waited with the rest of the outfit, Charley was still watching Feather through his Army field glasses. As the little cowboy reached the front of the Jersey Lilly, he was met by two members of the New Comancheros.

Charley watched as they talked and could tell by the friendly faces that Feather was doing a pretty convincing job.

Feather was eventually allowed to dismount. One of the men took his horse to a hitching post and tied it off, while the other led Feather up the steps to the porch, then over to the door.

Feather was ushered inside by Fernando. Most of the men had moved over to the bar, which ran parallel to the back wall. Their leader — the man in the leather outfit — stood slightly in front of them all, and he chuckled loudly when Fernando shoved Feather toward him, removing the little cowboy's revolver as he did.

Feather made a grab for the weapon, but his hand landed on an empty holster. He shot a look to the man who'd taken his weapon.

"Just who do you think you are, mister, takin' away a man's gun like that?" he said.

The large man took one step closer to Feather, until he towered over the much shorter man.

"They call me Zeke Cassidy," said Cassidy. "And I will ask you to direct anything you have to say only to me, and me alone."

Feather stared at the man. He was trying to gain some insight into this bull moose of a human by looking directly into his one eye. Instead, he only saw death.

One of the other men anxiously waved his hand for recognition. When Cassidy pointed to him, he stepped forward.

"Zeke," he began. "This here's a Whitney-ville Walker Colt," said the one called Ortega. "This is the weapon that they used to issue to every rookie Texas Ranger."

Feather saw Zeke Cassidy's large fist coming his way, but he didn't quite move fast enough.

Charley lowered the binoculars and turned to the others.

"How long's he been in there now?" he wanted to know.

Holliday pulled his pocket watch from his vest pocket and glanced at the face.

" 'Bout an hour, by my old Nelly here," he said. "But sometimes she can run slow."

"Anyone else?" asked Charley.

"Holliday's pretty close ta right," said Roscoe, holding out his own pocket watch for Charley to see. "It's never lost nor gained a minute since you give it to me on my fiftieth birthday."

"What was so special about yer fiftieth?" Holliday wanted to know.

"That was my thirtieth anniversary with

310

the Rangers," said Roscoe. "Charley give it to me."

The door to the Jersey Lilly's back room opened and Zeke Cassidy peeked inside. The judge was laying on the mattress of his bed. His eyes were closed and he was breathing hard. Feather's head was hanging down; he had been tied securely to a chair nearby.

From Charley's vantage point, he was still watching the front of the building with the field glasses. His stomach took a good jolt when one of the men came out of the front door, walked down the steps, then loosened the cinch on Feather's horse. He went on to unsaddle it right there, letting the leather-covered tree and stirrups drop to the ground. Then he led Chigger over to the first corral, removed the horse's harness and bit, and turned it loose with all the other horses.

Charley lowered the binoculars.

"Roscoe, Rod, Holliday," he said. "We're going in."

Before Charley and the others could make a move, Kelly spoke up.

"Just you hold on right there, Charley Sunday," said the woman. "What about

Henry Ellis and me? Did you forget your own plan that quickly? Now it's our turn to go on down there."

"They've just turned out Feather's horse into the corrals with the other horses. That has to mean —"

"That don't have to mean anything more than they're putting the horse up for the night. Did they put Feather's horse in the small corral or the bigger one?"

"The smaller one, Miss Kelly," said Charley, knowing what she was leading to.

"Well, don't most folks who build a large and a smaller corral use the big one for their herd and the smaller one for their personal horses?"

"Yep," said Charley, "s'pose they do."

"Then you'll have to agree with me, Charley, when I say isn't it just possible that Feather was invited to join them for supper? Maybe even to spend the night there? Now, you know who you're dealing with, so why's my idea not worth thinking about? C'mon, Charley," she urged. "Let Henry Ellis and me do what you trained us to do."

"Please, Grampa," said Henry Ellis, who was now standing between the two. "I know we'll be all right. I really do."

Charley rubbed his stubble, eyeing the two by half closing his other eye.

"It'll be all right, Charley," said Rod. "They won't harm a woman and child."

Charley drew in a large breath, then he expelled it real slow.

"All right," he finally said. "But instead of acting like you're a pioneer woman who's looking for her lost husband, all alone with just your son . . . You'll now be accompanied by your grandfather."

Before she could object, he continued.

"I'm going in there with you, too."

The redone vehicle, now posing as a covered wagon, rolled along peacefully, being pulled by two horses. Charley was in the passenger's seat, wrapped in a blanket and trying to look even older than he was. Beside him, dressed in a heavy coat, calico dress, with matching bonnet, was Kelly, who drove the team. Behind them, with his legs and lower torso still in the wagon, but with his face poking through between them, was Henry Ellis.

As they neared the Jersey Lilly, Roscoe, still some distance away, lowered the spy glasses and turned to Rod and Holliday.

"I sure hope this works," he said softly. Then he nodded to the others, and the three of them got to their feet and mounted their horses.

"Just remember what Charley told us ta do," he said. Then the three of them split up in different directions, riding away slowly.

Kelly drove the covered wagon straight for the Jersey Lilly. They all watched as one of the New Comancheros turned around and went inside the building. Then, as they drew even closer, a different man came back outside and said something to the others.

When the team reached the space in front of the saloon, two men stepped forward and took control of the horses' harness and bits. Fernando stepped in front of them. He looked up, eyeing the young woman, the boy, and the older gentleman.

"Is there something we can do for you, ma'am?" he asked. His eyes flicked back and forth between Kelly and Charley.

"Yes," said Kelly. "It seems that my husband has gone missing. He was scouting ahead for us yesterday, and he never came back to our campsite last night."

"What's he look like?"

"Tall. In his late twenties. Brown hair, blue eyes. He's wearing a gray wool coat, a rough, leather waistcoat, and a tan Stetson hat. His horse is a black, brown, and white pinto," she added.

"Since none of us know how to make more than our mark, would you care to come inside so you can write that description down on paper for us?"

"Ta tell the truth," said Charley in an older man's voice, "if ya got anything ta wet a man's whistle with inside, I'd kinda like ta come along, too."

Thinking to himself about just how easy this was turning out to be, Fernando answered:

"That will be fine, *Viejo,*" said Fernando. "And as long as you are both coming inside, you may as well bring with you the *muchacho.*"

Charley climbed down from the wagon. Fernando assisted Kelly, while Charley gave Henry Ellis a hand getting down. Then Fernando stepped back and he let the boy lead the way.

The threesome entered the saloon with Fernando behind them.

"Go and bring the *Jefé,*" he asked one of the men, who got up, then entered the back room.

The three of them stood together in the center of the room with all eyes staring. Finally, the door to the back room opened and Zeke Cassidy stepped out. He glanced at Charley and the boy, but gave Kelly a

315

really good looking over.

"Why didn't any of you idiots tell me there was a young lady with them?" Cassidy asked all the men present.

"Sorry, *Jefé,*" said a few embarrassed voices.

Cassidy's eyes continued to roam over Kelly's body.

"Are you married to this old . . . man?" he asked her.

"No," she said. "He's my husband's grandfather. I just told this kind gentleman . . ." she referred to Fernando ". . . that my husband has gone missing. We were searching for him when we saw your small settlement."

"I can send some of my men out to look for him," said Cassidy. "Would that help you, ma'am?"

"No," said Charley in his old man's voice. "We'll be all right lookin' fer him ourselves. But would you happen to have some spirits for sale? I could sure use a drink."

"What's to yer liking?" said Cassidy as he moved on around the bar.

Outside, one of the men sleeping on the porch got a quick gun barrel to the head. The same thing happened to the second man. They were both left where they were because they still appeared to be sleeping.

Another man, who was enjoying a smoke beside the corral, suddenly pitched forward onto his face. A Bowie knife's handle was protruding from his lower back. The killing had been so silent that none of the others had even turned around. A hand reached in and removed the bloody knife.

From behind another rustler, a thin piece of baling wire was slipped around his neck and pulled tight before he could make a sound. The wire remained taut as blood began to flow from the man's nostrils. By the time his eyes closed and his body slumped, Roscoe released his grip on the wire and stepped away.

The third and final horse thief flinched as the noose of a thick rope fell around his neck and tightened quickly. Rod was at the other end of that rope, and he'd looped the rope over a corral fence before he'd thrown it. All that was left to do was for Rod to jerk the noose, as hard and as fast as he could, and the man's neck snapped just as fast as if he'd been dropped through a trapdoor.

The three of them gathered at the side of the building. Rod looked up the street to the hotel. He could see that all the horses were still tied where they had been an hour earlier. He suspected the gang members who had been out all night stealing horses were resting by day, leaving only the few they had already dispatched, plus several more inside, to guard the stolen horses.

It was Holliday's idea to approach this dilemma from the rear of the building. They moved around to the backside of the Jersey Lilly, where they discovered the wooden addition that made up the back room.

Holliday was chosen to look inside because he was the tallest, so he went to the room's side window and stood on his tiptoes, leaning his chin over the bottom of the window frame until he could see inside. He held that awkward position for as long as he could bear it, then fell back on his heels. The others gathered around him.

"Well," said Rod. "What did you see?"

"Anyone in there?" asked Roscoe at the same time.

"Feather's in there, tied up. And the judge is sprawled out on a bed."

"Anyone else?" Rod wanted to know.

"That was it," said Holliday. "Just them two."

"Well, c'mon, then," said Rod. "Let's go see if there's a way all three of us can get inside."

Inside the front room, Zeke Cassidy was offering Kelly and Henry Ellis some fresh cider from behind the bar. Charley was already sipping on a half a glass of rotgut whiskey that Cassidy had poured for him moments earlier.

"Thank you, sir," said Kelly, taking the glass of cider from his hand.

"It's Zeke, ma'am," said Cassidy. "You can call me Zeke."

"And I thank you, too," said Henry Ellis, when he got his glass. He immediately chugged it down.

"Boy, was I thirsty," he said, setting his container down on the bar.

"If any of you would care to refresh your drinks, just let me know," said Cassidy. His eyes continued to stay focused on Kelly.

"If you folks'd care to spend the night with us, I can also offer you some fine horse meat steaks," said Cassidy.

" 'Fraid not," said Charley. "We still got some daylight left, and we oughta continue our search."

"I told you earlier that I'd have my men do the searching for you," said Cassidy. "Here," he said to the woman, "let me pour you another glass of cider."

He moved over to take Kelly's glass so he could pour her a refill, but his hand brushed against hers, and remained there for another moment.

Henry Ellis noticed the contact immediately.

Kelly threw a glance to Charley, then pulled her hand away gently.

"I'll have some more cider, too, mister," said the boy, holding out his empty glass.

"Anything your heart desires, son," said Cassidy. "So won't you change your mind and join us for supper?" he asked them all again, though his eyes never left Kelly.

"Sorry," said Charley, "but we gotta be gettin' on down the road."

"*Jefé,*" said one of the men in the room. "The *Viejo* carries a revolver in his boot. The same kind of *pistola* the other one had."

Charley threw a roundhouse right and clipped Cassidy a good one on the jaw.

The leather-clad leader dropped to one knee, but no more. He got to his feet while he held out a hand to keep his men back.

"Another Ranger, are ya?" he said, moving in on Charley.

"No, sir," said Charley, "It's ex-Ranger. And where is my partner?"

"I'm right here, Boss," said Feather, who had just opened the door to the back room. He held one of Holliday's Colts.

One of the rustlers made a move for his gun, and Feather shot him point blank. The outlaw dropped to the floor — dead.

Zeke was on his feet, facing Charley.

"I'm sorry that you're such an old man, mister," he said. "Because I really don't like hurting old folks."

Charley brought up his left boot, connecting with the leader's crotch.

Zeke's eyes crossed, and he went all the way down this time.

By then, Rod, Roscoe, and Holliday had entered behind Feather. They fired their weapons with ease, picking off the rest of the rustlers who were in the room.

Rod joined Henry Ellis and Kelly at the bar.

"Are you two all right?" he asked.

"I'm just glad I'm not Charley," said Kelly.

She nodded toward the fight in progress in the center of the room.

Cassidy got to his feet again. He faced off with Charley one more time. The difference in the two men's size was very apparent when they stood side-by-side.

"It really ain't a very fair match," said Roscoe, moving up behind Rod.

Cassidy took Charley by the arm and his opposite leg, then lifted him over his head.

Charley's eyes bugged out when he realized he was being held above the giant's head.

"Do something," Charley yelled to his

cohorts down below.

"Do what?" Roscoe yelled back.

Cassidy began to twirl Charley around over his head.

The dizziness showed in Charley's eyes.

"Whooooah," he said.

"What do you want us ta do?" yelled Holliday.

"Shoot the son-of-a-bitch," yelled Charley.

Bullets came from all sides — one from Rod. Another from Roscoe. A single shot from Feather, and one from Holiday.

Cassidy set Charley down gently, then he turned back to the others. He was still standing. Blood trickled from his wounds. His eyes were glassy.

That's when Charley reached for the Walker Colt, still in his boot.

Hearing Charley cock the gun, Cassidy turned again. He began moving toward Charley once more. Then came the final four bullets, fanned off by Charley, that bracketed Zeke Cassidy's heart.

With all that lead in him, Cassidy was still able to take another step across the floor, before toppling onto the table used for card games. His weight broke all four legs of the table and softened his final fall, just enough.

Still in all, when Charley, who was on the floor, looked over to the man dressed in what was now shredded leather . . . Cassidy's eyes still showed signs of life.

"Cassidy," said Charley. "If you don't die right here, and right now, we'll have to take you to a place where they'll hang you. Do you want that? That'll be one hell of a job, you know, hauling your body . . . anywhere."

To everyone watching, Zeke Cassidy appeared to have understood Charley's words — except he actually heard nothing. His eyes may not have closed with his death, but he had unquestionably drawn his final breath.

CHAPTER TWENTY-FIVE

1961

"What are you doing up so late, Noel?"

Those were the first words out of the girl's mother's mouth as she stepped through the front door. She was followed by a rush of cold wind.

"It's Christmas vacation," said Noel as she bounded toward her mother and was scooped up into her arms.

"I'm sorry, darling. I forgot," said Evie, setting down her purse so she could get a better grip on her daughter.

"Grampa Hank is still telling us his story," said Josh from his feet-up position on the couch.

"And it's a good one," added Caleb.

"Did you know Grampa Hank's grampa Charley knew Judge Roy Bean, personally, Mommy?"

"I seem to remember your father telling

me all about it," said Evie with a wink to Hank.

"Well," said Evie, "just let me put my keys away and take off my coat, and I'll sit in with you for the rest of the story."

She set Noel down and moved off into the kitchen.

The little girl went straight to Hank, hopping up onto his lap.

"I hope you're comfortable there, little one," said Hank. "I'll be just fine, too, just let me get the kinks out."

He tried to stretch a little, but the girl's weight was preventing him from doing so.

Noel wiggled her body into place in Hank's lap.

Evie came out of the kitchen, now wearing her regular housecoat. She found a place on the couch Josh had commandeered and made him move his feet, before she sat down.

"I'm ready," she said.

"All right with me," said Hank.

CHAPTER TWENTY-SIX

1900

In spite of the news that the Cropper Brothers had struck the westbound while it pulled into the Juanita depot that afternoon, and stolen an Army payroll, the outfit was having a special supper together in Flora Mae's place. It was to celebrate the fact that they had saved the day for Judge Bean, and that Charley now had his ranch back.

They all sat at a round table, brought in for the occasion by Flora Mae.

"So, the judge says to me," Charley was telling the others, "that he's been thinking of taking some time away from Langtry. He wants to go to San Antonio, tie on the biggest drunk he's ever had, then go back home to Langtry and die in his own bed."

As bottles were poured and glasses lifted, it was Henry Ellis, with his buttermilk held high, who gave the toast.

"To my grampa," he began. "The greatest

grampa in the state of Texas. He can out-ride, out-rope, out-drink, out-draw, and out-shoot just about anyone I can think of. He's also warm, friendly, strong, and . . . healthy," added the boy.

Flora Mae raised her glass.

"I'd also like ta make a toast ta Charley," she said. "He tells the truth, unless he's tellin' one of his windys. He's as honest as the day is long, so ya better catch 'im in winter when the days're real short, rather'n summer, when the days are real long. And he's smart, so smart he dang near let two city slickers cheat him out of his ranch and cattle."

Rod was the next to raise his glass.

"But he redeemed himself in Langtry, Flora Mae. Plus, he got his ranch back the proper way . . . by using the law and not violence. Oh," he went on, "I admit a few men have been killed since then, but that had nothing to do with Charley having his ranch stolen . . . it was from helpin' a friend in need."

Holliday raised his glass.

"Ol' Charley could bring about a change in the weather, if he'd only give it a try," said the old trick-gun artist. "I ain't never seen a man so blessed. I'd bet a nickel, if I had one, that Charley's got a special in with his Lord, a mite more'n most of us do."

"That's wrong, Holliday," said Charley, laying his hand on the gunman's shoulder. "The Lord don't love any one of us any more than the other . . . plus, it was the Lord that helped me put this outfit together, not me alone. So if there's any one of you who doesn't think they're as equal in God's eyes as those around him, I advise they have a talk with their own Lord."

Feather and Roscoe touched their glasses in a private toast, while Henry Ellis tipped back his buttermilk and gulped until his glass was empty.

Kinney County sheriff, Willingham Dubbs, entered Flora Mae's Pool Hall & Bar, just a little before the supper was about to break up.

He wore a rain-streaked slicker, with water dripping from his storm-drenched Stetson. When the outfit saw him, the room became very quiet.

"Evenin', Willingham," said Charley.

The others nodded their recognition.

"Did you find out anything more on the robbery today while you were out at the depot?" asked Charley.

"Yes, I did," said the sheriff. "You know," he went on, "West Texas has always had a kind of 'they can do their thing, we'll do ours' with the Cropper Brothers. And as long as they didn't steal that much, or kill anyone, we never really took 'em that serious."

"Are you trying to say that our outlook changes when it comes to the Cropper Brothers, Willingham?"

"Yes, it does, Charley," was the sheriff's answer. "The Cropper Brothers, and their gang, stole the entire Fort Clark payroll . . . all one hundred and fifty thousand dollars of it. And in doing so, an Army paymaster and two Army guards were killed."

There was a reaction from every person in the room.

"Well, we better get a posse tog—"

"Several civilians were also killed, Charley."

The sheriff signaled for Charley to come closer.

When the old rancher arrived at the sheriff's side, he could see that the sheriff had been crying.

"What is it, Willingham?" he asked. "What's wrong?"

The sheriff leaned in as close as he could before whispering, "Your grandson's parents were on that train, Charley. They had just disembarked and were on their way here to surprise you all for Christmas."

He gripped Charley harder with his hand.

"There was some shootin', and they somehow got caught up in the middle of it."

"Are you saying . . . ?" whispered Charley. His eyes were watering up.

"I'm saying that your daughter, Betty Jean, and her husband Kent, are dead, Charley. The Cropper Brothers' Gang killed them both."

Charley glanced over to where Henry Ellis was still sitting. The boy was laughing and having the time of his life.

Charley turned back to the sheriff. A full-blown tear had formed in one of his eyes, and now it broke away, sliding slowly down his cheek.

"How am I gonna tell him, Willingham? How am I going to do that?"

A crack of thunder rolled nearby. A heavy rain could be heard as it began falling overhead.

Charley continued to stare at his grandson.

CHAPTER TWENTY-SEVEN

1961

Hank stopped talking for just long enough to pull his handkerchief out of his rear pocket and blow his nose.

His listeners had tears streaming down their cheeks.

No one spoke. Just the sound of sniffling.

Evie turned to the others.

"Maybe it's about time to put the TV dinners into the oven," she said.

"Sounds like a good idea to me," said Josh, getting up and heading for the kitchen. His mother followed.

Caleb wiped at his eyes, then he got to his feet and followed his mother and older brother into the kitchen.

Noel, still sitting in her grandfather's lap, looked up at the old man with questioning eyes.

"It's just a story, Grampa," she said with a whimper. "You can change it back, can't you? Make it so Henry Ellis's mommy and daddy don't die?"

"I'd really like to do that, darlin'," said Hank, still holding her in his arms as he stood and started for the kitchen. "But since this is a true story I've been telling you, I'm afraid it won't be that simple."

"What kind of TV dinner do you want, Grampa?" shouted Josh as Hank and Noel entered the room. "Salisbury steak or fried chicken?"

"Salisbury," said Charley. "With catsup."

Charley set the girl down in a chair at the kitchen table, where she immediately began to play with the salt and pepper shakers.

"Don't do that, Noel," said her brother Caleb. "You know how Mom feels about us playing with stuff at the table."

Evie glanced back over her shoulder and gave her daughter "that" look.

Noel stopped her fidgeting and sat up straight.

Hank sat down next to her.

"You spilled a little salt right there, honey," said Hank. "You better grab a pinch and throw it over your shoulder."

"Why's that?"

" 'Cause it's bad luck," cut in Caleb. "Just like throwin' your hat on a bed."

"That's really bad," said Josh, who was

monitoring the dinners. "A hat on a bed is really bad luck. Grampa Hank taught me that before you were born, Noel."

"Well," said Noel, "I don't wear a hat, so I'll never have any bad luck."

"You wear one when it rains," said Caleb.

"But I have a place to hang my rain hat. Right over my raincoat and rubber boots in the mud room."

"Does anyone have any questions about the story so far?" asked Hank.

"I've got one," said Caleb. "Why did those Cropper Brothers have to kill Henry Ellis's mom and dad?"

"It was a mistake," said Hank. "They just got caught up in the middle of the payroll robbery. The sheriff said later that they tried to get out of the way, but witnesses testified that they ran the wrong way when the shooting started. They could have run into the depot itself, but instead they ran to the front of the building where the robbery was taking place."

"Will someone get the boxes for the TV dinners out of the trash?" said Josh. "I forgot how long they're supposed to be in the oven."

"I'll do that, Josh," said Noel as she ran to the trash container and retrieved the TV dinner boxes.

"It says right here, heat for forty-five minutes. Uh," she caught herself. "This one here is different. It says heat for thirty-five minutes, stir gravy, then heat an additional ten minutes."

"Caleb, Noel," said Evie. "Go and get the TV trays out of the closet and set them up in the living room where we were sitting. Grampa Hank'll finish telling you his story while we're eating supper."

"Just set them out on the table, Noel, with the cook times facing up. That'll help me to know just whose dinner is ready to come out first."

CHAPTER TWENTY-EIGHT

1900

"Bring-ing in the sheaves, bring-ing in the
   sheaves,
We shall come rejoic-ing, bring-ing in the
   sheaves;

"Go-ing forth with weep-ing, sow-ing for the
   Mas-ter,
Though the loss sustained, our spirit often
   grieves;
When our weep-ing's over, He will bid us
   wel-come,
We shall come rejoic-ing, bring-ing in the
   sheaves."

Charley stood back away from the other
mourners, with an arm draped lovingly over
Henry Ellis's shoulder.

The boy was having a hard time of it, but
it was Charley whose body trembled. It was

Charley who was having a problem holding back his tears. It was Charley who kept looking up at the freshly covered graves with their brand-new markers. They stood beside an older grave, with a marker that read:

WILLADEAN CLARKE SUNDAY
Born 1831 Died 1887
A Good Wife and Mother

There were four smaller graves nearby, plus an empty space beside Willadean's grave, and Charley's mind was on that day in the future when it would be him they were singing over.

It won't be long now, he thought to himself. *I'm sneaking up on eighty pretty fast, and I still got a lot more about living that I have to share with Henry Ellis before I go.*

He tousled the boy's hair, and when Henry Ellis looked up at him, he knew the boy was thinking about the same things that he was. *They would be together now . . . grandfather and grandson . . . for a lot longer than just visits every other summer, plus the occasional holiday.*

The boy has no home to go back to in Austin anymore. His roots are right here in Juanita, now, thought Charley.

Henry Ellis pondered what his life would

be like living in Juanita with his grampa: *No more private school. How will I handle the loss of my old friends? A totally different way of living — country, instead of city — is about to happen in my life.*

He thought about his parents: *There are more memories of Mother here at Grampa's ranch than there ever would be back in Austin. And Father always preferred the open country to the city, anyway . . . that's why he loved traveling to Mexico. It certainly won't bother either of them if I live down here with my grampa.*

Everything will work out just fine, Charley was thinking.

Plus, I'll get to know Grampa a whole lot better, too, the boy reflected.

The reception after the funeral was held in the ballroom of Flora Mae's hotel. Besides Flora Mae, the entire Texas Outfit was present, along with Roscoe and Charley's friends from town, Sheriff Dubbs, the Reverend Pirtle, and a bunch more whose names had slipped Charley's mind.

Folks had brought food from all around the county — a regular potluck. Great-looking dishes had been laid out on a long table, surrounded by salads, side dishes, and desserts.

No one was being served; they just lined up as if they were at a weekend barbecue and served themselves while walking through a line — then they found a place at the table and commenced to eating.

Kelly stood behind the serving table, pouring lemonade and serving punch from a large bowl. As Feather passed by with two full plates delicately balanced in his two hands, he asked her for a glass of punch.

Without realizing that he had no place to carry it, Kelly went ahead and poured him a glass, then went about looking for a place to set it.

"In my mouth," said the pee-wee cowboy. He opened his mouth just enough to snap his teeth at her, showing her where he wanted her to place the container.

Kelly shrugged, then she raised the glass to Feather's open mouth, and the man grasped the lip of the glass in his teeth, clamping down just right.

As Feather turned and started off toward the table, Kelly smiled, feeling quite proud of herself. Suddenly, there was a loud gasp from those around her, causing her to look up.

Standing before her was Feather, now in the middle of the room. Both plates of food were teetering in each of his hands, and he still held the glass of punch firmly between his teeth.

Slowly but surely, the glass started slipping. Actually, it was his false teeth that were slipping. Everyone just continued to stare, as the teeth — both uppers and lowers — slid all the way out, sending the glass of punch crashing to the floor, splattering punch in every direction.

"Ahh, hell," said Feather under his breath.

Then one plate of food began to totter — then the other. Finally Feather raised his eyes to the sky, mumbling something to his Lord. Just then, both plates of food slipped off completely, falling to the floor in a thunderous cacophony.

A crack of thunder outside, much louder than the crashing plates had been, exploded at the same moment. Lightning flashed all around.

"Lightning hit the telegraph office," someone yelled from where he stood by a window.

Smoke could be seen rising from a small building down the street.

"Consider this a fire alarm," yelled Sheriff Dubbs. "All of you who are members of the volunteers gather outside, right now."

Most of the men headed straight for the door, bumping one another out of the way in order to be first.

Among the volunteers were Charley, Roscoe, and Feather.

Confused, Holliday went over to the sheriff.

"Do you hafta be a citizen of Juanita ta help fight the fire?" he wanted to know.

"No, sir," said Sheriff Dubbs. "We'll take anyone we can get if it means savin' our town."

"Good," said the old trick shooter. "Rod, Kelly . . . any others who ain't connected to this town officially . . . get on out there and grab a bucket."

Henry Ellis found himself alone as the large room emptied out. Then a thought came to him: *I reckon I'm a full-fledged citizen of Juanita now, so why, in the devil's name, am I still standing here?*

CHAPTER TWENTY-NINE

Four days had passed since they had buried Henry Ellis's mother and father. Charley had decided that his grandson might just need a little more time to himself in order to get more of a grasp on what had happened, and to privately grieve if he felt the need.

The storms continued to come and go, delivering rain, hail, or just the heavy winds that were pushing the northern tempests in their direction.

The boy got up early. Even though the room was cold, he washed up in the pan of cold water beside his bed that Roscoe set there for him every morning. Then he dressed in his denims and a new wool shirt, pulling on his boots as an afterthought.

If I'm going to be living here in West Texas, I better start looking like a West Texan was what he was thinking to himself as he left the room.

He could smell the bacon frying as he bolted toward the kitchen. And when he entered the room, the other terrific aromas of Roscoe's cooking enticed him over to the table, where he sat down beside Charley.

The kitchen was overly warm, and the windows were already covered with a sheet of condensation. His grampa was already eating — washing down every other bite with a big gulp of Arbuckles coffee.

"It's good to see you, son," said Charley.

"It's good to see you, too, Grampa . . . Roscoe," he nodded.

"Since you're here, you must feel like you're ready to go back to work," said Charley.

"Work?" echoed the boy. "What kind of work?"

"How does hunting down a gang of bank robbers sound to you, son?"

Roscoe set the boy's plate in front of him, along with a steaming cup of coffee. This was the first time ever Henry Ellis had been offered coffee.

He took a sip. It burned his lips, but he held back any expression of pain.

"Just give me a minute to eat my breakfast," said Henry Ellis, "and I'll be right with you."

■ ■ ■ ■

Henry Ellis came through the screen door, off the back porch. He skipped the steps as he jumped down to the ground in the ranch yard. Roscoe and Charley were waiting for him. They were already in their saddles and holding the reins to the boy's horse.

On his way over to join them, he spotted the family graveyard beside the barn. He noticed the two new stones that were not there before, and couldn't help himself as he was drawn to them.

He stopped and stood outside the wrought-iron fence that surrounded the gravestones, and he read the two inscriptions on the stones. The first read:

KENT MICHAEL PRITCHARD
1868–1900
Husband and Father
R I P

The second stone had been engraved to read:

BETTY JEAN SUNDAY PRITCHARD
Daughter – Mother – Wife
1870–1900
A good wife and daughter.

Henry Ellis stood there for a moment or two longer. Seeing it engraved in stone had finally made it all real for him. Tears began to flow down both cheeks, and as much as he wished his sniffling would stop, it wouldn't.

He felt the gentle hand of Grampa Charley rest on his shoulder. He knew Charley would always be standing behind him, no matter what.

"Are you all right with it now, son?" asked Charley.

"I'll never be all right with it, Grampa," answered the boy. "Not until I find whoever did this —"

"Hold on, son," said Charley, cutting in. "They were caught in a cross fire. They could have been hit by the lawmen's bullets as well as those of the Cropper Gang. There ain't no reason to hold a grudge, son. These things happen. Sometimes it's best we forget and forgive."

"Well, I'm not going to forget, or am I going to forgive. I just hope you catch that Cropper Gang. Because, when you do, it'll make me a whole lot happier."

Within fifteen minutes, Charley, Roscoe, and Henry Ellis were trotting down the road toward the entrance gate. Roscoe dismounted and unlocked the gate. He let the others through, then he squeezed himself and his horse through the opening behind them. He locked the gate and remounted, kicking out after the others who had gone on ahead.

"Hey, fellas," Roscoe shouted, "wait fer me."

He reined up beside the two, and together, they rode toward town.

It was sprinkling lightly when they reached Flora Mae's place. The drizzle hadn't even had time to dampen their outer clothing before they had tied off their horses and entered the establishment.

Like the kitchen back at the ranch, and most other interior rooms in Juanita, the windows were sweating on the inside yet freezing on the opposite side of the pane.

Charley slid out of his sheepskin coat. The others did the same before crossing over to the bar behind Charley, where several others were sitting.

Feather was sleeping on one of the pool tables, while Holliday practiced his fast draw beside the bar.

Bud the bartender had some coffee simmering on the old potbellied stove next to the bar, and he set up two cups and poured when he saw Charley and Roscoe enter.

"Give my grandson a cup of that belly-warming brew, will you, Bud?" said Charley. "If he's going to be doing a man's work, he ought to be allowed to drink like one."

Roscoe leaned in. "You don't want Henry Ellis ta be drinkin' whiskey, now do ya?" said Roscoe.

Charley chuckled. "No, Roscoe," said Charley. "No whiskey. I'm just starting him off on coffee to begin with. When he proves he can handle it, I might be tempted to buy him his first shot of whiskey."

"Thanks, Grampa," said the boy. "But I don't think I ever want to try any liquor. I've seen what it can do to people."

He glanced over to Feather who was snoring like a lumberjack sawing logs.

"You mean him?" said Charley. "Ol' Feather ain't had a drink in a long, long time now."

"But that doesn't matter, Grampa," said Henry Ellis. "There's something different about Feather. He's not like you and Uncle Roscoe. You've seen him. He can take a drink when you least expect it. Why, I'll bet he's even been to a sanitarium before to help him stop . . . but that still didn't keep him away from the bottle, did it?"

"I have a lot of faith in Feather, Henry

Ellis," said Charley. "Now that he's staying on the water wagon, ol' Feather's back to his old ways, now that he gave up John Barleycorn."

The boy could only stare at Charley. What he was trying to say just wasn't getting through.

"Here ya go, Henry Ellis," said Bud, setting down a cup of coffee in front of the boy.

About then, one of Sheriff Dubbs's deputies entered the pool hall. He saw Charley near the bar and called over to him.

"Hey, Charley. Sheriff wants ta see you in his office. Says he's got some information on the Cropper Brothers' Gang. He thinks he knows where they're hidin' out."

Nearly everyone in the place, not just Charley, got up and followed the deputy out of the building.

While the deputy stood back and watched, Charley led them all out onto the street, then down the connecting boardwalk to the sheriff's office.

Willingham Dubbs, sheriff of Kinney County, was sitting at his desk talking with a smallish man in his late fifties, who wore black sleeve garters with a starched shirt and vest, plus a short-brim derby hat. Both men turned as Charley stepped through the door, asking the others to remain outside until he learned more.

"What's this I hear about you having some new information on the Croppers?" he said to the sheriff as he closed the door behind him.

Dubbs swiveled his chair around.

"Glad you could come on such a short notice, Charley," said the sheriff. "I'd like you to meet Mr. Beverly DeSoto . . . he's in charge of railroad track inspections."

"I supervise twenty-two men in this district . . . the Forty-third," said DeSoto. "They cover all exposed track between San Antonio to the east and Del Rio to the west. North and South, they cover the right-of-way from San Angelo to Eagle Pass."

"And they check the track —"

"Their job is to make sure nothing's wrong with the track and to keep it in good repair."

"Your deputy said you had some new information on where the Cropper Gang might be holed up. Is that true?" asked Charley, not really trying to hide his impatience anymore.

"If you'll give Mr. DeSoto a chance, Charley," said the sheriff. "I think he was about ta get ta that."

The railroad man looked first to the sheriff

and then to Charley, who was nodding for him to go on.

"I was about ta get ta that, Mr. Sunday. Just hear me out, will ya?"

"Go ahead, DeSoto," said Charley. "I won't interrupt you again."

"Well," DeSoto began, "two of my men were out scoutin' track yesterday, when they saw somethin' mighty peculiar. They were on a workman's velocipede . . ."

He coughed . . . "A handcar . . . headin' down toward Eagle Pass when they saw 'em."

"Saw who?" said Charley.

"They saw the Cropper Brothers. Damnit, Charley," said the sheriff. "They saw both Sam and Dale Cropper, hightailin' it up the rightaway. They were headed south until they cut off to the west, right about where Sam Marley built his homestead, a couple hundred yards from the water tower."

"They rode on up into that Dead Cat rock formation," said DeSoto. "The one that sticks up right there, just like someone dumped a pile of boulders. Right there, before ya get to the river."

"So you're saying they crossed the river into Mexico?" said Charley.

"No," answered DeSoto. "I'm sayin' they rode into them rocks is what I'm sayin'."

"Mr. DeSoto's employees told him the Croppers rode their horses right inta Dead Cat Rocks. That's what they're sayin'," said the sheriff.

"That place is full of caves, and there's plenty of water tanks, it bein' the rainy season as it is."

"Are we supposed to think the whole gang could be hiding out in one of those caves?" asked the sheriff.

"That, or they were just takin' a shortcut," said DeSoto. "But my men hung around . . . from a great distance, mind you . . . and those two never came out of those rocks in the whole hour my men were there."

Sheriff Dubbs turned to Charley.

"That's an awful long way to go," he said, "just riding a hunch. Besides, that's in the next county over. Maybe I should send the sheriff in Eagle Pass a wire, advising him before we make a trek like that."

"Willingham," said Charley. "You remember how Sheriff Jenkins, over there in Eagle Pass, bungled it the last couple of times you relied on his doing something for you that you should have done yourself."

"Yes, I surely do," said the sheriff. "And I reckon you're right, Charley. We gotta go over there ourselves, less'n we wanna take the chance that Jenkins bungles it this time, too."

"All right then," said Charley. "I got your posse all rounded up for you, just outside. Go take a pee, if you need to. I know I am. Get your horse and meet me out front in ten minutes."

The outfit had been on the trail to Eagle Pass, and hopefully the Cropper Brothers' hideout, for two hours. Only this time, it wasn't under Charley's guidance. They had all been deputized — even though that would mean nothing in a county other than the one in which they had been sworn in.

They were prepared to camp overnight if they found the need to. Roscoe had their food packed on a mule he'd brought along. They all wore their rain slickers. The weather had not changed and was continuing to produce storm after storm.

Charley had allowed Henry Ellis to ride along with them, mainly because Roscoe had also been deputized and no one would have been left back at the ranch to look after him. Kelly had also been sworn in, and she sat in her saddle at Rod's side the entire way.

They all rode along together for the next six or seven hours, and when they stopped in Del Rio to purchase extra ammunition, they also found a little Mexican café where they took their supper.

They could have all stayed overnight in several local Del Rio hotels, but Sheriff Dubbs told them hotel rooms weren't in his budget. So they all camped out in a local farmer's hay barn, with a roof that protected them when a big storm came along around midnight.

The farmer who owned the barn was an old friend of Stink Manning's. Stink had shown up after everyone else had been deputized and was told he couldn't go. But he begged Sheriff Dubbs to reconsider until the lawman gave in and deputized him, too.

When the first flash of lightning and its following boom of thunder exploded all around them, it woke half of the posse, including Charley and the sheriff. Henry Ellis stirred, but he didn't wake up. Within minutes, the rain was coming down — and it kept coming for the rest of the night.

Just before daybreak, Roscoe got up to start breakfast. Henry Ellis joined him, helping with the wood for the fire and stirring the batter for Roscoe's buttermilk pancakes after Roscoe mixed the ingredients.

When the coffee was ready, the aroma itself began waking the men. And by the time they'd finished their first cup, Roscoe was ready with the pancakes, butter, and syrup. He had also fried up some strips he'd sliced from the side of bacon he'd brought along, and he forked a few sizzling pieces into each man's mess kit as they stood in front of him to receive their portion.

By seven a.m., they were on the trail again, and the trail to Eagle Pass was just that — a wagon-rutted trail. And a muddy trail at that. Even though the rain had let up some, a sharp, northerly wind had picked up and was becoming quite abrasive to the men's faces and other exposed skin.

They tied their neckerchiefs over their noses and wrapped scraps of wool blankets around their necks, until it got so cold and uncomfortable they had to stop.

Feather had found an old railroad workers' shack, near the tracks that paralleled the trail, and the posse found safe harbor inside, where they stayed long enough to warm themselves up and gulp down more of Roscoe's coffee.

"If I'da known the weather was gonna be this bad," said Sheriff Dubbs, "I'da sent that telegram like I wanted to do in the first place."

"You're just getting spoiled in your old age, Willingham," said Charley. "Why, if a bunch of old geezers like Feather, Roscoe, Holliday, and me can do it, so can you. What are you now, Willingham? Fifty-five?"

"Forty-nine," said the sheriff. "Old enough fer my bones ta ache."

"Well, when those ol' bones of yours start aching again, just think of ol' Roscoe over there . . . and Feather, and Holliday . . . and me. Every one of us have got at least fifteen years on you, Willingham. So, when we all start complaining about the cold, just maybe someone'll give a damn about you."

Henry Ellis walked over to Charley.

"Grampa," he said. "Would you mind if I had a cup of coffee, too? I just need something to warm up my insides."

"I told you the other day, before we left Juanita, that as far as I'm concerned you're old enough to drink coffee. Now, go on. Get yourself a cup, before we have to go outside and mount up again."

CHAPTER THIRTY

The trail from Del Rio to Eagle Pass was more wagon ruts than anything else. What made it easier to follow, with all the mud that had accumulated in the deep gouges over the past month of bad weather, was that it ran parallel to the railroad tracks.

When Charley first saw Dead Cat Rocks, for some reason the formation looked much larger than he'd remembered it being. *Why, it's big enough to conceal a whole army, let alone fifteen members of a gang of bank robbers,* he thought to himself.

When the posse reached the water tower — an old wooden tank, atop eight braced six-by-six wooden supports, with a spout that could be lowered to refill the great engines that traveled the iron rails — the sheriff called for them to stop and dismount.

The remains of Sam Marley's homestead could be seen to the west of where they stood, with its weather-worn adobe bricks standing no more than three feet tall. A reminder of the original, dug-out shelter that had been there until the Comanches burned the Marleys out.

But it was the Dead Cat rock formation, which began several hundred feet beyond the Marley house ruins, that was sparking everyone's interest. Right now, there could be a gang of train robbers hiding in the crevices between those giant boulders, or holed up in one of its many caves.

"There's two ways of doin' this," said the sheriff. "We can just ride in slowly and sniff the place out . . . or we can split up, with half of us going around to the other side . . . and on my signal, we'd rush 'em from both sides. The second way is probably the best. It would take 'em by surprise."

"I got an even better way to get 'em out of there, Willingham," said Charley. "Split up, like you say, but only one-half of us rush in firing our guns. That should flush 'em out the other side, and right into the hands of the rest of our posse."

More than a few of the men spoke their agreement to Charley's plan.

"So it's Charley's plan," said the sheriff. "You, Brady, Clemmons, and Stillwell, take Holliday and Roscoe on around ta the other side of this rock pile. Charley, you and the rest of the boys stay here with me. We'll do the shootin', because it only makes sense that they'll run for the river once they hear our shots fired."

"First," Charley cut in. "Don't you think it might be wise to send someone in there to scout the situation before we commence with the shooting?"

The men exchanged questioning looks.

"That way, we'll at least get an idea of how many they are."

"An' I s'pose you're the one wants ta go," said the sheriff.

"Everyone stay right here," said Charley. "I'll be back before you know it."

He reined around. There was a moment of thought, then he reined his horse back to facing them.

"Henry Ellis," he called out.

The boy rode his mount over to where Charley was.

"Yes, Grampa," he answered.

Charley leaned in to the boy, as close as he could get.

"If anything happens to me, the ranch belongs to you. Understand? It was supposed to go to your mother, but that ain't the way it's worked out, is it?"

He reached over and put his hand on the back of the boy's neck and gave Henry Ellis a squeeze.

"I love you, son. But you already know that."

He looked directly into the boy's eyes for a long moment, then he turned and rode away toward Dead Cat Rocks.

Henry Ellis followed his grampa with his eyes, until the old Ranger disappeared behind a huge, granite boulder.

Charley nudged Dice deeper into the cluster of giant boulders, until he came across several pair of tracks that crossed the narrow path he had chosen.

He decided to follow the tracks, and he reined Dice in their direction.

The hoofprints went along for about one-fifth of a mile, before the ground in front of him turned from dirt to gravel.

Charley could still make out the shapes of the horseshoes in the small stones, so he kept on following.

Suddenly the prints disappeared. To the right, a flat rock veered off, leading to another passageway. Charley urged Dice up onto the even surface, and when he got to the other channel between the rocks, he picked up sign of the hoof-prints again, he dismounted, then kept on following.

Back where the posse was stopped, one of the townsmen who'd been deputized called over to the sheriff.

"Just how long are we gonna wait fer Sunday, Sheriff? What if something's happened to him?"

Roscoe moved in quickly, puffing his chest out and almost knocking the man down.

"Ain't nothin' happened ta Charley Sunday, mister," he said. "And if ya can't come up with something positive ta say, don't say it."

Roscoe moved over to Henry Ellis, putting his arm around the boy.

"And next time ya open yer mouth with somethin' distasteful, pay attention to who just might be listenin'."

The sheriff turned to Roscoe.

"That won't happen again," he said. "I promise you that, Roscoe."

The townsman nodded, pulling down the brim of his hat.

Deep in the rock formation, Charley was moving along slower. Every so often he would hear strange noises, causing him to hesitate.

As he rounded a slight bend in the pathway between the boulders, something caught his eye and he ducked back, so not to be seen.

Charley slid down to his belly. A closer look from ground level revealed the entrance to a large cave. It was from this opening that Charley heard the noises of restless horses, plus low mutterings of men talking.

He realized he had to get around to the opposite side of the cave's entrance before he could see better what was going on inside. And he knew he'd have to climb the almost sheer surface of the rocks beside him in order to do so.

He reached down and pulled his boots off, one by one, slipping his Walker Colt inside one of the stovepipes for safekeeping. Then, he started climbing up the rock to his left, with his fingers and toes both clinging as best they could to prevent his slipping. He finally reached a ledge he knew would take him where he wanted to be.

He crawled along slowly on the outcrop, stopping completely one or two times as a pebble came loose and bounced down the sides of the rocks, landing on the path below.

When he was finally opposite the cave's entrance, he lowered his head as far as he could, then looked across the gap, peeking inside.

He could only make out one horse and one guard, just inside the opening. But beyond the one guard there was a fire going. Its flames lit up the walls of the cave, revealing it to be much larger than Charley had expected.

He counted fourteen horses tied to a makeshift picket line. Plus, there were just as many men, it appeared, sitting around the fire, talking and drinking coffee.

Beyond the fire, it looked to Charley as if the grotto went on forever, at least until the fire's light began to fade. It eventually went to black, completely.

Charley watched for a while. He counted again and noticed there were two men less than there were horses.

"Hold it right there," came a voice from directly above him. "Hand me your gun, an' start climbin' down. There's someone in that cave who'll be wantin' ta meet you, mister."

"Ain't got a gun," said Charley. "It slipped outta my hand while I was climbing and dropped into a crevasse that was too deep for me to retrieve it."

"An' what happened to your boots?" said another voice. "Did they drop inta the same cre—"

"I took 'em off so's I'd get a better grip on these rocks," said Charley. "I don't remember where they are. Down there somewhere."

He indicated the path below.

"Well, you start climbing down, mister, and keep your hands where we can see 'em."

"Where else could I keep 'em, you two are above me," said Charley under his breath.

He slid himself backward across the shelf he had crawled over to get there. Then he turned himself around and began descending in the same manner he'd climbed up. When he got to the bottom, very close to where he'd discarded his boots, he planted his two feet and looked up.

The two gang members had already started down behind him, with the second man laying back to keep Charley covered.

When the first man's boots hit solid ground, he drew his gun and aimed it at Charley. Then he called out to his friend who was still up in the rocks.

"I got him covered, Pete," he said. "You can come ahead now."

As the man started his climb down, the other one appeared to be watching his friend's every move. That was when Charley spoke.

"Mind if I put my boots on, fellas?"

Those inside the cave heard the two shots echo back and forth between the walls of the narrow rock canyons that made up the Dead Cat rock formation. They all stood up and went for their horses.

Outside, Charley waited for the gang to show themselves. He could hear their horses whinnying and snorting as the gang members mounted up, and the sounds of the horses' hooves as they began galloping.

But they weren't galloping toward the cave's entrance. They were galloping toward the back.

Charley got to the entrance just in time to see the final few horses disappear into the blackness at the back of the cave.

Even though he was still in his bare feet, Charley ran as fast as he could after the outlaws, firing off a few more shots in their wake. And when he rounded a bend in the darkened tunnel, he could see the light of another opening — the gang's escape route — with the last rider breaking away into the outside gloom, doing his best to catch up with the others.

Charley's final shot hit the reluctant rider dead center, and he tumbled out of his saddle, hitting the dirt — along with several cactus plants — as he rolled to a stop.

The sheriff decided that the posse would camp at the base of Dead Cat Rocks for the night. Charley had appeared, leading Dice, with two bodies slung over his saddle. After he dropped them off, he mounted up, then with Rod riding with him, they circled the rock formation until they came to the cave's other entrance, hidden behind more giant boulders to keep out prying eyes.

They found the third body about sixty yards from the cave's second entrance.

"How did you manage to hit this one?" said Rod. "You told us you had to leave your horse behind, and you never said anything about taking your rifle with you."

"I used my Walker Colt," said Charley. "Samuel Colt never made a better sighted pistol."

That night, after another nice meal prepared by Roscoe and Kelly, the posse sat around talking about Charley's chance meeting with the Cropper Brothers' Gang. And how, if that rear entrance had been on the eastern side of the Dead Cat rock formation and not the western side, they would have had them all in custody right now, hands down.

Someone had brought along a harmonica, and another had concealed his fiddle in a bag that he tied to his saddle. By the time the mess kits had been cleaned the music got under way — and the men, along with Charley, Henry Ellis, and Kelly, sang old cowboy songs into the wee hours of the night.

CHAPTER THIRTY-ONE

It stayed dry all night, so finding the tracks of the Cropper Brothers' Gang wasn't that difficult to do.

Following them was a different story. Not because it had started to rain again, and the heavy drops were beginning to wash away the hoofprints, but because the tracks led directly to the banks of the Rio Grande.

When the posse arrived at the river, they all knew the game was over. Even so, the Cropper Gang had set up their own camp on the Mexican side, and they jeered the posse from across the water's flow, knowing there was nothing the Texans could legally do about it.

"But there's something I can do about it," Charley was telling the sheriff. "I can go in alone —"

"No, you can't, Charley," said the sheriff. "You've been deputized, and the law says —"

"The law says that I can't, because officially, I'm part of a law enforcement agency. And law enforcement in our country ain't supposed to cross international borders while in pursuit of anyone."

"That's right, Charley," said the sheriff. "Sometimes I forget that you were in law enforcement yourself for a lot of years."

"Un-deputize me, Willingham," said Charley with a stern look.

"What?" said the sheriff.

"Un-deputize me . . . and while you're at it, un-deputize Roscoe, Feather, Holliday, and Rod. I just can't stand here while the lawbreakers that we're after are as close to us as they are, Willingham."

"It can't be done, Charley," said the sheriff. "It's gotta be done official-like . . . when our hunt is all over."

"Either you un-deputize us, Willingham, or we'll un-deputize ourselves. Now, what'll it be?"

The sheriff shook is head. Then he called the rest of the outfit over. Kelly and Henry Ellis came along out of curiosity.

When they were all standing in front of the sheriff, facing him, the law officer raised his right hand.

With some confusion, the others followed his lead.

The sheriff lowered his hand.

"Put yer hands down. That's only fer the swearin'-in ceremony, damn it. I'm not quite sure what I'm supposed ta do ta undeputize ya."

"How 'bout if we take off our badges and hand 'em back to you, Willingham?" said Charley. "Think that'll work?"

While the sheriff was getting even more flustered, five deputy badges landed in the sand at his feet.

"So that's it?" he said.

"Pretty simple, wasn't it, Willingham?" said Charley. "Now if you want to take the others and head back to Juanita, go right ahead."

"I want to go with you, Grampa," said Henry Ellis.

"Me too," added Kelly. "When you speak of the Texas Outfit, you can't leave me and Henry Ellis out of it. We're part of the outfit, Charley. We want to go along with you. Like always."

"All right," said Charley. "You can be your husband's responsibility, Miss Kelly . . . but who's gonna watch after Henry Ellis?"

A big smile was growing across the woman's face.

"That's why I'm going to be there," she said. "To watch over Henry Ellis."

Charley smiled. He shook his head.

"Sometimes you can be very conniving, Miss Kelly."

He winked.

"And so can you, Mr. Sunday," she said, winking back.

When the posse turned for home, heading for the road on which they had come, they had to pass Dead Cat Rocks to get there. As they rode by the rear entrance to the gang's hideout cave, Charley and the outfit split off from the others and spurred their mounts straight into the stony hillside, which appeared to consume them all, as if the rock formation were a living creature.

By the time the remainder of the posse was passing the ruins of Sam Marley's adobe, a quick look over the shoulder showed Dead Cat Rocks was standing just as silent and foreboding as it had been when they'd first observed the unique stone configuration.

Inside the cave in Dead Cat Rocks, Charley led his outfit through the darkness until the gray light from the inside entrance lit up the old camp used by the Cropper Gang.

Charley told everyone to loosen their horses' cinches but not to unsaddle them. Then he had them tie the animals to the rope picket line the robbers had left behind in their haste.

They all spread their bedrolls on the floor of the cave, following Charley's example.

"All right," said Charley. "You can all sleep until dusk, then, after we eat, we're goin' across the Rio and get those *hombres.*"

"We gonna ride 'em down right there in Mexico?" asked Roscoe, "or are we gonna just chase 'em back over here where we got legal jurisdiction?"

"We don't have legal jurisdiction on our side of the river anymore, Roscoe. We un-deputized ourselves . . . Remember?"

"Then, what do you aim to do, Charley?"

"We'll just follow 'em on across the river and bring 'em back the same way," said Charley. "Just like we done when we were Rangers."

"But we was still breakin' the law when we done that back in the old days," said Roscoe. "How's this time gonna be any different?"

"Roscoe," said Charley. "Ain't it true that no one ever bothered us about that law, once we got whoever we were chasing back across the border and into our custody?"

"That's true, Charley," said Roscoe. "But that was in the middle of the 1880s . . . we're in the twentieth century now."

"Just the wee early part of the twentieth century, Roscoe," said Charley. "Still feels like the nineteenth to me."

"Well, I'm still goin' with ya, pardner, whether I like what yer doin' or not."

"Why, thank you, Roscoe," said Charley. "I wouldn't have it any other way."

They left the protection of the cave just a little after nightfall. As they urged their horses out of the cavern's rear entrance — the way that they had entered — an icy blast of stinging sleet battered them head on. They knew it was still cold outside the confines of the cave, but they weren't expecting this.

Henry Ellis rode up beside his grampa, blinking away the ice crystals that the sleet was depositing on his lashes. A knitted neck scarf had been wrapped tight around his neck, something Kelly had done, and his right hand was gloveless.

"Where in tarnation is your right glove, son?" Charley asked gruffly.

The boy looked up to him. He appeared to be holding back tears.

"I musta lost it, Grampa," he answered. "I musta left it back in the cave somewhere."

"Well, here," said Charley, slipping off his own right glove and handing it to the boy.

"Take this one . . . but don't lose it, for heaven's sake."

They rode along in the sleet for another few yards before Charley continued.

"Now get yourself back to where Miss Kelly is. I don't want you up here where you could get hurt."

The boy reined around and went back to where he had come from in the column of riders. Charley blew on his bare right hand, then he stuck it in the pocket of his sheepskin coat, which he wore underneath his oilskin slicker.

The sleet made seeing anything at a distance nearly impossible. When they came to the river's edge there was no way of knowing the depth of the water, so Charley just took a chance and spurred Dice into the near-freezing current.

He moved out into the river's flow with the rest of the outfit following. God had been with him in his choice for a crossing, because the water never got deeper than the bellies of the horses.

As they came out on the Mexican side, with the horses' hooves clattering as they slipped and slid on the shoreline pebbles, Charley signaled once again for the group to gather around.

"All right," he whispered. "We'll be attacking on foot, so everyone'll have to dismount. Kelly, Henry Ellis? I'm putting the two of you in charge of the horses."

Charley dismounted. The others did the same. Charley had more to say. He continued in his low whisper.

"Rod, Feather, you two go wide around to the left. Roscoe, Holliday . . . you two go to the right and stay wide of the gang's camp. I'll stay right here until you've all had enough time to get into your positions. Then I'm going to fire off a shot as a signal, and I want every one of us to charge that camp a-whooping and a-hollering, just like we Rebs done in those final battles we had with the Yanks."

"Ya sure ya don't want us ta fire our guns, Charley?" whispered Holliday.

"No sir, I don't," answered Charley. "I don't want us taking any chances of hitting our own people in this damn storm. I figure we'll surprise 'em enough with our rebel yells, and that should give us enough time to fight our battle on foot . . . with our fists and Bowie knives."

"Can we shoot 'em if it looks like they're gonna shoot us?" Feather wanted to know.

"Only if you're close enough," answered Charley. "Like I said, I don't want us shooting our own people. Now, move out like I asked you to. When you've gotten to where you think you should be . . . wait. You'll hear my signal shot soon enough."

Everyone followed Charley's orders, heading out in separate directions after handing their horses' reins to either Kelly or the boy. When Charley handed Dice's reins to him, Henry Ellis held out the right-hand glove Charley had given him earlier.

"Here, Grampa," he said. "You'll be needing this now more than I will. It takes two hands to fight a man . . . only one to hold on to a few horses."

Charley hesitated.

"I mean it, Grampa," Henry Ellis said again. "Take the glove."

Charley did not speak. The tears rimming his eyes were the only expression he showed. He took the glove and slipped his hand into it.

"Thank you, Henry Ellis" were his only words. Then he moved up beside Rod, and the two took a few more steps together until they were only outlines behind the sheet of blasting ice particles.

Kelly moved up beside the boy. She motioned for him to follow her behind the protection of several large boulders. As the last horse cleared the edge of the rocks, the shot from Charley's gun split the air.

Kelly and Henry Ellis stayed behind the boulders with the horses. Their ears became their eyes as they listened to the yelling and war cries being made by Charley and the others.

Henry Ellis wished that they were using their guns instead of fists and knives. At least the sound of gunshots would give him a better idea of how the battle was progressing.

Then it was over, quicker than it had begun. The Rebel yells and war cries just stopped. And after that, only the ongoing rush of the wind could be heard.

The silence went on. No sounds at all came from the bank robbers' camp — or where Henry Ellis thought it should be. He exchanged glances more than once with Kelly. The horses were beginning to show their restlessness, pawing the ground — snorting.

"Don't be alarmed, it's us."

The two whipped around, and there stood Charley and Rod. The others were drifting in from behind them.

"What happened, Grampa?" yelled Henry Ellis as Rod moved past the boy to take Kelly in his arms.

"What happened?" said the boy once again.

His eyes were locked on to his grandfather's eyes. Charley moved toward him, then stopped.

In Charley's hand was the glove. He held it out for Henry Ellis to take.

"I reckon I won't be needing this for a while, son," he said. "Take it back. I know you're colder than I am."

"Grampa," Henry Ellis said one more time, only much more forceful, "Please . . . tell me?"

Charley shook his head.

"They weren't there. They must have run off in the night because the camp wasn't anywhere close by."

Feather tramped up through the wet grass.

"No way ta keep trackin' 'em, Boss," he said. "The ground is too grassy over here . . . an' it's wet, too. There ain't a sign of 'em anywhere. Nothin' at all ta tell us which way they went."

"Then you may as well tell the others that we'll be heading home," said Charley. "If we're lucky, we may run into 'em on our way back."

They weren't lucky. Even though they followed the railroad tracks back to Del Rio, and again on to Juanita, they never saw a sign of the Cropper Brothers and their gang.

CHAPTER THIRTY-TWO

Charley had everyone stop at the Juanita/ Spofford railroad depot, where he conferred with the station master for a few minutes concerning the possible whereabouts of the Croppers. Then he called the Texas Outfit to line up behind him for the remainder of the journey to Juanita.

They rode into town, single file, looking like the defeated bunch of ex-posse members they were. On Charley's order, they broke up and drifted toward Flora Mae's place, while Charley and Henry Ellis spurred their mounts over to the sheriff's office. Once there, they dismounted and tied off their horses.

"I don't see no Cropper Brothers wearin' cuffs strollin' in behind ya," said Sheriff Willingham Dubbs as Charley and the boy entered the office.

The sheriff sat behind his rolltop desk in his brown-leather swivel chair, located between the rifle closet on the wall and the first jail cell. There were three cells in all, and all of them were unoccupied.

"I hope to have those cells filled for ya by the week's end," said the sheriff. "I got word that the Croppers didn't stay in Mexico too long before they decided ta make their way back here."

"I know," said Charley. "We spent overnight in the gang's old camp in the cave, then crossed the river the following morning with hopes of capturing them by surprise. But they weren't there, Willingham. I didn't peg 'em right. They musta come back across the Rio while we were sleeping, then bypassed us without us knowing it. That's the only way I can figure it all out."

"Thank you, Charley," said the sheriff, "for at least bein' honest with me. Now that you're back, will you let me deputize you like before? I can really use you and your outfit's help in this matter."

"How about we hang our hats over in Flora Mae's place for a while? That all right with you?"

"Sure, Charley," he answered. "And, if anything comes up, I'll send one of my deputies over ta get y'all."

Charley and his outfit had spent most of

the afternoon playing billiards and lounging around Flora Mae's establishment.

Now suppertime was rolling around and Charley asked Flora Mae if he could buy meals for everyone in the house, just like he did with drinks when the glasses had gone dry.

"You're always pickin' up everyone's tab," said Flora Mae. "It's about time you let us buy you a meal fer once."

"C'mon, you tired excuses fer best friends," she called out to the others. "Everyone chip in. We're gonna all buy Charley and Henry Ellis's supper tonight."

There was agreement from the group as they gathered around the proprietor, handing her coins and bills until they were stacked high on the table in front of her.

Flora Mae scooped up all the money and put it in her purse before heading to the hotel's kitchen in the other building up front.

"Looks like I shook enough money outta you skinflints ta pay fer everyone's supper . . . including mine."

She headed off down a hall, leaving them all to wonder what had just happened.

They were all finishing up their dessert of apple pie when the door burst open and one of the sheriff's deputies came running into the room.

"Charley . . . and all the rest of you folks," he yelled. "Sheriff Dubbs wants you over at his office. He's got something he wants ta tell y'all."

Everyone scrambled, grabbing their coats, then pushing their way past the deputy on their way out.

The sheriff was waiting on the sheriff's office porch, as Charley, Henry Ellis, and the rest of them came running down the street. Once there, they gathered around him.

He raised both hands to calm them down.

"Whoa . . . Whoa down now, you crazy people. I didn't want ta start a stampede."

The members of the Texas Outfit began to settle down as Charley moved to the front with his grandson. The others gave the sheriff their attention.

"It's nice ta see that ye're all willin' ta come a runnin' if it looks like I might need yer help. But what I wanted ta tell ya has nothin' ta do with the Cropper Brothers."

"Then why did ya call us, Sheriff?" asked Holliday. "I thought that was the main reason we was hangin' 'round Flora Mae's 'stead of goin' home."

"It was, Holliday," said the sheriff. "But,

ye're gonna like what I hafta say just as much."

"Well," said Feather. "Get on with it."

"The railroad wants ta throw all of us a little gratitude party," he began. "Fer what we all done, possein' up like we done, and damn near capturin' that band of nogoods."

Charley stepped in closer.

"I'd feel a lot better about attending a party if we *had* captured that gang of no-goods."

"Yeah, it feels like someone's gettin' cheated when ye're praised fer somethin' like this before it's even happened," said Roscoe.

"Tell you what, Sheriff," said Charley. "Why don't you tell the railroad to hold off on that party until we really do capture the Croppers?"

A clatter of hoofbeats drew their attention to the other end of the main street, where a rider could be seen racing toward them at a full gallop.

The man reined up, sliding his horse to a stop in front of Charley and the sheriff.

"You're gonna love this, Sheriff Dubbs," said the man. "The Croppers just hit the San Antonio Special, about six an' a half miles out from the station."

"Did they get away with much?" asked the sheriff.

"That's just it," said the man. "The mail car clerk and the conductor are refusin' ta open up his slidin' door, so they're all hangin' around, dickerin' about it."

Within minutes, the sheriff and Charley were galloping back toward the train station, followed by the outfit and some others. The cowboy who'd brought the message was leading the bunch as they kicked up a swirl of twigs and mud chunks behind them.

A bright flash of lightning flickered all around, followed by a loud crash of thunder. It wasn't that long before the gray clouds overhead opened up with another pounding rain.

When they got to the depot, the messenger pointed east.

"About six an' a half miles down that-away," he shouted. Then he dismounted, tied off, and ran toward the station.

"Ain't ya comin' along with us?" shouted the sheriff over the noise of the thunder and the rain on the depot's tin roof.

"Nope," yelled the man from the front door. "I done my job by comin' in ta town ta get y'all. It'll be up ta you boys ta handle it from now on."

The sheriff shook his head. He turned to Charley.

"Ain't that just like some people these days?" he said. "Willin' ta do half a job but can never finish the whole thing. C'mon," he shouted. "Let's put some leather into it."

He spurred away, following the railroad tracks, with Charley and the others right behind.

Steam was leaking from a few of the valves around the wheels of the large locomotive. The silver and black behemoth was stopped, along with the several cars it pulled, dead center on the tracks that led away from Juanita.

Activity was centered around the mail car, hitched directly behind the locomotive's wood box. The remainder of the cars, both freight and passenger, were strung out behind, with the passengers leaning just as far as they could out the windows to get a better look at what was going on up by the mail car.

Sam Cropper and his brother, Dale, sat horseback, facing the sliding door on the left side of the railroad car. Sam was busy talking to whoever was inside.

A rifle exploded through the crack between the door and its frame, with the bullet creasing Sam Cropper's hat right down the middle, sending the floppy, wool head-piece flying in the wind.

"Now, cut that out in there," yelled Sam. "Now I gotta send one of my men off ta fetch that damn thing before I catch cold out here in the rain with nothin' ta cover my thinnin' hair."

"Next one'll be even closer, if ya don't back off a little more like I been askin' ya to."

Sam raised one hand, the other pulled back on his horse's reins, signaling the animal to ease off and back away slowly. Dale did the same with his horse, until the two brothers had joined the rest of the gang who were situated farther away from the mail car than the brothers had been.

The sheriff and his posse, now made up of Charley, Roscoe, Rod, Kelly, Feather, Henry Ellis, and Holliday — with one deputy and several more townsmen who had been there when the sheriff swore them all in — slowed to a stop. They dismounted and, in minutes, were on their knees behind some pecan trees, watching the scene play out across a field.

"I wish there'd been a way to get closer," whispered the sheriff. "I'm havin' one hell of a time hearin' what they're sayin'."

"That's all right, Willingham," Charley whispered back. "I got real good hearin'. I can understand every word that's coming out of their mouths."

Henry Ellis crawled over to where his grandfather was exchanging whispers with the sheriff. Charley put his arm around the boy and pulled him to his side, as close as he could get to him.

"Did you have something you wanted to ask me, son?" said the old man.

"I just wanted to know where you want me to go when you start moving in for the capture?" he asked.

"Well," he began. "That's something better left up to the sheriff, don't you think? He's in charge of this posse."

"Ah, hell . . . I mean, heck, Charley," said the sheriff. "You know as well as I do that I depend on you, more than I do myself, to come up with a plan in situations like this one."

Charley turned to Henry Ellis.

"Whatever happens, Henry Ellis, I want you and Miss Kelly to stay back here in these trees . . . and don't you move. No matter what happens over at the train. Promise?"

Henry Ellis lowered his eyes.

"I promise, Grampa," he said. "But, I was —"

"You was what?" said Charley.

"I was just wondering when I'll ever be allowed to —"

"You're still too young, son. And even though you've had to shoot someone before in self-defense, or while protecting a good friend . . . that was because you had to, not because you were facing him one-on-one like it's done on a battlefield, or in a gunfight."

Charley tousled the boy's hair. He smiled.

"When the time comes that I feel you're grown up enough to ride with us into a squabble like the one that's about to happen, I'll let you know, boy. You can bet money on it . . . I'll let you know."

With that, Charley got to his feet. He turned to find Dice, then he mounted up.

"Just where in heaven's name do you think you're going, Charley Sunday?" asked the sheriff.

"Oh, I thought I'd ride on over to that train . . . see if I can stir anything up."

He nudged Dice out into the open, walking the horse directly toward the train.

The Cropper Brothers and their gang had all eyes on the door to the mail car, so they had no idea someone was coming up from their rear.

Charley got closer and closer, and still no one had noticed his presence.

When he reached the point where he still had all of them in his peripheral sight, he reined Dice to a stop, pulling his Walker Colt from his boot in one slick movement.

From his position, Charley continued to watch the standoff play out. First Sam Cropper would demand something from those inside the mail car. Then someone inside the car would shout back an answer to Cropper's stipulation.

Then Sam would signal for one of his men to fire on the car with a pistol. And just as routinely, a rifle barrel sticking through a crack in the sliding door would roar back with a couple of shots of its own.

By the number of bullet holes in and around the mail car's sliding door, Charley figured this tit-for-tat game had been going on for some time.

Charley knew that if he stayed where he was, someone would notice him in due time. So he nudged Dice over toward the rear end of the train, and because the gang's attention was riveted on the mail car, no one was watching as he slipped around to the other side of the conveyance.

Charley walked Dice along the sides of

the railroad cars until he came to the mail car's opposite sliding door. None of the robbers had thought to surround their quarry, so he was alone on the back side.

He nudged Dice over closer to the sliding door, then he reached over and knocked on the small window, with its glass still intact.

It wasn't more than a few moments until the conductor's perspiring face appeared at the window. Charley held up his deputy's badge for the man to see.

The conductor turned to discuss the matter with the mail clerk, then both of them unlocked, then slid the door open just wide enough so Charley could get through to the inside of the car.

The interior of the mail car was hot and stuffy. The two railroad employees had everything closed up tight, except for the crack in the door they were using for communication, and the occasional return of gunfire.

Charley helped the conductor slide the large door he'd come through closed. The clerk locked it, then returned to his position on the other side of the car, where he could see the Croppers through the crack by the door.

As quiet as he could be, Charley introduced himself.

"I'm Charley Sunday," he said. "One of the deputies in the posse that's after that gang out there."

"Where is the rest of the posse?" asked the clerk.

"Up there behind the gang, on that tree-lined hill," Charley told them. "Keepin' outta sight, like me, until we can get more information on these dirty buzzards."

"They weren't that lucky this time, mister," said the conductor. "They didn't expect me to be in here with Alex when they hit us."

"They're used to it bein' one man in the mail car," said the clerk. "And this time they got two."

"Two brave ones, at that," said Charley. "What made you decide to stand your ground?"

The conductor turned and faced Charley.

"Well, first we're carryin' a load of raw silver from one of the mines north of Langtry. S'posed to deliver it to the smelter in Sabinal."

"But most of all," said the clerk, "I reckon we just got tired of givin' in to the Croppers every time they stop the train."

"And you're putting up a fight just to save that raw silver, are you?"

"Well," the conductor finally said, "rumor

389

has it that the Croppers are killin' innocent folks these days. I don't rightly know how Alex over there feels about bein' a living target for that gang, but I surely don't want no part of gettin' killed without puttin' up a fight."

"Why are *you* here, mister?" asked the conductor. "Only one gun barrel at a time's able ta shoot back at 'em."

"Like I said, I'm just here to collect information."

He turned to the door he had come in.

"So, if one of you could just unlock this sliding door . . . I'll make myself scarce and get outta your hair for a while."

He slid the door open, then he jumped onto Dice's back outside.

"Keep that door closed and locked, no matter what happens," Charley told them.

"Oh," said the conductor. "We know that."

He nodded, then pulled the door shut behind him.

Twenty minutes later, Charley had managed to skirt the gang as before. He was once again at the top of the low, tree-lined rise overlooking the train robbery, sitting his saddle beside the sheriff and the rest of the outfit.

The scene below them hadn't changed

much since Charley had first ridden down nearly an hour earlier. But now that he'd had the chance to observe the layout, he felt he had a better understanding of just how to handle the situation.

"What I think we're going to have to do, Willingham, is simply back that train up . . . all the way to Juanita, if we have to."

"Back it up?" said the sheriff. "An' just how do ya expect ta do that?"

The engineer and his fireman lay unconscious in the cab of the locomotive. Two members of the gang were guarding them at gunpoint. No one was talking. They were both trying to listen to the muffled voice of Sam Cropper, who continued to shout his threats to those behind the closed door of the mail car.

Without any previous sounds, two Walker Colts appeared behind the ears of the two gang members. The sounds of the weapons being cocked was all it took for the outlaws to realize they should lay down their own weapons.

Charley and Feather moved on into the cab. It was a tight fit, but they were able to exchange positions with the gang members. Feather motioned for both of the men to turn around, and when they did, both he and Charley laid their gun barrels across the men's heads, producing a double whack that Charley figured would wake the devil himself.

The two gang members were shoved out of the cab, then Charley took the controls. At the same time, Feather signaled with his hand, and the rest of the posse members who had snuck around to join them began climbing onto the train from the same side.

Charley closed a steam release valve and waited. When he figured he had enough pressure, he reversed gears and gave it the throttle.

With a giant chug, which included a couple of spine-rattling screeches, the drive wheels turned, causing the train to lurch backward.

The conductor and clerk inside the mail car grabbed for something to hold on to. As the locomotive chugged once again, the mail car moved another few feet to the rear.

The Cropper Brothers and their gang were all stationed right outside the sliding door. They edged their horses back as the third chug was distinctly heard, coming from the engine up front.

Then a fourth chug, and a fifth.

Sam Cropper glanced toward the locomotive at the head of the train. Before he could say anything, he saw the prone bodies of his two men lying on the ground beside the left drive wheel.

The mail car clerk fired off several shots from inside, which made the robbers back off even more.

The train had started to roll backward, and posse members began to appear from everywhere on the train, firing their weapons at the gang.

Even though they were confused, the Cropper Brothers and their gang knew that the sudden movement of the train could only be controlled from the locomotive. So, on a signal from Sam, they all reined their mounts around and spurred out toward the engine.

Charley and Feather, still in the cab, had been joined by Roscoe. They all huddled down, preparing for an onslaught by the gang.

The rest of the posse turned their weapons on the pursuing gang as the train kept gathering more speed. One gang member tried a running transfer from horse to train car, but he was knocked out of his saddle by one of Holliday's better shots.

Another man tried the same, leaping from his saddle to the platform between the engine's cab and the stacks of wood in the fuel box behind it.

One of Charley's well-placed conical bullets caught him in the belly before he concluded his desperate relocation, and he fell beneath the locomotive's wheels, leaving an echoing scream as his final word.

The train went faster and faster in the reverse direction, and the robbers began to pull away until the train was on its own — a wood-burning missile that was proving to be uncatchable.

They had left the Cropper Brothers' Gang well in their wake.

By the time they rolled to a stop at the Juanita station — still pointed in the wrong direction — the sheriff found Charley, who was being congratulated by everyone around him for eluding the Cropper Gang. He reminded him that their whole purpose had been to stop a robbery in progress and capture the Cropper Gang.

"Well," said the old cowboy, "at least we got it half right."

It had been left up to Henry Ellis and Kelly to get the horses back to the Juanita depot. When they showed up a half hour or so after the train had come to a rest in front of the station, Charley, the sheriff, and darn near the whole posse had tipped back a few in celebration.

"Don't you fellers get too stinky on me, now," said the sheriff. "We still got another job ta do."

There were some verbal complaints from certain posse members, but even so, the sheriff continued.

"We still hafta ride guard on this train until we get it ta Sabinal. I'm havin' a livestock car attached so we can bring our horses with us. And you might wanna slow down on yer celebratin', because I've been told it's a long hard ride 'tween Sabinal an' back here."

As tired and liquored up as some of them were, Charley and his Texas Outfit rode along on the train, guarding the silver shipment all the way to Sabinal. That was where they dropped off the shipment and unloaded their horses for the ride back to Juanita.

Only one time on the way to Sabinal did something upset Charley. That was after they had just passed through Uvalde, and the rain had started to come down even harder. Henry Ellis thought he saw a small band of horsemen riding parallel to the train. He had turned away to call for his grampa to come and see, but when he turned back, the rain had obscured everything within fifteen feet of the car in which he was riding.

On their way back home, the leftover posse members looked like a stiff bunch of funeral-goers riding in single file after the burial, as they followed Charley and the sheriff along the trail to Juanita.

The pup put on a show for them when they arrived back at Flora Mae's Pool Hall & Bar. He raced from Henry Ellis, to Charley, to Roscoe, then into the center of the room where he twirled around, barking and whining, before repeating the same greetings to the sheriff, Kelly, and the rest of the outfit. They were all straggling in, one after the other, from the hitching posts out front, batting water from their hats and slickers and sounding like a flock of wet chickens.

"I'm fer a good bath an' a warm night-time of sleepin'," said Feather.

"Me too," echoed several of the others.

Charley called over to the owner.

"Flora Mae," he said. "Would you mind if we all stayed here for another night? We're gonna have to come back into town again tomorrow morning, anyway."

"Be my guests, Charley," she said. "I'm runnin' a tab on everything ye're eatin' an' drinkin', too."

Charley moved over closer to the woman.

"Are you serious, darlin'?" he asked. "I thought you were givin' from your heart when you said we could stay here. And now that we're giving of ourselves for the town . . ."

"That was before you were here a second night . . . and a third . . . and a —"

"All right, all right," said Charley, jumping in to silence her. "I'll make you a deal. I'll pay any charges after the first night we stayed here. How's that?"

"Includin' the bar bill."

"Including the bar bill," confirmed Charley.

Chapter Thirty-Three

That night, when Charley, Roscoe, and the boy had finally settled in for a restful sleep, Henry Ellis's voice rose above the silence of the room to ask his grampa a question.

"Grampa?" he whispered.

"Humph," said Roscoe as he rolled over, turning his back to them.

"Grampa?" whispered Henry Ellis, just a little bit louder this time.

"What is it, son?" came the old man's reply.

"When I die, will I go to heaven?"

"Why, sure you will, Henry Ellis," answered Charley.

"That's good. Because I want to be able to see Mother and Father again . . . and I know they're both in heaven."

"Now where in the world did you get the idea that you wouldn't be goin' to heaven, son?" Charley whispered. "Tell me."

The boy raised his eyes to the ceiling —

thinking.

"Oh," he began. "Probably because I killed those men."

"That was a while back, son," said Charley. "And you killed them while saving my life both times, didn't you?"

"Yes, sir," said the boy. "I did."

"Then there's nothing more to worry about. As long as a feller kills another man . . . a bad man . . . who's trying to kill a good man . . . I'm pretty sure the Good Lord has forgiven you, way before your finger had even pulled the trigger."

Henry Ellis pondered what Charley had just said, then he turned his head toward his grandfather.

"That gives me peace of mind, Grampa, it really does."

He scooted over in the bed he was sharing with Charley and cuddled up closer to him.

Charley wrapped his arms around the boy, pulling him as near as he could.

"If you ever have one of those easy questions again," he whispered, "don't be afraid to ask me."

"I won't," said the boy. He pulled the covers up over both of them.

There was a blinding flash of lightning outside the hotel room, followed by a tremendous clap of thunder. The rain began again, making a gentle pattering sound on the porch roof just outside the windows.

Charley was racing his mount, just as fast as it could run, heading for the adobe ruins that were still about a quarter of a mile away.

Comanche arrows and the occasional rifle bullet whistled past him in his bid to get to the only cover on the vast plateau that surrounded him. Puffs of black-powder smoke appeared every so often, coming from behind the ruins' walls. Charley knew his fellow Rangers, Roscoe Baskin and Feather Martin, had already concealed themselves behind the pile of adobe bricks, which had at one time been Roaker's Wells — a stagecoach stop and passenger rest before the Indians had attacked and burned it to the ground several months earlier.

The Comanche were having a difficult time of it, giving up their old ways. Even though their chief — Quanah Parker — had signed a treaty that would send all Comanches to a reservation in Indian Territory.

This must be one of the last raiding parties left, thought Charley. Most of the Comanches in Texas had turned themselves in at the nearby forts, but there were still several small bands who hadn't gotten the message — or had just refused to believe that their warring days were over. They still held out and kept on killing the white man.

That's who these fellers are, thought Charley, just as an arrow slammed into his horse's neck beside the pommel of his saddle. While still riding at a breakneck speed, the Ranger reached forward and jerked the arrow free, tossing it aside.

Several more wooden projectiles whizzed past him, and his friends up ahead returned more fire, knocking two nearby Indians from their running horses.

Charley removed his neckerchief, wadding it up, then packing the horse's wound to prevent more bleeding.

Charley's Walker Colt had run out of its conical bullets long before the chase had even begun. It was his own choice to go out scouting just after the trio had decided to make their camp at Roaker's Wells.

Now, as he hunkered low in his saddle, rein-slapping his mount to get more speed out of her, he figured that he may have scouted just a little too far away from their camp. Coming over a low rise, he'd run directly into the small hunting party, who were coming up the rise from the other direction.

Out of instinct, he emptied the Walker Colt of every bullet it held, killing four of the Comanches outright. The others had been taken by such surprise it gave him time to reverse direction and spur out for the camp.

Then they were after him, whooping and hollering with every breath taken, all while firing their arrows, and the one rifle they had between them, at the departing Texas Ranger and his rapidly galloping mare.

When Charley figured he was getting close enough to the adobe ruins, and those who were defending his getaway, one of those arrows buried itself into some more solid horse flesh, directly behind the saddle. The flint arrowhead sliced just deep enough to puncture an equine kidney. The horse let out a shriek, lost its footing, and threw Charley to the other side of the adobe wall he was preparing to jump.

As the animal rolled to a stop beside another portion of the crumbling wall, Charley picked himself up and dove in beside his two fellow Rangers, who were still popping off shots at the advancing Comanches.

Now it was the Indians who had to reverse direction, and as they rode away, back toward from where they had come, Charley grabbed an extra Winchester and assisted his friends in finishing off the last three Comanches. That left only their confused horses, all running in different directions on the flat surface of the sandy ground.

Charley awoke in a sweat. He had to pee.

He tiptoed down the hall to the water closet, but to his dismay, it was in use. The rain was still coming down, so he decided to stop by the room where he slipped on his slicker over his longjohns before he made the trip downstairs to visit the outhouse. Just the thought of standing there over that sawed-out black hole, in the near freezing darkness, made him think about cracking a window and relieving himself on the porch roof below.

But what if Henry Ellis woke up? Or Roscoe — that was even worse. Both of them were so modest that even on the trail, they both had to hike away from what they believed were prying eyes. That made stopping for a quick pee, anywhere, into something much bigger than it was ever meant to be.

He pulled on his boots, so he'd be able to keep his feet dry, while at the same time provide a holster for his Walker Colt.

Then it was down the stairs and out the side door. He stepped into the freezing alleyway that ran between Flora Mae's Pool Hall & Bar and the rear of a small warehouse that faced the next street over.

As Charley opened the outhouse door to enter the wooden cubical, he noticed that there was a lamp glowing in the back room of the warehouse. He made sure he peed as quietly as was possible, and he listened, through the rain, to some low voices that appeared to be coming from that back room, across the narrow passage.

The only words that he could make out were, *railroad, Del Rio,* and *Cropper Brothers.* The rest he had to fill in with his mind.

When he stepped out of the lopsided structure, he noticed that the lamp in the back room of the warehouse had been extinguished. He also could not hear any more anonymous talking, so he ducked under a working rain spout and went back inside.

"Is that you, C.A.?" came Roscoe's hoarse voice as Charley re-entered their hotel room and began to remove his slicker and boots.

"I've just been downstairs for a quick pee," whispered Charley as he found his bed and climbed back in.

"Hell," whispered Roscoe. "If ya wanted a quick pee . . . and a dry one . . . all you had ta do was raise the window and piss on the porch roof down below."

The following morning, after Charley, Roscoe, and the boy had finished breakfast with Flora Mae, Charley and the others stopped by the sheriff's office. Charley wanted to find out just who it was that owned the warehouse that backed up to Flora Mae's establishment.

"I can get that information for you, Charley," said the sheriff, "just as soon as the bank opens. Farley Workman keeps that kind of information locked up in his real estate office that's right next door to the bank. Pretty smart of old Farley, owning the bank like he does, to connect his real estate business to the bank building. Guess who ends up makin' all the loans?"

"Well," said Charley, "when you find out, can you leave that information with Flora Mae? The three of us're going to ride out to the ranch and check to see if everything's all right."

"Are you takin' yer pup back with ya?" asked the sheriff.

"No," said Henry Ellis. "The pup'll still stay here with Flora Mae. We'll be coming right back to Juanita for another night."

"No word on the Croppers yet, Charley," said the sheriff.

"Of course not," he said. "They could be anywhere after that trick we played on 'em yesterday."

"Well," said Charley, "knowing Sam Cropper like I do, Sam'll want to get back at us for making a fool of him."

He started for the door.

"Oh, Willingham," he called back. "When you find out that information for me, could you also relay it to Rod Lightfoot and his wife. They're still sleeping up in their room at Flora Mae's as far as I know."

"I'll do 'er," said the sheriff.

Charley closed the door behind all three of them.

Henry Ellis never thought that the ride out to his grampa Charley's ranch could get boring, but it seemed like he'd made that same journey one too many times over the past few weeks. Maybe it was the weather that bored him. He had no recollection of ever seeing sunlight since he'd left Austin on the train to head down to meet up with his grampa in San Antonio.

And gee, he thought to himself, *the time has sure gone by fast. A full week has already passed since we buried my parents. Shouldn't someone be checking back with the school officials in Austin, or at least finding out where I'm going to be living, now that I'm an orphan?*

Except he hadn't been orphaned. He still had Grampa Charley . . . and Uncle Roscoe . . . and Feather. And his pup. Plus, Flora Mae, and all the other members of the Texas Outfit.

He nudged his horse up next to Charley, Roscoe, and Feather.

"Grampa," he said, "I know it might be too soon for me to ask, but . . . where will I be living . . . now that Mother and Father . . . ?"

He couldn't speak anymore. He took a deep breath, then he continued.

"And where will I be going to school . . . ?"

He began to tear up. His words stuck in his throat. He looked away from his grampa's face. He knew that talking about what he really needed to talk about would be just as painful for Charley as it was for him.

"Why," said Charley, rubbing his nose, "you'll be living with me, of course. And Roscoe, too," he added. "And you'll be going to school here in Juanita. Damn," he said. "I mean darnit. I've got to get you enrolled in school, Henry Ellis, before your Christmas vacation is over. Plus, I need to contact your old school in Austin . . . tell 'em what happened and let them know you'll be moving down here with me."

He suddenly reined up.

"We got a lot of things we have to get done, son, so let's not be loafing around. C'mon," he said.

Charley spurred Dice and away he went,

with Roscoe and the boy following.

The ranch house was still a mess, left that way since it had been occupied by Ben and Eleanor Campbell and their hired gunmen. The threesome had come back to the kitchen after looking the place over.

"I'll ask Flora Mae if she can recommend someone who can clean this place up. And she oughta know who to talk to in town about getting you signed up for school, too. Oh, I almost forgot . . . we've got to get you some new school clothes."

"Grampa," said Henry Ellis, "Grampa, can't we just take it one thing at a time? Next, you'll have us riding that train all the way back to Austin to go shopping for my school supplies."

That set Charley to pondering. Finally he said, "That's it, Henry Ellis. That's what we have to do."

"You mean, ride the train all the way up to Austin to go shopping for my school supplies?"

"No," said Charley. "No. We . . . the outfit . . . the posse . . . whatever. We should be riding *on* the train the next time the Cropper Gang decides to rob it."

"And you, Grampa . . . and Roscoe and Feather, should be in the mail car, right there, right along with whatever the Cropper Gang wants to rob. We can bait the trap," said the boy.

"We can what?" asked Charley.

"We can lure 'em in with some crackerjack bait," said Henry Ellis, "and it doesn't even have to be money or gold."

"Go on," said Charley.

"All we have to do," the boy began, "is to start a rumor that the train will be carrying something very, very special."

"And what would that be?" asked Roscoe.

"Let it get out that a very expensive gold shipment will be on the train. And let 'em know that you three will be guarding that shipment. Just don't let anyone know that the rest of us . . . the outfit and the posse . . . will be on the train, too."

"And we could hitch a livestock car on to the train," said Roscoe. "Just like we done the other day, ta haul our horses . . . just in case."

"Hauling horses could give us away," said Charley. "I vote we don't take 'em."

"Yeah, but . . ." said Roscoe.

"Yeah, but what?"

"Yeah, but what if they get away from us, and leave us all stranded out in the middle of nowhere without our horses? What about that?"

"We'll just board the next train headed back to Juanita and try again at another time," said Charley.

"That makes sense," said Roscoe, scratching his head. "Yeah . . . that should work."

CHAPTER THIRTY-FOUR

Arrangements were made with the railroad, the sheriff, and the Juanita newspaper for the phony shipment to take place. Colin Livers, the newspaper editor, wrote a front-page story about a one-hundred-thousand-dollar shipment, consisting of old and damaged coins, plus used bills of all denominations, that were going to be shipped to the mint in Philadelphia, where they would be destroyed.

"What about the soldiers?" asked Livers, when he showed the rough draft to Charley.

"Soldiers?" said Charley. "What soldiers?"

"Shipping old coins and bills falls under the federal government's jurisdiction," said Livers. "If this were really happening, there would be a small detail of U.S. soldiers accompanying the consignment."

"How many men is that?" asked Charley.

"It would depend on what they are guarding," said the editor . . . "In your case . . . a hundred thousand in cash money . . . probably six to ten troops."

"I've got the bodies," said Charley. "Now, where do you think I might find some uniforms to fit 'em?"

"I have a friend who does business with the quartermaster's office over at Fort Clark," said Livers. "Just maybe, she could help you find some U.S. Army uniforms."

"She?" said Charley. "Since when does a woman do business with an Army quartermaster?"

"Ida Jane Bronson is a seamstress, Mr. Sunday, and a damn good one," said Livers. "And she does business, all right. Besides contracting with the Army to repair all their uniforms over at the fort for the past thirteen years, she's been known to whip up a few uniforms from scratch . . . special order, of course."

Charley's smile grew into a wide grin.

"I think I'll be wanting to speak with this Ida Jane Bronson, just as soon as we're done here, Mr. Livers."

Ida Jane Bronson was a few years older than Charley, but her nimble fingers could still sew a seam straighter than any of the modern-day machines designed to accomplish the same thing.

She was also a handsome woman for her years, and she knew how to compliment a gentleman when conversing — just as she had always done ever since starting her own business when she was fourteen years of age, sewing gold buttons on officers' uniforms in Washington, D.C., some years before Texas had become a Republic.

Presently, she made Juanita her home. Semi-retired, she picked up odd sewing jobs now and then, along with repairing the uniforms at Fort Clark.

"You want me to make you eight U.S. Army uniforms?" she asked. "Do you know how long it would take me to make you just one uniform?"

Charley shook his head.

"N-no, ma'am," he answered.

"A much longer time than you'd be willin' to wait," she said. "That's for sure."

"Well, uh," said Charley, "I'm going to need 'em before the month's out. I know that for sure."

"Then, how about you letting me see what I can do for you, over at the fort. I'm willing to bet you that Sergeant Novall will loan you . . . or rent you . . . all the uniforms you need."

"Sergeant Novall?" said Charley. "Now, just who is Sergeant Novall?"

"He just happens to be the supply sergeant over at Fort Clark . . . That's who he is."

"And you know him well enough that he'd go out of his way to lend . . . or sell me . . . the uniforms I need?"

Charley cleared his throat.

"Just how well do you know this . . . this Sergeant Novall, if I may ask?"

"Well enough," she said with a wink. "Bernard," she yelled. "Bernard!"

She moved over to the foot of a very small stairway.

"Bernard," she shouted one more time. "There's someone down here want's to talk over some business with you."

Moments passed, then a corpulent, middle-aged, full-bearded soldier, dressed in his full-length, faded-red union suit — with just one suspender hastily draped over his right shoulder to hold his trousers up — came down the stairs, one foot at a time, doing his best to pull on his left boot.

By the time the man reached the floor downstairs, he was facing Charley awkwardly, still trying to shake away the grogginess that accompanied the headache he had when he awakened with a throbbing hangover.

"Now do you think I know him well enough, Mr. Sunday?" said Ida Jane Bronson. She winked again. "Ain't he a beaut?"

Ida Jane introduced the two men. Then Charley discussed the plan with Bernard, in detail, trying his best to describe the sizes of the members of the outfit. Eventually the supply sergeant told Charley to have his men drop by the sewing shop, one at a time, the next day, and Ida Jane would take their measurements.

"Will you be in need of a uniform for yourself, Mr. Sunday?" asked Bernard. "If so, I'll get your sizes before you leave today."

"You'd better go ahead and fix me up," said Charley. "And give me an extra stripe or two, so my men will know I'm still giving the orders. Now," he added, "if you can get all these uniforms to a Master Sergeant Tobias P. Stone, over at the fort, he'll make sure they're delivered to me and my men, without your having to risk your neck anymore than you have to."

"Sergeant Stone?" said Bernard. "Why, I know Sergeant Stone. Is he going to be part of all this?"

"That's right," said Charley. "I just got the sergeant's letter yesterday saying that he'd be more than glad to join us for this operation."

"If you don't mind my askin', Mr. Sunday," said Bernard. "But how would you like to save on one of them uniforms?"

"How do you mean?" asked Charley.

"Well," said Bernard, "if you let me go along with you fellas, too, I'd throw in my own soldier boy outfit for nothing."

"Are you any good with a gun, Bernard?" asked Charley.

"I ain't fired a rifle since I've been at the fort, Mr. Sunday, but I was a damn good marksman during the war," said Bernard.

"What if I say that I'll think on it. The closer we get to the day we do this, I'll know more about where we stand, as far as the guard detail."

"Thank you, Mr. Sunday," said Ida Jane. "Ever since they stuck him in the quartermaster's office, he hasn't felt like a real soldier. You, know . . . no one ever fires a gun when they're the supply sergeant."

The members of the outfit stopped into the sewing shop throughout the following day. Ida Jane would take their measurements, then sit them down for a cup of tea, and have a chat to get to know them better. She only had trouble one time — that was getting Feather's sizes. He squawked like a bantam rooster when she tried to measure his inseam.

■ ■ ■ ■

In the meantime, Charley had Henry Ellis and Kelly cut up pieces of old newspapers, all in the exact shape of paper currency. They were also told to go down to the general store and buy as many different sized washers as they could get — enough to fill at least twenty gunnysacks. And if they didn't come up with enough washers, they were to go down by the creek and gather as many small, flat stones as they could find, to use as a filler.

The military garb was "in the works," at least that's what Ida Jane told Charley every time he dropped into her shop to check.

Sheriff Dubbs worked right alongside Charley and the Texas Outfit, planning every move they would be making during the actual event. The sheriff even offered his services, and those of his two deputies, if Charley figured he might need them in some way.

A month earlier Charley had sent off a letter to the warden at the Huntsville State Prison, asking if Mitchell Pennell might, by chance, still be incarcerated there. But in his reply, the warden told Charley that Pennell had been pardoned for what he had done some months earlier, to help Charley out of his situation in Mexico, and Pennell and his new wife, Elisabeth, had settled in nearby Liberty, Texas. And that he, the warden, would forward Charley's letter on to the address Pennell had filled in on the papers that were all part of the acceptance of his release.

From the very beginning they all knew that they couldn't let the Army in on what they were planning.

"Too many damn departments," is what Charley said about it. "Just too big of a chance that our plans'll get leaked if we involve the Army." So they never included the Army at all.

But the railroad was a different story. In order for the whole plan to be executed like clockwork, the railroad had to be deeply involved. But only a select few who worked for the company would need to be included in the covert scheme.

One busy morning, Flora Mae received a telephone call on her crank phone asking her to have Charley drop by the sheriff's office when he could. Charley waited until he had some time, then he walked on down to Sheriff Dubbs's office by himself to find out what the sheriff wanted.

"All right, Willingham," said Charley as

he entered the door. "What is it that's so important that I gotta walk all the way down here to find out what you want? Couldn't you have relayed the message through Flora Mae, over that telephone gadget?"

"Come on in, Charley. Shut the door," said the sheriff.

He got up from behind his desk and led the old rancher to a chair, right beside his desk. And while Charley sat himself down with a confused look on his face, the sheriff returned to his own chair and sat across from Charley.

"What is it, Willingham?" asked Charley. "Has somebody spilled the beans about our plans to nab the Cropper Gang?"

"No, sir," said the sheriff. "Nothin' as bad as that. It's just that one of my deputies arrested a man this morning on a vagrancy charge. I got him back in a cell right now."

"So," said Charley. "What does that have to do with me?"

"Probably nothin'," said the sheriff. "I even found an old circular on him, and this fella is one bad actor."

"His name wouldn't happen to be somethin' like Mitchell Pennell, now would it?" said Charley. "Because, if it is . . . I know the man quite well."

"Would you care to see him?" asked the

sheriff. "Make a personal identification?"

He turned in his chair before Charley could answer, calling back into the cell area.

"Laban," he yelled. "Laban, could you and Matt bring that new prisoner up here to the office? Right now."

There were the sounds of boots on the wooden floor, the jingling of keys, and several noises resembling a blacksmith's hammer striking a raw piece of meat.

This was all followed by one of the deputy's voices saying, "Are we goin' ta hafta go through all this again, every time we move ya?"

There were a few more stumbling sounds, then deputies Laban Burlap and Matt Jenkins brought the prisoner down the hall toward the office.

Both deputies looked as if they'd taken a few good punches to the face, and were still struggling to keep the rowdy prisoner in line, when they entered the room. They stopped in front of the sheriff, who still sat calmly behind his desk.

"That's him, Charley," said the sheriff. "You sure you still think you might know this hooligan?"

Charley slowly got up from his chair. Then he walked around so he was facing the huffing troublemaker. He reached forward, grabbing hold of the man's chin, then he lifted it up so he could look him directly in the eye.

It was Mitch Pennell for sure. And when he recognized Charley, his angry expression changed into a wide grin.

"Charley Sunday," he said. "Damn, it's good ta see you, you old bastard."

Charley's rock-hard fist sent him flying back into the arms of the waiting deputies. Mitchell Pennell was out cold.

The sheriff looked up to Charley, playing with a toothpick he had just stuck between his teeth. He shook his head slowly.

"Sum'bitch never saw that one comin', did he, Charley?"

Now they'd added three more to the Texas Outfit: Sergeant Stone, Mitch Pennell, and Bernard Novall — the errant supply sergeant. Within two days, Sergeant Stone had delivered the uniforms to Ida Jane at her shop. The men then showed up, one by one, to try on the uniforms. If something didn't fit just right, Ida Jane would correct the mistake with a few quick stitches of her sewing needle and thread, until all the uniforms were hanging on a rack and tagged with each man's name. Ready to go.

Still following Charley's orders, Henry

Ellis and Kelly arranged the newspaper cuttings into neat stacks and bound them in the middle. Then they were stuffed into gunnysacks labeled U.S. GOVERNMENT, just like the ones containing the washers and rocks, and stored in a back room at Flora Mae's place.

When Kelly and Henry Ellis showed Charley the make-believe cargo, the ex-Ranger was delighted. So elated, in fact, that he asked the two if they wouldn't mind riding along in the passenger car to keep their eyes out for any members of the Cropper Gang that might be riding along with them inside the car, and to help keep the passengers at ease during the attack.

When everyone figured that they had prepared enough, Charley gave them even more homework to do. He showed them a schematic of the train and its cars, then asked them to memorize it just so everyone would know where the others would be stationed — at least where their positions would be when the Croppers stopped the train.

That was when Colin Livers, the newspaper editor, was given the word, by Charley, to go ahead and publish the made-up story about the cash money shipment, with the precise date mentioned several times in the article.

To make it appear to be the real thing, even more, Charley and the outfit would have to start their journey in Del Rio. That was so the Croppers would be able to hit the train anywhere they chose to along the railroad line, between there and San Antonio. Leaving from Del Rio was also being done just in case the Croppers had spies watching. The story in the paper stated that the shipment would originate out of Del Rio.

The deserted line shack, where the Cropper Brothers and their gang had been holed up in since the wrong-way train debacle, had a roof that leaked and a stove that barely heated anything — food or human beings. They were all miserable, and some were even talking about leaving the gang.

That changed abruptly when Dale Cropper showed up one day with a copy of the Juanita newspaper containing the story about the shipment of a hundred thousand dollars of spoiled currency that was going back to the mint in Philadelphia. Sam told them all this would be their next holdup. Planning for the event began immediately.

The date for the shipment was fast approaching. Charley and the others knew they had to be in Del Rio before the train would stop to pick up its consignment, plus the guard detail of lawmen dressed as U.S. Army soldiers. So when everything had been packed away into Charley's old two-seat buckboard — the one that had been converted into a chuckwagon for the cattle drive from Colorado the year earlier, and recently into a covered wagon for Kelly to drive — they all were allowed to celebrate. That was because, Charley told them, there would more than likely be some of them who wouldn't be coming back.

So, they had another "wing-dinger" in Flora Mae's place. Everyone involved was invited — even Henry Ellis was allowed to attend. And that's something Charley wouldn't normally allow when he, personally, planned on getting pretty darn drunk himself. *But the boy is old enough now to see his grampa in all his glory, isn't he?* he thought.

While they were drinking, Flora Mae's bartender, Bud Rawlins, edged over to Charley, nudging him.

"Mr. Sunday," he said. "Flora Mae said you were the one to ask this question, so here goes. Do you think it would be at all possible if I rode along on this one with ya?"

"Do you mean, as one of the Texas Outfit?"

"As anything, Mr. Sunday," said Rawlins. "Just as long as I can be a part of capturing the Cropper Gang."

"Just two things might keep you from it," said Charley. "One is, I know you can't shoot worth a damn, because I saw you practicing one day a while back. And second is that we don't have any uniforms left, and no time to get you another. But" — Charley stopped, just long enough to smile — "you can ride along in the passenger car with Kelly and my grandson . . . keep an eye out from inside there."

"Thank you, Mr. Sunday," said Rawlins. "I thank you with all my heart and soul."

"I'll tell Flora Mae you're going to be with us. I hope you have a horse."

The bartender shook his head.

"No, sir, I don't."

"Then it's a good thing we're taking the old chuckwagon along with us. You can ride in there with Roscoe, Kelly, and Henry Ellis. I'm sure you'll enjoy their company."

The rain had stopped completely by the time they started out on their journey to Del Rio. Instead, the weather had become extremely cold. Along the way, Feather was prone to say, "It's just too gol-dern chilly ta

425

snow." The clouds remained overhead, and they were still as gray as ever, but it stayed dry for the entire day and half of the night it took them to travel between Juanita and Del Rio.

They made their base camp in an old, abandoned livery stable, on the far side of town. A perfect setting for them to don their uniforms and to finish up the last touches on Charley's chuckwagon: they painted it Army green, then added U.S. ARMY on both sides, plus the tailgate, using a stencil Kelly had made for the money bags.

The livery stable also gave them a place to sleep before the big day. And a lot of them took full advantage of that. Roscoe was in charge of the grub, as usual, and he'd made sure he had brought along some special items for the group — including several bags of peppermint candy and the ingredients to whip up a batch of corn bread.

CHAPTER THIRTY-FIVE

1961

There was very little cleanup when TV dinners were served. Noel found a paper sack under the sink and used it to collect everybody's aluminum tray. Then she put the utensils in the kitchen sink to soak. Josh and Caleb folded the TV trays and put them back on the stand, then they rolled them back into a small closet near the vestibule.

When everyone had completed their chores, they took their old seats in the living room and waited for Grampa Hank to pick up the story from where he left off.

"Where is Grampa Hank?" said Noel after she'd noticed his absence.

"I don't know," said Evie. "He was here a minute ago."

"He might have just gone to the bathroom," said Josh.

"Well, I wish he'd get back soon. I wanna hear the rest of his story."

"Well, lemme see, now, just where was I?"

It was Hank's voice. Every head turned as the old man sauntered back into the room and sat down, facing his audience.

"Does anyone remember exactly where I left off?" he asked again.

Noel's hand shot up in the air.

"Noel," said Hank. "Be my guest."

"Well," said the girl, moving over to where Hank was sitting, then climbing up into his lap once more. "Grampa Charley and his friends were just about to board the train in Del Rio."

"That's right, darlin'," said Hank, giving her a hand up.

CHAPTER THIRTY-SIX

1900

The guard detail of U.S. Army soldiers just seemed to appear on the main street of Del Rio, Texas. They were surrounding a strange-looking green wagon with a canvas covering. It had U.S. ARMY stenciled on both sides, plus the tailgate. It was being pulled by two shabby-looking brown mules.

As the detail marched up the street toward the train depot, quite a few local citizens gathered around to watch. It wasn't too often that so many American troops were seen in one place together in Del Rio, unless it was inside a saloon. The spectators, along with their jubilant children, followed the detail all the way to the station.

When the train pulled in — almost on time — the bartender, Kelly, and Henry Ellis were the first passengers to board.

Charley, wearing the stripes of a master sergeant, had his men load the gunnysacks into the mail car. Then he gave the order for the other soldiers to take their positions on the roof of the mail car and on the other railroad car roofs in front of, and behind, the mail car.

A conductor — employed by the railroad, but in on the whole plot — waited until all the soldiers were settled before giving the engineer the go-ahead signal.

Bud Rawlins, Kelly, and Henry Ellis waited on the platform between cars after boarding. They found they would only have a view of the mail car when the train went around sweeping curves. Otherwise, Kelly advised, they should probably stay inside the passenger car where Charley wanted them to be.

The engine released some steam, and the drive wheels were put into gear. Within moments, the locomotive began to move, pulling its load of cars — one of which contained the bait for the Cropper Gang — on down the tracks, until it grew smaller and smaller, and finally disappeared from sight.

Laban, one of the sheriff's deputies, moved swiftly through the door of the sheriff's office, then stopped when he saw the sheriff sitting at his desk.

"Something I can do for ya?" asked the sheriff.

"I just came from the bank, Sheriff, and old Farley Workman showed me the ownership records on that old warehouse you wanted me ta get for you."

"And . . . ?" said the sheriff.

"And," said the deputy. "That old warehouse is owned by . . . Flora Mae Huckabee. The title's clear."

"Go get your horse, Laban," said the sheriff. "I need you to run that information out ta Charley Sunday at the depot."

"Uh, that train they was all goin' ta be on has already left the station, by my recollection."

Willingham glanced at his pocket watch.

"Then find that train. Charley's in the mail car. Just make sure he gets that message."

Laban bolted out the door, leaped to the cross-rail of a hitching post, then straddled his saddle, dropping into it. He spurred out, rein-whipping his mount down the length of the street, until they both disappeared into a cloud of fog that had begun to form at street's end.

Laban nudged his horse into a high-speed run across the wide-open Texas landscape. Overing and undering, he kept the animal

431

on a straight path, all the way to the depot.

As the young deputy slid his horse to a stop in front of the train station, he could see that the eastbound was long gone. He dismounted and found a baggage handler.

"Hey, how long since the eastbound pulled outta here?"

" 'Bout seventeen minutes ago," answered the man.

Laban turned to his horse, and with a slap on the rump to get him moving, the deputy pony-expressed into the saddle and was on his way before the baggage handler knew what had happened.

The eastbound train moved rapidly down the tracks, still gaining momentum. Black smoke spewed from its stack, leaving a dissipating tail of smoke in its wake.

The large drive-wheels of the locomotive turned faster and faster, finally settling into a refreshing speed as they hummed along the tracks.

Inside the mail car, Charley and Roscoe, both dressed in military uniforms, rode along in silence, with the mail car clerk standing at the sorting table nearby, doing his job.

On the roofs of the train cars, Rod, Holliday, Feather, Sergeant Stone, Mitch Pennell, and the supply sergeant lay flat on their bellies with their rifles right beside them.

The wheels of the cars rolled along with no problems, sending their clickety-clack rhythm resonating through the floor of the passenger car.

Inside that car, Kelly and Henry Ellis sat in their seats, eyeing everyone else riding in the car. They were doing their job. Nothing appeared to be out of the norm with the two of them on watch.

The hooves of Laban's horse dug into the damp ground beside the shiny rails. Every so often the horse would veer a little bit to the right, kicking up gravel from the bed beneath the tracks.

The Cropper Gang, led by Sam and Dale Cropper, edged their horses through some tall cactus before coming to a clear trail that would lead them to the spot Sam had chosen for the ambush.

Charley, standing side-by-side with Roscoe in the mail car, pulled his pipe from a pocket and began to prepare a load. The clerk, over at the sorting desk, happened to glance around. When he saw Charley's pipe, he threw the ex-Ranger a disgusting look.

"I don't think the mail clerk over there cares too much about you havin' ta smoke in here," whispered Roscoe.

"I don't give a hoot what he cares, Roscoe."

He scratched a match on the U.S. Army belt buckle he was wearing and held it over the bowl of tobacco, drawing in the sweet flavor, then letting the smoke trickle out through his nostrils.

The wheels of the passenger car continued to turn with the steady sound of steel on rail. Above them, on the small platform between cars, stood Henry Ellis. He was trying to catch a glimpse of the mail car as the train swept around a wide curve in the tracks.

Suddenly, the door behind him opened and Flora Mae's bartender stepped out on the platform beside him.

"Oh, sorry, Henry Ellis," said Bud Rawlins. "I thought I'd come out here for a smoke. If you don't mind."

"That's all right," said the boy. "I was just leaving."

Henry Ellis slipped back into the passenger car and took his seat beside Kelly.

"What's up?" she asked the boy.

"Nothin' much," said Henry Ellis. "Except Bud just stepped outside for a smoke."

Kelly smiled, accepting what the boy was telling her.

"The only thing funny," said Henry Ellis,

"is that as long as we stayed at Flora Mae's, I never saw Bud smoke anything . . . not even a roll-your-own."

The galloping hooves of Laban's horse were now pounding across a small bridge. And as they got to the far end, the deputy could see the tail end of the locomotive's smoke, hanging low above the flat land that surrounded. He jabbed his spurs into the horse's flank, trying to make him go faster.

Up the tracks, a short distance in front of the train, the Croppers and their gang had stopped. They all had their heads turned in a westerly direction, when the faint sound of a train's whistle cut through the air. That caused everyone to take notice.

"Break it up, men," said Sam Cropper. "Dale, take some of the boys to the other side of the tracks. Me an' the rest of the men will stay here on this side. Now move!"

The gang broke off into two factions. Dale and his group crossed the tracks and found cover in a small grove of pecan trees. Sam led his men over behind an outcropping of rocks where they could conceal both themselves and their horses.

Bud Rawlins came back through the door of the passenger car. He passed Kelly and the boy, then took a seat on the opposite side of the car beside a window, leaning back and feigning sleep.

"Did you notice that he didn't have that awful tobacco smell about him when he passed us by?" whispered Henry Ellis.

"To tell the truth, I didn't," whispered Kelly. "Do you think he's up to something?"

"He's just acting very suspicious," the boy whispered back.

The train was approaching a narrow gap between some rocks. Laban knew that if he didn't board the train right then, he would be out of luck. So he nudged his horse over and spurred through the gravel until he was close enough to grab hold of a ladder attached to the rear of the last car. Then he transferred from saddle to train with ease. His horse veered off, and he immediately started up the ladder.

When Laban reached the roof of the final car, he flattened out on his belly and took a look up ahead of him. What he hadn't been able to see from ground level stared him in the face from his roof-top perch. Soldiers . . . United States Army troopers . . . were spread-eagled on top of the first three cars behind the engine. *That must be where Charley Sunday is,* he thought. *I'll just go on up there, introduce myself, and give him the sheriff's message.*

He got to his knees, but that was as far as

he went. A bullet, fired by one of the soldiers in front of him, glanced off his forehead on the right side, and the deputy passed out cold.

On his stomach on the roof of the mail car, Holliday re-cocked his rifle, blowing smoke out of the chamber.

"There's one member of the Cropper Brothers' Gang that won't be giving us any more trouble," he said.

"Get down," hollered Feather as Sergeant Stone physically shoved the old gunfighter's face down on the roof.

At that point, gunshots could be heard coming from both sides of the tracks. The make-believe soldiers flattened out even more as the sound of galloping hooves joined the gunfire.

Inside the mail car, Charley was looking out through a horizontal gun port.

"It's them, all right," he said. "Looks like our little scheme is working out just fine."

Like clockwork, two gang members rode up on either side of the locomotive, pointing their pistols at the engineer and fireman.

The engineer got the message and immediately shut down the throttle. The train began to slow.

Inside the mail car, Charley turned to

Roscoe and the clerk.

"They're here," he said.

Both he and Roscoe pulled their Walker Colts.

On the roof of the mail car, the members of the outfit lay still. All were apprehensive as the train continued rolling to a stop.

What they didn't see was Laban, the deputy, clawing his way toward them, inches at a time. Blood flowed freely from the wound on his forehead.

Inside the mail car, Charley was still looking out the horizontal gun port. From this vantage, he could see Sam Cropper and his portion of the gang, riding along beside the train, their horses gradually slowing to a walk as the engine slowed the train's movement even more.

Then there was the irritating screech of steel sliding against steel as the brakes finally locked and the train came to a halt. As Charley stepped back from the narrow gun port, Sam Cropper put two expertly aimed bullets through the port, crashing through anything that got in their way once they were inside.

Shots started to ring out on the other side of the car. Roscoe made it to the horizontal gun port on that side. He took a look, then shouted back to Charley.

"It's Dale Cropper and the rest of 'em on this side, Charley."

The two men exchanged looks.

In the passenger car, Henry Ellis glanced over his shoulder.

Bud Rawlins's seat was empty. The boy looked up just in time to see the bartender disappear through the door at the far end of the car. Henry Ellis turned to Kelly.

"You stay here. I'm going after him."

Before she could stop him, the boy ran toward the rear of the car. Then he cautiously peeked outside, using a small vertical window at the side of the door.

Feather, still laying flat on the roof of the car next to the mail car, felt something tugging on his pants leg. He turned to see the bloody face of the deputy.

"I got a message for Charley Sunday," gasped Laban through the stream of blood coming from his head wound. "I-it's from the s-sheriff."

Henry Ellis stood beside the rear door to the passenger car. He was still watching Bud Rawlins through the vertical slit of etched glass beside the door.

Out on the platform, between the two cars, Bud Rawlins was working at the lock on the door of the car behind him — the door to the car in front of the mail car.

Sam Cropper and his men edged up closer to the mail car's sliding door.

"Whoever's in there," yelled Sam, "this is a holdup. Open the door."

A rifle barrel poked through the vertical gun port and fired. The gang's horses reared back at the sight and sound of the black-powder explosion.

Inside the mail car, Roscoe fired off a second shot through the port.

Charley did the same on the opposite side of the car.

Outside, Dale and his men backed way off, dismounted, and took cover behind some rocks.

Up on the roof, Feather slid flat-bellied over to a ventilation pipe that was protruding through the roof. He got as close to the opening as he could, then called out quietly.

"Charley . . . Charley Sunday . . . Can ya hear me?"

Inside the mail car, Charley heard his name being called. He looked to the ceiling.

"I can hear you, Feather," he said, just as quietly. "What's going on?"

On the roof, Feather continued talking into the ventilation pipe.

"Sheriff's deputy just got here. He gimme a message for ya."

Inside, Charley answered, "What is it,

Feather?"

On the roof: "He said the sheriff told him ta tell ya that Flora Mae owns the warehouse. Whatever that means."

Back inside the mail car, Charley only had moments to figure out the connection.

"Flora Mae's bartender," he pondered. "Bud Rawlins."

Roscoe turned.

"What's that, C.A.?"

"The bartender. He's the connection."

"Ain't he up in the passenger car with Kelly and Henry Ellis?"

Charley looked up to the ceiling.

"Feather? Are you still there?"

"Yeah, Boss, I'm still here," answered Feather.

"Count off thirty seconds. Then open fire."

"You got it, Boss."

Charley turned and ran toward the front door of the mail car. He stopped just long enough to unlock the lock, then he started moving through to the outside.

With a bullet to the lock on the car in front, Charley entered. Between the cars, Bud Rawlins had stepped back and drawn his gun when he'd felt the handle turning on the car door behind him. Now he stood with his back to the passenger car door, his weapon cocked and ready.

As Charley stepped out onto the platform, Bud Rawlins stopped Charley in his tracks.

"Hold it right there, Sunday," said the bartender. "Set that old hogleg of yours down, and be quick about it."

Charley did what the man said. He knelt down, placing his Walker Colt on the platform beside his feet.

"You just saved me a lot of time, Sunday. Openin' the door for me like you did."

"I always like to oblige a man who's turned on his own, Rawlins. Conspiring with the Cropper Brothers . . . now, that about takes the prize."

"Well, the only prize you're going to get, Mr. Sunday, is this piece of lead, right between your eyes."

He thumbed back the hammer of his gun.

The door behind him flew open and there was a quick, swirling movement behind him. Rawlins cried out in pain, and the gun discharged. Then Bud Rawlins toppled forward, his body slipping through the opening between the two platforms. He grabbed for the coupling, but he hadn't the strength to hold on. The continuation of the fall took him to the rail bed below.

About then, all hell broke loose as the counterfeit soldiers started shooting from the train car roofs.

Charley stood facing the passenger car door and the person in front of it. Henry Ellis stood there, looking back to his grandfather. In his hand he held a large pair of bloody scissors.

"I needed a weapon, Grampa. And the only thing Kelly and I could come up with were these scissors she found in her purse — the same ones we used to cut up the newspaper with for bait."

"Thanks," said Charley. He stooped to pick up his Walker Colt and was down the side steps in a single leap.

Henry Ellis watched after him for a moment, then bent down to retrieve Bud Rawlins's revolver, which had landed on the platform. The boy checked the cylinder, then jumped to the ground, running after Charley.

Charley reached the gang's position within seconds. He immediately shot Sam Cropper out of his saddle. Then he waded into the fracas with gun blazing. A gang member jumped him from behind and Charley tossed him off easily, before putting him down permanently with a bullet from his Colt.

In the meantime, Sam Cropper had managed to crawl his way to the sidelines of the fighting, where he got to his feet and started to run away.

A single bullet to the shoulder brought him to his knees. As he was struggling to get to his feet, he looked up.

Standing directly in front of him was Henry Ellis. The gun in the boy's hand was still smoking.

Cropper began to sweat. He raised his hands as high as his wounded body would let him.

"You ain't thinkin' about killin' me, are you, son?" he asked.

Henry Ellis took a step closer. He cocked the gun, aiming it at Sam Cropper's forehead.

"You killed my parents, back at the depot," said the boy.

"They musta been caught in the cross fire, boy," said Sam Cropper. "Someone else shot 'em. It's true."

"You, your brother, your gang . . . even somebody shooting back at you. It doesn't matter. It was you that killed them, just the same."

"Are you sure you want to do this, kid?" said Sam Cropper.

"Are you *really* sure you want to do it, Henry Ellis?"

The boy turned slightly. His grampa was

standing only feet away.

"Killing Sam Cropper won't bring your mother and father back, boy," said Charley. "Remember, I lost my daughter, too. And I ain't going to kill the man."

Henry Ellis glanced at Sam Cropper, then he looked back to Charley.

"But he killed 'em, Grampa . . . Someone's gotta pay."

"I s'pose I'll have to leave that choice up to you, then, son."

Charley took a step in closer to his grandson.

"But if I'm remembering correctly, you aren't too proud of the other men you've killed. Plus, getting rid of Sam Cropper will only add another demon to those you already have . . . the ones that haunt you every time you close your eyes at night to go to sleep."

Sam Cropper, still on his knees, his hands covering his bleeding wounds, continued to look back and forth between Charley and the boy.

Charley stared directly into Henry Ellis's eyes, searching for the forgiveness he knew was inside the boy.

Finally, Henry Ellis let the gun slip out of his hand. It fell to the ground.

"I can't do it, Grampa," said Henry Ellis.

"When it comes right down to it, I just can't do it."

"Then," said Charley, "why don't you go back to the passenger car . . . see how Kelly's getting along. I'm sure Rod would like to know that."

Still making direct eye contact with his grandfather, the boy nodded.

"I'll do that, Grampa. I'll go and see how Miss Kelly is doing . . . Thank you," he added.

He turned back, heading for the steps to the passenger car.

Charley waited for a quick moment to make sure the boy made it to the platform, then he nudged Sam Cropper.

"You can't be that bad off that you can't walk. Now, get the hell up!"

Cropper struggled to his feet, and with a jab of Charley's Walker Colt's barrel, Sam Cropper stumbled toward the side of the mail car, where the Texas Outfit, dressed as soldiers, were rounding up the last of those who were still living.

Roscoe slid the side door wide open. The clerk was opening the opposite door at the same time. When Charley was able to take a look through the car, from side to side, he could see more men in Army uniforms rounding up more train robbers over there.

Rod and Feather stood with guns out, both pointed at Dale Cropper, who had already been put under arrest.

Henry Ellis walked down the aisle inside the passenger car, pushing his way through the chaotic jumble of people who had been aroused by all the confusion.

"Everything's all right, folks," he shouted at the top of his lungs. "It's all over now. The Cropper Gang has been taken into custody. They're all under arrest."

By the time the boy reached where Kelly was sitting, the passengers had begun to calm down. He slid into the seat beside Mrs. Rod Lightfoot, who pulled him even closer. She let his head slowly fall onto her chest, then Henry Ellis Pritchard began to cry like he'd never cried before.

CHAPTER THIRTY-SEVEN

The parlor of Charley's ranch house had been decorated for the Christmas holiday. The large tree stood in one corner. It had been strewn with shiny ribbon, homemade ornaments, cranberry strands, and garlands. On each outer limb, a candle burned brightly as Flora Mae lit the final candle from a burning stick.

The outfit, Roscoe, Feather, Rod and Kelly, Holliday, Sergeant Stone, and Mitch Pennell, were sitting in a circle, drinking cider and eating cookies. They had just finished singing a carol, when Flora Mae moved in with a suggestion.

"How about this one next?" she said. "I'll start it off, then you can follow along."

She began, "Si-i-lent Night . . ."

Everyone stopped talking and began to sing along with Flora Mae.

"Ho-ly Night. All is calm . . ."

Outside, it was indeed a silent night. Snow

was falling, and strains of the carol could still be heard softly seeping out of the ranch house, into the cold, crisp night.

Henry Ellis stood beside his grampa Charley, with snowflakes softly falling all around them. They had just placed two small Christmas ornaments on the snow-covered graves of Kent and Betty Jean.

"Merry Christmas, Mother . . . Father," said the boy.

Charley put a gloved hand on his daughter's headstone.

"Merry Christmas, darlin'," he said in a raspy whisper.

He rubbed his fingers over his daughter's engraved name, then turned to his wife's headstone. "Merry Christmas, Willadean," he said.

Then he turned to the boy.

"Come along, Henry Ellis," he said, wiping at his eyes. "They're all waiting for us inside."

Charley Sunday took his grandson by the hand, and together they started walking back through the snow-covered, horse-and-buggy-filled ranch yard, to the snow-covered ranch house, only a few yards away.

The singing continued inside.

"Sleep in Heav-en-ly Peace,
Sleep in Heav-en-ly Peace . . ."

EPILOGUE

1961

Grampa Hank's story was over. He stood up to stretch while the children stayed sitting with their mother.

Hank found himself walking over to the Christmas tree. The multicolored, blinking lights cast a kaleidoscope of hues across his wrinkled countenance. He stopped for a moment to re-hang one of the decorations that seemed to be slipping. He glanced out the front window to see snow falling.

"It's snowing," he said. "Why don't you kids come over and take a look?"

Evie grimaced as Noel jumped out of her lap. The girl joined her brothers, who were already at Hank's side watching the neighborhood turn white.

"It sure is pretty," said Josh.

"Yeah," said Caleb. "It sure is."

By then, Evie had joined them all beside the tree.

450

"Your great-grandfather and I have a surprise for you children," she said. "If you can get this house cleaned up in short order, Grampa Hank is going to sleep over."

The kids turned in her direction.

"We can do that, Mom," said Noel.

"I'll go get the vacuum," said Caleb.

"Now, if Josh'll just run out to Grampa Hank's car and bring in his overnight bag."

Hank handed his keys to the older boy, and Josh was out the front door in a flash.

Evie turned to Hank, placing her fingers on his stubbled cheek.

"I don't know how to thank you, Hank. Whenever you're with the kids, they're angels. Every time you tell them a story about the old days, they're on their best behavior for at least the rest of the month."

"Mom?" It was Noel's voice. "We're going to go out in the front yard and let it snow on us."

"Just be careful, sweetheart," said Evie. "And stay off the sidewalks . . . they're probably icy."

The door opened, then closed, and they were gone.

"You know what?" said Hank. "This'll be the second White Christmas I've spent with family in my entire life."

"I'll get some sheets and blankets for you,

dear. When the kids come back inside, they can clear off the couch, then help me make up your bed. And don't let me forget to bring out a couple of pillows from the linen closet for you."

The employees of Thorndike Press hope you have enjoyed this Large Print book. All our Thorndike, Wheeler, and Kennebec Large Print titles are designed for easy reading, and all our books are made to last. Other Thorndike Press Large Print books are available at your library, through selected bookstores, or directly from us.

For information about titles, please call:
(800) 223-1244

or visit our website at:
gale.com/thorndike

To share your comments, please write:
Publisher
Thorndike Press
10 Water St., Suite 310
Waterville, ME 04901